BBC

DOCTOR WHO

BBC CHILDREN'S BOOKS

UK | USA | Canada | Ireland | Australia
India | New Zealand | South Africa
BBC Children's Books are published by Puffin Books,
part of the Penguin Random House group of companies
whose addresses can be found at global.penguinrandomhouse.com.
www.penguin.co.uk www.puffin.co.uk www.ladybird.co.uk

First published 2017
This paperback edition 2019
001

Murder in the Dark written by Jacqueline Rayner, *Something at the Door* written by Mike Tucker,
The Monster in the Woods written by Paul Magrs, *Toil and Trouble* written by Richard Dungworth,
Mark of the Medusa written by Mike Tucker, *Trick or Treat* written by Jacqueline Rayner,
The Living Image written by Scott Handcock, *Organism 96* written by Paul Magrs,
The Patchwork Pierrot written by Scott Handcock, *Blood Will Out* written by Richard Dungworth,
The Mist of Sorrow written by Craig Donaghy, *Baby Sleepy Face* written by Craig Donaghy
Illustrated by Rohan Eason
Copyright © BBC, 2017

Printed and bound in Great Britain by Clays Ltd, Elcograf S.p.A.
A CIP catalogue record for this book is available from the British Library

ISBN: 978–1–405–94279–9

All correspondence to:
BBC Children's Books
Penguin Random House Children's
80 Strand, London, WC2R 0RL

BBC

DOCTOR WHO

TALES OF TERROR

Illustrated by Rohan Eason

PUFFIN

CONTENTS

THE FIRST DOCTOR

MURDER
IN THE DARK

Written by Jacqueline Rayner

All that could be seen through the darkness were two glowing eyes and a fiercely fanged mouth. Dodo yelped – before bursting out laughing. She ran forward, the Doctor and Steven following more slowly.

'It's only a jack-o'-lantern!' she called. 'Now I can see why people used them to see off evil spirits. They're dead creepy.'

More pinpricks of fire-lit eyes glowed in the distance, and Dodo ran on ahead. 'I think they're marking a path,' she said. 'Yes, I'm sure they are. Let's follow them!'

It would be a lie to say the Doctor and Steven were enthusiastic about this course of action, but since returning to the TARDIS was their only other option, they carried on after Dodo as she called back a running commentary.

'I think I can see a house in the distance . . . The path's leading towards it, I think . . . Ooh, it's a big house – a mansion! I wonder who lives there? Hang on, I can see someone at a window. It's –'

She'd briefly gone far enough ahead to be out of sight of her companions. As her scream rang out, Steven leaped forward. Within seconds he'd caught up with her, and he placed a comforting hand on her shoulder as she buried her face in his chest.

'What happened?' he asked urgently, scanning the dark for any imminent threat but finding nothing.

'Oh, Steven, it was horrible! A monster!'

'Where?'

Dodo lifted her head and looked back towards the mansion. 'Oh, it was there, Steven. It was! A face at the window! A monstrous face! With only one eye! I thought it was . . . well, you'll laugh at me, but I thought it was a Monoid.'

Steven did laugh, but it was a half laugh, intended to be reassuring rather than mocking. 'A Monoid! Well, I don't know where we are, but I don't think it's Refusis Two! Anyway, there's nothing there now. There's not even a light. I don't think anyone's at home.'

'It *was* there, whatever it was. It pulled back the curtain and I saw it.'

The Doctor, breathing rather heavily, had joined them now. He too dismissed Dodo's fears. 'A Monoid? Oh, goodness me no. You're imagining things, child. Imagining things!'

'Maybe . . .' said Dodo, knowing that she wasn't. It might not have been a Monoid – one of the green, one-eyed adversaries of a recent adventure – but it had been *something*.

The three carried on together towards the mansion, Dodo too nervous now to run ahead alone. The jack-o'-lanterns led them to a huge door of black wood, a lion-head knocker looking uninviting in the flickering light from the pumpkins.

Dodo raised a hand towards the knocker, then pulled away, scared. 'I don't think I want to,' she said. 'Maybe we should go back.'

'Nonsense, child!' said the Doctor. 'We need to prove there are no monsters here!' He reached past her and gave a firm *rat-a-tat-tat* with the metal ring.

The door swung open with a horror-film creak. A figure stood in the doorway, and it was the Doctor's turn to give a sharp intake of breath. Embroidered robes, a mandarin hat and a blank, pale face. But the face was so blank, so pale . . .

The Doctor snorted with laughter and turned to Dodo. 'For a moment I thought . . . But it's just a mask! Just a mask. They're all masks!'

'Why, it's a fancy-dress party!' Dodo beamed with delight. 'How super.'

The masked mandarin spread out a hand in invitation, and the three friends entered the house. The Doctor pointed out a figure wearing a green ogre costume, the mask's single eye seemingly staring at them. 'There, you see! That is no more a Monoid than this fellow is the Celestial Toymaker, or that gentleman over there –' he gestured at a man wearing a ten-gallon hat – 'is one of the gunfighters we met recently!'

They were in a huge hall, lit by a thousand candles. Masked figures in costumes stood all round the edges of the room – not milling about, as might be expected at a party, but watching and waiting. In the centre of the room was a ring of children, each also in costume, as still as statues. The door creaking shut behind the new arrivals was the only sound to be heard.

And then music exploded into the hall. A masked figure dressed as a gypsy violinist was scraping his bow wildly against the strings, and the music coming from the fiddle echoed around the space, louder than seemed possible. The children were up, dancing – a tiny witch was waltzing with a small scarecrow, while a bandaged mummy hopped from one foot to the other and a black cat galloped around all of them. The adults moved too – although they weren't dancing; they were still just observers – and a vampire came over to the newcomers to offer them goblets of deep red fluid. 'Bat's blood,' he whispered, his fanged mask muffling his voice, and Dodo turned to the Doctor in alarm.

'Just fruit punch, my dear,' he told her, having sniffed it, and the three drank deeply.

Dodo watched the violinist appreciatively. 'I tried playing the violin at school,' she said. 'I didn't get much further than "Twinkle, Twinkle, Little Star". Wish I'd stuck with it. He's fab.' But, as she spoke, the music stopped. The violinist froze, and everyone else froze too.

'I think the music's controlling them,' Dodo whispered to the Doctor, suddenly scared.

'You're right,' said the Doctor, unconcerned. 'Well, in a way. Have you never come across the game Musical Statues?'

She grinned. 'Oh, of course! Hey, I wonder if they'd let me play?'

Although still whispering, her voice must have travelled in the silence, for a moment later an Egyptian pharaoh had taken her hand and was dragging her into the centre of the room, among the still-rigid children. When the music started again, Dodo danced with the rest of them, taking the hands of a girl dressed as a ballerina and a ghoulish boy draped with chains.

The music stopped again. All froze – except one small red devil who carried on jigging regardless. The pharaoh who'd brought Dodo into the game took the boy by an arm and removed him from the dancefloor. Dodo felt sorry for him – how embarrassing to be the first player out! – and as the dancing began again she looked for the boy (his costume made him easy to spot), and saw him being led out through a far door.

The game continued. More and more children failed to hold their poses and were led one by one from the room. Soon only Dodo and six others were left. When the music stopped once again, the little ballerina beside Dodo had been in the middle of a pirouette and now started to wobble. Wordlessly, an adult zombie grabbed her by the arm and began to drag her away. The ballerina gave a gasp of pain, and Dodo, indignant, leaped forward in her defence. 'Hey, you're hurting her!'

The zombie ignored Dodo – but one of his fellows didn't. Another zombie now took Dodo's arm, pulling her in the same direction. 'Hey!' she said again.

He looked at her, but the eyes she saw appeared to be as

lifeless as the mask they gazed through. She shuddered and stumbled along beside him.

Suddenly his hand was ripped from her arm. 'Let her go,' Steven demanded.

The zombie turned to face the newcomer. 'But she moved,' he said, and Dodo almost laughed – it sounded whiney, petulant, and made her remember that all they were doing was playing a game, and she'd lost. These were just people and this was a Hallowe'en party, not a monster's castle. Not every place they landed in the TARDIS contained a threat.

'He's right, Steven. I did move,' she said with a shrug.

The zombie beckoned and she followed him out of the room, although Steven, still looking wary, now accompanied them.

They went into a smaller room – smaller than the huge hall, that is; it was still about eight times bigger than the largest room in Dodo's house back on Earth, the room her great-aunt still insisted on calling the 'best parlour'. Funnily enough, there was a slight great-aunt smell here: a faint mixture of lavender and candle wax, the scent of dull Sunday afternoons in Wimbledon. She turned to say something to Steven, but he was already being led through another door, and Dodo realised that all of the children in this room were girls. At the zombie's insistence, she took a seat on the floor next to her ballerina friend. 'What happens now?' she whispered. The girl just shrugged her shoulders.

A green-wigged witch and a skeleton with fluorescent painted bones walked into the centre of the circle, each holding a basket. The witch put a hand in her basket and drew out an apple, shiny, red and green.

The apple from 'Snow White', Dodo thought. *Safe on one side but poisoned on the other.* She fought from shying away when the witch offered it to her. But it was just an apple. Just an ordinary apple. She took it.

Then the skeleton stood before her and dipped its fake finger bones into its own basket and drew out a knife. A huge, sharp knife. She gasped, but the skeleton began to laugh – a disquieting sight as its grinning jaws never moved – before turning the knife round and offering it to her handle first.

'It's a game,' the ballerina told her, as she too took an apple and a knife. She sounded slightly exasperated at this teenager who was behaving more like a scared child than the actual children present. 'You have to peel the apple all in one go, without breaking the peel. Then you throw the peel over your shoulder and it'll show you the initial of the person you're going to marry.'

'Oh, that sounds like fun!' said Dodo, even though she

wasn't entirely certain she wanted to get married to anyone. You probably had to stop travelling through time and space if you got married, unless your husband or wife was incredibly understanding.

She began to peel her apple. The first time she tried, the knife slipped slightly halfway round and left her with a sadly short and limp piece of peel of no use to anyone. The witch, after tutting at the waste, was finally persuaded to let her have another piece of fruit.

The little ballerina, meanwhile, had finished hers in record time, the first of the girls to do so. She flung the long green strand over her shoulder, calling out, 'Apple peel, please reveal, who will be my love!'

The other children shuffled over to look at the result. 'It's a T!' they decided eventually.

The ballerina went off in ecstasies. 'Maybe it's Tommy! Or Timothy! Or Tony!'

Other girls completed their peeling and found out they would marry a D–, or an M–, or an S–. Dodo tried to block out their excited screams as she concentrated on her own task. Finally she had a single, unbroken spiral of apple peel. Copying the others, she called out, 'Apple peel, please reveal, who will be my love!' and threw it over her shoulder. She turned round. And gasped.

The peel hadn't landed in the shape of a letter. There, clearly in front of her, was an outline of a skull.

'What is it?' asked one of the others. 'A weird sort of A, maybe?'

Dodo just shook her head, staring.

'Maybe a Q gone a bit wrong?' said another, sparking off an argument as to whether there were any boys' names that began with Q.

But there was no way it was an A or a Q. It was quite clearly a skull, an impossibility of curves and shadows making a death's head out of the single line, and she couldn't understand why the children weren't seeing it as she was.

Married to . . . death?

No. That made no sense.

Perhaps her future held no wedding, but only death?

She shivered. 'What a silly game,' she said. 'I hope the next one's more fun.'

'I think you'll find it will be,' said the skeleton.

When all of the girls had finished, the remnants of apple were cleared away, and a new figure entered the room. He wore no mask, but there was no sign of his face – instead a shirt, topped with a ruff, covered his head, giving the impression of a decapitated man. A model head was carried under one arm.

'Ooh, the headless horseman!' said Dodo.

'He hasn't got a horse,' the ballerina pointed out, but Dodo ignored her.

The witch and skeleton carried a carved wooden chair into the centre of the circle and the horseless headless horseman sat on it, placing his head on his knees. The chair was carved from ebony, with back and seat padded in red satin, and gave the impression of not being a chair so much as a seated coffin.

I'm being ridiculous now, thought Dodo as that crossed her mind. *Whoever heard of such a thing?* She smiled at the man and sternly told herself not to let her mind run away with such silly notions.

'A man has died,' announced the horseman, and Dodo kept smiling, because obviously this was part of the game and not a pronouncement of actual death. 'We do not know how. The only clue left behind was the body itself.'

The girls in the circle giggled and shuddered.

'It is our job to make that dead body talk and so discover the truth. Let the autopsy commence!'

There were little shrieks of nervous excitement as the room was plunged into darkness. 'First the eyes!' said the man, and Dodo also shrieked as two slimy objects were suddenly dropped into her hands.

'Here, take these,' she said to the inky blackness on her left-hand side, where she knew the little ballerina to be, and the ballerina gasped as the spheres were passed on to her. 'Don't worry,' said Dodo. 'I've played this one before. It's just peeled grapes or something.'

'They're too big to be grapes,' the girl pointed out.

'All right, maybe they're . . . I don't know, apricots. Or plums. Ugh!' This last was as something new was passed on to her: a mass of slimy strands. 'Spaghetti, I bet,' she said, as the horseman announced, 'Now his guts!'

The game continued, with more and more slimy and strange items being passed round – 'His liver! His fingers! His heart!' – until they got to the grand finale: 'His brain!'

Something cold and clammy, a lump of bumps and ridges, landed in Dodo's outstretched hands. 'Cauliflower?' she said out loud.

There was a deep, rumbling, unpleasant laugh. Suddenly a number of candles flared to life around the room. The light was hazy, but Dodo could see clearly that in her hands she held something grey and wrinkled.

It was not a cauliflower.

She looked up at the headless horseman, who was still laughing away. The laughter was coming only too clearly from the severed head sitting on his knees.

At this point, Dodo realised that this really wasn't a normal party after all. She screamed.

Steven had also ended up in a separate room, herded together with all the boys who had played and lost at Musical Statues. From the ceiling hung strings, evenly spaced out, each with a pink-iced ring-shaped doughnut tied to the end. Steven's upbringing had been worlds apart from Dodo's twentieth-century childhood and Hallowe'en parties were something he'd never come across before, so he just stared, bewildered, at this display, wondering if it was some eccentric form of interior design. But when a masked cowboy shouted 'Go!' and all the boys ran forward, their hands clasped firmly behind their backs, it didn't take him long to work out that this was a game where they had to try to take bites of the swinging doughnuts using just their mouths. Not caring much for games or for cakes, he stayed where he was.

Some doughnuts had been nibbled, but it was a few moments before the first full bite was managed. 'I did it!' cried a small boy dressed as an astronaut. (Steven approved of the costume, even though for him the spacesuit seemed laughably primitive.)

'I did –' The next cry of triumph became a shout of disgust. All around the room boys were yelling as their teeth pierced the doughnuts and a red substance ran out.

'What on earth is that?' demanded Steven.

'Jam,' said the cowboy. 'Just jam. Doughnuts have jam inside. Didn't you know?'

'I've never seen a child react like that to jam!' said Steven. He took a step forward, but the cowboy blocked his way.

'It's just jam,' the cowboy repeated.

'Jam isn't that runny,' said Steven. He made to step round the cowboy, but was blocked again. Behind the cowboy, a man in a vampire mask was removing the remaining doughnuts, while the boys, some still looking upset, sat back down, cross-legged, on the floor.

'The game is over. It was jam,' said the cowboy. He indicated that Steven should also sit on the floor. Reluctantly, unsure what course of action he should be taking, Steven complied.

The vampire and cowboy now pulled a large tub of water into the centre of the room. Apples floated on the surface. Again, Steven had little idea what this represented. Bath time for fruit?

The cowboy asked the spacesuited boy to join him, but Steven leaped to his feet and barred the boy's path. 'Oh no,' he said. 'I think I'd better try this one out first. Just in case there's anything nasty on offer.' He marched up to the tub and looked down at the apples. 'So . . . what am I supposed to do exactly?'

'It's apple-bobbing,' said the young astronaut. 'You have to pick up an apple using only your teeth.'

'What is it about all these games and only using your teeth?' muttered Steven. He leaned over the tub – and two pairs of arms grabbed him. Steven, caught by surprise and off balance, was unable to prevent the vampire and cowboy from tying his wrists together.

'Just to make sure you don't cheat,' said the cowboy. His mask was fixed in a permanent grin, and Steven was sure the same smug expression was spread across the real face beneath.

'I'm not a cheater,' Steven growled through gritted teeth. He knelt down, baring his teeth, and set his sights on an apple.

The apple also bared its teeth.

Steven yelled as a dozen pieces of fruit clamped their jaws on to his nose, his ears, his cheeks. Somehow, they were dragging him down, into the water. An apple wedged itself in his still-open mouth; he tried to breathe but his head was underwater now.

But space pilots need cool heads, and Steven was not one to give in to panic. He stopped thrashing about, relaxed, and as he was drawn deeper into the tub he raised a knee on to its rim and pressed down hard. It wasn't an easy or elegant move, but it succeeded. Steven ended up on his back, very wet, with the upturned tub on top of him, but he could breathe again. A spreading pool carried the fanged apples across the room, and as Steven pushed himself up on to his knees he was delighted to see that some were already nipping at the toes and ankles of the vampire and the cowboy.

Then he heard a scream. *Dodo!*

Steven got to his feet and slipped and slid his way to the door. 'Dodo! I'm coming!' he shouted, before realising he had no way of opening the door with his hands still tied behind his back. 'Hold on!'

The door was opened from the other side and Dodo stood in front of him. 'Oh, Steven! I'm so glad to – what happened to your face?'

'Untie me, would you?' he said, turning round and holding up his wrists as best he could. 'We need to find the Doctor! Something pretty odd is going on around here.'

'You're telling me! I just found myself holding someone's br– Argh!' she cried out as she was grabbed from behind by the headless horseman, his head now under his arm.

But she'd loosened the ropes enough that Steven was able to shake his hands free. He grabbed hold of one of the biting apples and flung it at Dodo's captor. The body let go of Dodo – and let go of its head too. Shrieking, the head rolled away, as the boys from Steven's room and the girls from Dodo's started flinging things – mainly apples, but also the occasional body part – at the horseman, the vampire, the cowboy, the witch and the skeleton.

'Come on, let's get the Doctor,' said Steven, holding Dodo's hand to help her through the throng.

'But the children . . .' she began.

'They seem to be coping fine. Anyway, we can help them best by finding the Doctor.'

Together, they ran out into the huge hall. To their astonishment, it was almost exactly as they'd left it. The Doctor was sipping from a goblet, chatting to a Frankenstein's monster. Dodo and Steven hurried over to him. 'Doctor!'

The Doctor put up a hand, as if they were children needing to be taught not to interrupt their elders. 'In a moment, in a moment. Now, my dear sir –'

'Doctor!' Dodo grabbed hold of his coat sleeve. 'It's important!'

Tutting and shaking his head, the Doctor apologised to the monster – 'Excuse me, my dear fellow' – and turned to them. 'Well? What's so important, hmm?'

'There's something really scary going on, Doctor,' said Dodo.

He looked at her with tolerant pity. 'My child! This is a

Hallowe'en party. Being scary is the whole point!'

'Not like this,' said Steven. 'I was attacked by apples!' He saw the Doctor's face, half disbelieving, half almost-laughing. 'It wasn't funny! Listen.'

They told him what had happened, and were about to head off to investigate further when a voice boomed out, 'Time for our final game!'

Everyone fell silent at the announcement and turned to the speaker, a figure covered completely by a sheet, a cartoon-like ghost.

'Murder in the Dark!' the ghost continued. 'Join us, everyone!'

The far door opened and all the children ran back into the room, laughing and excited, not a hint of the confusion or chaos or fear Dodo and Steven had just been telling the Doctor about.

'Everyone will select a role at random.' The masked figures began circulating through the crowd of children, holding out upside-down top hats full of white discs.

'I don't want to play,' said Dodo, when a hat was offered to her. The masked ghoul continued to thrust the hat at her. 'No! I won't!'

'I think you'd better,' said Steven from behind her. She turned to see two masked Roman soldiers menacing the

Doctor with their all-too-real-looking short swords. He had taken a disc and so had Steven. Reluctantly, Dodo did too. She just had time to see it had no word on it, just a question mark, when all the candles went out.

There was a scream. Long, piercing, but whether a man's, woman's or child's she couldn't tell. Then she felt someone bump into her.

Almost immediately the candles spontaneously started burning again.

Now Dodo herself shrieked in horror. In those few moments, things had changed.

The three of them – herself, Steven and the Doctor – were completely surrounded by every masked figure. The gunfighter, the headless horseman, the ghost, the gypsy violinist, the skeleton, the mandarin, the one-eyed ogre – all of them. And beyond that circle . . .

Every single child was lying on the floor.

'Are they . . .?' Dodo whispered, unable to utter the word 'dead'.

'It's just make-believe,' said Steven. 'It's just part of the game. Play-victims.' He sounded convincing, but she knew he was trying to convince himself as much as her.

'Who is the detective?' boomed the sheet-covered ghost.

Silently, the Doctor held up his disc. The word

DETECTIVE was written clearly on it.

'And now, Doctor, you have to find the murderer. Not too difficult. You only have two suspects.'

Dodo looked down at the disc she held, the one with the question mark on it. She turned it over. On the other side, it read MURDERER. Steven held out his. It was identical.

'Examine your suspects, Doctor,' said the ghost. 'Then make your decision. But be sure of your answer. Only one of your friends can walk free.'

'And what happens to the other, hmm?' demanded the Doctor.

'The guilty must be punished.'

'This is ridiculous!' shouted Steven. 'Neither Dodo nor I have hurt anyone. The Doctor knows that. Everyone knows that!'

'But it's the rules of the game. You accepted our invitation, joined our party. That means you must play by the rules. Or else. So decide. Who killed the party guests? One of your friends must be punished; the other will walk free.'

Dodo felt sick with fear. She choked back a sob of panic, and reached in her pocket for a handkerchief.

There was something else in there. Horrified, she pulled out a small blue bottle. It had a skull and crossbones on it.

'Was it Miss Chaplet with poison in the punch?'

'Someone must've put this in my pocket when they bumped into me!' cried Dodo. 'It's not mine!'

'Or Mr Taylor with drugs in the drink?'

Steven wordlessly pulled an identical blue bottle out of his pocket.

The ghost yelled, 'Decide, Doctor!'

The surrounding crowd took a step forward, hands outstretched, ready to grab the guilty party.

'It was me!' Steven suddenly said. 'I did it. That's your answer, Doctor. Please.'

Dodo felt an indescribable rush of gratitude, but of course she couldn't let him do that. 'No,' she said urgently. 'Doctor, it was me. I . . . I poisoned them.'

The Doctor looked at her, met her eyes. 'I'm sorry, my dear.' Then he turned to the ghost. 'Very well,' he said. 'I have my answer. The murderer is . . . you!' But it wasn't Dodo he indicated, or Steven. He spun round to face the masked mandarin, and ripped the rubber from his face. Below was a face almost identical to the mask – a face Dodo recognised. A face they'd last seen only a short time ago, when they'd escaped his world of toys and tricks. The Celestial Toymaker.

'Hiding in plain sight, hmm?' the Doctor said. 'But who else could it be? Who else would twist games like this?'

'Well done, Doctor,' said the Celestial Toymaker. 'But

your answer is invalid. My toys –' he made a gesture and all those surrounding them pulled off their masks to reveal crude dolls' faces with dots for eyes and nose, a semi-circle for a mouth – 'know that games must follow the rules to the very end. They are waiting for your decision. Steven or Dodo?'

'Games must follow the rules, hmm? Well, if they must, they must. But I have a request. A music request! "Twinkle, Twinkle, Little Star!"'

The Celestial Toymaker looked as though he thought the Doctor had lost his mind. So did Steven.

But Dodo suddenly got it! She grabbed fiddle and bow from the gypsy violinist, and began to frantically scrape out the only tune she knew. All the dolls took a step towards them.

'We're playing Musical Statues again!' declared the Doctor. 'And when the music stops –' obediently (and relieved) Dodo stopped playing – 'all the players must stop moving!'

All the dolls froze, and the Doctor cried, 'Dodo, Steven, run!'

The three of them fled through the frozen figures, and through the children on the floor, which were now revealed to be nothing more than floppy ragdolls of cotton and thread.

'This is not Musical Statues! This is still Murder in the Dark!' they heard the Toymaker yelling at his creatures as they dashed through the huge wooden door. 'Get after them!'

But the Doctor, Steven and Dodo were already on the path. The jack-o'-lanterns were still lit and they hurriedly retraced their steps away from the mansion towards the TARDIS.

'How did we get away?' said Dodo when they stood in safety at last. 'Did we win the game? I thought the Toymaker destroyed his world and everything in it if he was beaten.'

'We won Murder in the Dark,' said the Doctor. 'I rightly identified the killer – the Toymaker himself. But starting a new game confused things for long enough to let us get away.'

'Oh, I see,' said Dodo, who wasn't entirely sure she did. But being back in the TARDIS was all that mattered. 'You know, when we beat him last time, I thought it'd keep him off our backs for a bit longer than this.'

'For those such as him, time is nothing,' said the Doctor. 'He could have spent a thousand years planning this since we last met, although only days have passed for us.'

'You'd think he'd have made a better job of it, if he'd been planning it that long,' put in Steven. 'A twisted kids' party!'

'But he nearly got us!' Dodo pointed out.

'Oh nonsense, nonsense,' said the Doctor. 'It wasn't as near as all that. Anyway, we got away. That's the important thing.'

Dodo shivered. 'Let's never come here again.'

'Definitely not!' agreed Steven.

But had either of them glanced at the scanner screen, they would have seen a flashing blue light, an outline of another police box appearing.

The battle between the Doctor and the Toymaker would never end . . .

2

THE SECOND DOCTOR

SOMETHING
AT THE DOOR

Written by Mike Tucker

'Och, I dinnae believe it. How many rooms are there inside this wee box?'

Ben laughed. Jamie's confusion at the TARDIS was understandable. Ben considered himself an up-to-date twentieth-century London man and the TARDIS perplexed him; he couldn't imagine what a young Scottish piper from the battlefields of Culloden in 1746 must make of it.

'We've stopped counting,' said Polly. 'Ben and I did a bit of exploring when we first came on board.'

'And you nearly got us lost in the process!' Ben chastised her.

Polly stuck her tongue out at him. 'We found our way back eventually.'

'Yeah, only because the Doctor came and got us,' Ben replied.

'Well, that was because it was all new then! This time I know *exactly* where I'm going. Come on.'

Grabbing hold of Jamie's hand, Polly set off along another corridor, the walls peppered with the strange circular indentations that were a common feature of the TARDIS. Before he followed them, Ben took the time to get a good look at his surroundings. While he had only been teasing Polly, the truth was that she had been choosing corridors at random and had no real idea as to which way she was leading them. If Ben had been in charge of this little expedition, he would have come up with some kind of system: one left turn, one right turn, one left turn – or something like that. Polly was just choosing which corridors they went down on a whim.

Fortunately, the Doctor's habit of collecting unusual objects from every conceivable time and place stopped the endless passageways from looking identical. Even here, a long way from the time machine's control room, there was an antique coal scuttle propped against one wall, and what appeared to be a unicycle sticking out of a packing crate. The Doctor didn't keep a very tidy ship.

Once he was satisfied that he had remembered enough recognisable features to be able to find the way back when the time came, Ben set off after his shipmates.

Polly's infectious laughter rang through the corridors ahead.

By the time that Ben caught up, Polly was struggling to open a door. This door was quite unlike all the others they had tried. Where they had been uniformly metallic and flat, this one was made out of dark wood and had a fancy piece of stained glass set into a circular window.

'It won't budge,' said Polly, heaving against it with her shoulder. 'Ben, come and open it for me.'

Before he could oblige, Jamie had stepped forward and pulled Polly to one side. 'Out of the way, lassie. You need a highlander to do this for you, not some Sassenach.'

A few weeks ago, Ben probably wouldn't have let an insult like that pass, but travelling with the Doctor had smoothed some of his rougher naval edges. Besides, if the newcomer wanted to make a fool of himself in front of the lady . . .

'All right, let's see you do it then.' Ben folded his arms and leaned casually against the wall of the corridor.

Jamie made a show of rubbing his hands together in preparation, then threw himself against the door. His calf muscles bulged as he pushed against it with all his strength. He failed to make any impression on the unyielding door.

Ben, who was watching in amusement, was just about to offer to show Jamie how it should be done when, to the

surprise of everyone – especially Jamie – the door swung
abruptly open.

Ben stifled a laugh as the young Scot tumbled through
the open doorway, followed by a loud crash from the room
beyond.

'Jamie!' cried Polly. 'Are you all right?'

She, too, vanished through the doorway, and Ben quickly
followed her. The room they found themselves in was dark
and dusty. Polly was trying to haul Jamie to his feet.

'Very elegant,' teased Ben, giving him a helping hand.

'Aye, well, I wasn't expecting it to open so easily.' Jamie
looked embarrassed, brushing the dust and cobwebs from
his shirt. 'What is this place, anyway?' He looked around
curiously. 'That desk looks like the Doctor's control . . .
console.' He struggled to remember the unfamiliar word.

'Hey, Ben, he's right, you know.' Polly was also staring
around in astonishment. 'It *does* look like a smaller version of
the control room.'

Ben had to agree. It did indeed look very similar – only,
instead of the familiar white walls and gleaming controls,
here everything was dark wood and stained glass. Before Ben
could suggest that they exercise a little caution, however, Polly
had already made her way over to the central console-like
desk and opened one of its six hinged panels.

There was a hum of power and the room was flooded with light.

Polly gave a squeal of delight.

Ben wasn't quite so enthusiastic. 'Are you sure you should be messing about with things like that, duchess?'

'Oh, come on. It's not like I'm going to press any of the buttons now, is it?' Polly replied.

Jamie was staring at the rows of illuminated switches that had been revealed by opening the panel. 'What do you suppose all this is for?' he asked.

Ben shrugged. 'Back-up navigational controls or something. I guess that the Doctor can operate the TARDIS from either this control room or the other one.'

'And that?' Jamie nodded at a circular mirror set into a silver stand protruding from the top of the wooden console.

Ben frowned. 'It looks like a shaving mirror.'

'Do you think this is where the Doctor comes to trim his beard?' Polly laughed.

'The Doctor doesn't have a beard,' Jamie pointed out.

'*This* Doctor doesn't,' Polly said. 'Who knows if any of the previous ones did?'

Ben and Polly had recently witnessed the Doctor changing his entire physical appearance. Ben wouldn't have believed such a thing to be possible, except that it had happened right in front of his eyes.

Ignoring the puzzled expression on Jamie's face, Polly started to explore the room. Ben looked around in admiration; the TARDIS certainly wasn't short of surprises. Trust the Doctor to have two control rooms. He wondered what else they might find if they explored the TARDIS for long enough . . .

'Ben! Come and look at this.' Polly's excited voice brought him back to earth. She was kneeling in front of a large wooden chest on the far side of the room.

'What have you found now, duchess?'

Leaving Jamie, who was still staring in perplexed fascination at the coloured lights blinking away inside the console, Ben wandered over to Polly. She was pulling something out of the chest and, as he approached, she held out what she had found, her eyes shining. Ben took it. It was a wooden board, its surface scuffed and faded. Each edge was decorated with crudely painted symbols depicting the sun, the moon and other unidentifiable planets. The central portion of the board was taken up with the twenty-six letters of the alphabet, the numbers zero to nine, and three words: 'yes', 'no' and 'goodbye'.

Ben frowned, not knowing what it was that he was looking at. 'I don't get it, Pol. Is it some kind of board game?'

'Better than that!' She scrambled to her feet, now holding out a small glass tumbler also engraved with planetary symbols. 'It's a Ouija board!'

Ben rolled his eyes. 'A Ouija board. Oh, for Pete's sake, Polly . . .'

'Don't be so mean.' Polly snatched the board back from him. 'After all that we've seen recently, I'd have thought that you'd be a little more open-minded.'

'I'm very open-minded,' said Ben firmly. 'But the supernatural?'

'Who's to say that the supernatural isn't as real as everything else we've encountered? A few weeks ago, you'd have scoffed at the idea of aliens or robots, but now you know that *they're* real.'

Frustratingly, Ben didn't have a good answer to that. He watched impatiently as Polly closed the lid of the chest and set the board down on top of it.

'You're not going to set that up here, are you?' he asked.

'Why not?' said Polly.

'I thought you wanted to explore.'

'Well, we have explored,' stated Polly. 'Now I want to try this.'

Ben sighed. He knew from experience that once Polly got an idea in her head she wasn't easily dissuaded.

'OK, duchess, you win, but do me a favour – let's do this back in the other console room, rather than here, all right?'

Polly looked at him in surprise. 'Why?'

'I dunno . . .' Ben glanced down at the board, with its strange cosmic symbolism. There was something unsettling about it. Something that made his gut clench. He was aware of Polly's eyes watching him, aware of how foolish it would sound if he voiced his uneasiness. More annoyed with himself than with Polly, he scooped up the board. 'I just want to get back, OK?'

Before Polly had a chance to argue, he started towards the door, nursing the suspicion that finding the Ouija board was something that they were all going to regret.

Some time later, the three companions finally found themselves back in the familiar surroundings of the main control room. Polly would have been the last to admit it, but Ben had been right about her casual regard to exploring. If it hadn't been for his careful remembrance of their route, they would have all been totally lost. Fortunately, Ben's unerring sense of direction had brought them right back to where they had started.

As they entered the gleaming white control room, Polly did have to admit, though, that returning here had been an equally good idea. She would never tell Ben, of course, but she too had experienced a shiver of nervous unease when she had first set eyes on the strange decorations of the Ouija board.

'There's no sign of the Doctor,' said Jamie.

'Well, that's probably a good thing,' replied Ben. 'I can't imagine him being too happy about us doing this.'

'Why not?' said Polly indignantly. 'It's *his* board.'

'Or something he took from some ferocious monster.'

'What does it do, anyway?' Jamie took the board from Polly and peered at it curiously.

'It's a means of contacting the spirit world,' explained Polly. 'Of communicating with the dead.'

Jamie's face fell and he practically threw the board back at her. 'Och, I dinnae want anything to do wi' demons or ghosts.'

Polly rolled her eyes at him. 'You're as bad as Ben. Both of you are too scared to try anything new.'

'I didnae say that I was scared,' Jamie protested.

'Yeah, hold your horses, duchess.' Ben was equally put out. 'I never said I wouldn't try it.'

Polly stifled a smile. She knew that neither of the boys would want to look frightened in front of her. 'Well, then, help me set it up,' she declared.

It didn't take long to find a small card table and a couple of battered chairs and set them up alongside the TARDIS console. Polly got them all to sit round the table in a circle, then placed the glass upside-down on the wooden board.

'Right, we all put one finger on the glass,' she instructed.

Sharing a dubious glance, Ben and Jamie did as they were told.

'Now then, close your eyes.'

Ben didn't look happy about that. 'Hey, why do we –'

'Just do it, Ben!'

To Polly's satisfaction, both men obeyed. She took a deep breath and shut her eyes too. 'Are there any spirits here in this room?' she intoned.

Ben sniggered, and Polly opened her eyes to glare at him. 'If you're not going to take this seriously . . .' she warned.

'All right, all right. I'm sorry.' Ben placed his finger back on the glass.

Polly took another calming breath. 'I ask again, are there any spirits in this room?'

The console room suddenly became uncannily silent; the clicks and beeps that made up the constant background hum dropped in pitch until they were virtually inaudible. At the same time, Polly was aware that it had become much, much colder. She shivered.

'Hey, I can feel the wee glass moving!' exclaimed Jamie.

Heart pounding, Polly realised that Jamie was right. She too could feel the glass starting to slide across the board as if it had a mind of its own.

'I don't believe it,' murmured Ben.

Urging him to be quiet, Polly watched as the glass slid from letter to letter.

T . . . A . . . R . . . D . . .

'TARDIS,' she whispered. 'It's spelling out TARDIS.'

'But why?' Jamie asked.

'I think it's asking if we are in a TARDIS,' said Polly. 'Yes! Yes we are. Where are you?'

The glass started to move again.

V . . . O . . . R . . .

'VORTEX.' Ben looked up from the board. 'The Time Vortex?'

'It's not finished yet,' Jamie said, as the glass started to move faster and faster across the board.

As Polly kept track of the letters being spelled out, a cold chill of horror rippled down her spine. The three friends stared at each other nervously.

WE WILL DEVOUR YOU.

This was a decidedly sinister turn of events, but before they could make any decisions about what to do, the glass started to jerk and jump beneath their fingers, then flew from the board and shattered against the ceiling.

Polly cried out, throwing her arms up over her head as broken glass rained down on her. Ben and Jamie were forced to scramble backwards as the Ouija board bucked and rattled violently, before launching itself from the card table and flying across the room, making a noise like a screaming animal.

Jamie ducked as the board swooped down at his head like an angry wooden bird. As he struggled desperately to stop it from crashing against his head, Ben snatched up one of the wooden chairs and smashed it hard against the floor, shattering it into fragments. He picked up one of the broken legs and swiped it at the spinning board, trying to get the board away from Jamie before it could cause serious injury.

Seemingly aware of this new attacker, the board turned its attentions towards Ben, flying directly at his face. That was exactly what Ben had wanted. Now that it was safely away from Jamie, he didn't have to hold back. Steeling himself, he swung the chair leg at it with all his might.

There was a deafening crack and the wooden board split in two. The halves clattered to the floor. The horrible, cat-like screeching stopped and the room fell silent, apart from the hum of the console, once more.

■

'How could you all be *so* stupid?'

Ben didn't think that he had ever seen the Doctor so angry. The scruffy little man was pacing round and round the console, wringing his hands in agitation. Jamie was staring at his shoes. Polly looked like she was about to burst into tears.

'Don't you realise how incredibly dangerous this could have been?' cried the Doctor. 'It could have the most appalling consequences.'

'Surely there's no harm done?' said Ben, trying to calm things down. 'I mean, it's only a stupid game, and, besides, it's broken now, isn't it?'

'A *game?*' The Doctor stared at him as if he was an imbecile. 'You really don't have the slightest idea of what you have done, do you?'

With a sudden shock, Ben realised that the Doctor wasn't just angry; he was frightened. Very, very frightened.

'We're sorry,' sobbed Polly, her eyes brimming with tears. 'We didn't mean for things to get out of hand like that.'

The Doctor's manner changed abruptly, as though he'd just realised that his anger wasn't helping anyone, and he placed a comforting hand on Polly's shoulder. 'No, of course you didn't.' He sighed. 'Let's get this mess cleaned up, hmm? We must simply hope that we haven't attracted too much attention to ourselves.'

'Attention?' Ben frowned. 'Attention from who?'

The Doctor fixed him with a piercing stare. 'Let's just say that we are rarely alone in our travels through the Time Vortex, and that some of our fellow travellers are things that we do not wish to become too closely acquainted with.'

Without a further word, the Doctor set about cleaning the broken glass and splintered wood from the TARDIS console.

It was only much later, when he was lying on the bunk in his quarters, that Ben really started to think about what the Doctor had said, and about the final sentence spelled out by the Ouija board.

WE WILL DEVOUR YOU.

He'd never really considered it before, but if the TARDIS was a ship of time, then the Vortex really was the equivalent of an ocean, and it stood to reason that there might be other creatures living within that ocean. While he couldn't bring himself to accept the supernatural like Polly and Jamie could, he had to concede that his short time with the Doctor had forced him to reconsider some of his beliefs. It was more than possible that using the Ouija board might have brought them to the attention of some unimaginable alien being somewhere outside the ship – something that wanted to devour them.

His thoughts were interrupted by the sound of footsteps outside the door of his room. He stilled his breathing, trying to determine who it might be. The footsteps were soft, furtive, as if someone was trying hard not to be heard.

After the day that he had just had, Ben was in no mood for any further surprises. He slid from his bunk and quietly slipped on the shoes he had discarded earlier. He eased open the door of his room, peering out into the darkened corridor beyond. The Doctor never seemed to sleep, but was all too aware of his companions' needs, and tended to keep the habitation sections of the TARDIS on a regular cycle of 'day' and 'night' lighting.

Although the corridor seemed deserted, Ben could still hear the steady footfall, and he was certain that he had caught a glimpse of a figure moving swiftly at the far end of the passageway. Whoever it was, they were making their way towards the control room.

Quietly pulling the door to his room shut, Ben set off after the stealthy figure. He was quite aware that this might turn out to be nothing more than the Doctor quietly wandering the corridors of his ship. Perhaps he was being deliberately quiet so as not to disturb his shipmates' sleep?

As he approached the door to the console room, he became aware of the sound of controls being activated, and there was the all-too-familiar grind of the TARDIS engines as the ship began to materialise. Ben had pulled himself from his bed for nothing; it was just the Doctor taking them on some new adventure.

He stepped into the control room, intending to ask where they had landed this time, only to stop short in shock.

The figure standing at the hexagonal console wasn't the Doctor at all.

It was Jamie.

'Hey, mate. What are you doing?' asked Ben warily. There was something wrong with the Scot's entire manner. For starters, there was no way that he should have had the faintest idea of how to operate the ship.

Jamie's face cracked into a horrible, leering smile at the same moment as the doors to the TARDIS shuddered under some enormous impact.

THUD! THUD! THUD!

Ben clapped his hands over his ears as the deafening blows echoed around the room.

THUD! THUD! THUD!

Seemingly oblivious to the tremendous battering the TARDIS was getting, Jamie stretched out a hand towards the door control.

'Ben. Stop him! Don't let him open the doors!' The

Time Lord, alerted by the unexpected sound of his ship materialising, had appeared in the doorway. He held a large leather-bound book in his arms.

Spurred on by the urgency in the Doctor's voice, Ben hurled himself towards the console, grasping Jamie's arm and pulling him away from the door control. The highlander snarled at him, his face twisted with rage.

The terrible banging on the door increased in tempo. *THUDTHUDTHUDTHUDTHUD!*

'Doctor, what's happening?' A terrified Polly had appeared at the Doctor's side, woken by the strange noises from outside the ship.

'Help Ben with Jamie!' shouted the Doctor. 'I have to get the TARDIS moving again.'

He hurried forward, placing the heavy book down on the console and busying himself at the controls. As he did so, Jamie gave a horrible cry of fury and struggled to release himself from Ben's grip.

'Duchess, I could use a hand here!' yelled Ben.

Polly ran to help him, grabbing hold of Jamie's other arm. Between the two of them, they managed to pin him against the wall.

The Doctor danced round the console, operating the controls like a concert pianist. As he reached for the lever that would put the TARDIS back into flight mode, Jamie arched his back and gave a huge, terrible bellow of anguish.

Ben and Polly stumbled backwards as something enormous and dark burst from Jamie's mouth, boiling up into the air above the console like a vast swarm of bees. As the monstrous thing left him, Jamie collapsed in a heap on the floor. Polly scrambled forward to try to help him, but Ben couldn't take his eyes from the writhing, spitting being that swirled angrily above the Doctor's head.

Looking up in triumph, the Doctor slammed down the dematerialisation controls, and the raucous wheezing, groaning noise filled the room once more. At the same instant he snatched up the leather-bound book from the console, wrenched it open and read aloud from one of the pages.

Ben couldn't hear what the Doctor was saying, but the words had an immediate effect on the swarm. It began to swirl ever faster. Long black tendrils reached out to swipe at the chanting Time Lord.

Undeterred, the Doctor lodged the book in the crook of one arm and raised his other hand, index and little fingers making some occult sign. Eyes closed, his lips continued to move, repeating whatever incantation it was that he had found in the book.

With a screech of alarm the boiling creature reared up,

hovering like an angry, intelligent cloud. For one horrible moment, Ben thought that it was poising to attack the Doctor – but then it dived towards the console and poured itself through one of the grills that dotted the surface.

Within seconds the creature was gone and, with one final rattle of the doors, the room was silent and calm once more.

The Doctor opened one eye. Satisfied that the creature had departed, he let out a deep sigh of relief.

'Where did it go?' asked Polly, astonished.

'Back out into the Time Vortex via the telepathic circuits.' The Doctor placed the book back on the console and hurried over to help her to make Jamie comfortable.

'Never mind where it went to. How did it get in here in the first place?' asked Ben.

'Oh, it came in through Jamie's subconscious,' said the Doctor, as though that explained everything. 'The Ouija board opened a doorway, and the creature used Jamie's mind as a place to hide itself, waiting for an opportunity to stop the ship and let others of its kind on board.'

'To devour us.' Polly shuddered.

'Yes, I got the impression that was the general idea,' said the Doctor with a sad smile.

'Well, it's a good thing you had that book of spells to drive it off,' said Ben, clapping the Doctor on the shoulder.

'Spells, Ben?' The Doctor looked at him in disappointment. 'I would have thought that you'd been travelling with me for long enough now that you didn't believe in magic any more.'

'But the incantation . . .'

'Well, yes, ancient Gallifreyan does sound a *bit* like magic if spoken in the right tone. Particularly if you don't know what it actually means.'

'But it worked.' Ben pointed to the vents in the console. 'The words you spoke banished it . . .'

'Well, it would seem to suggest that the universe is full of lots of different species that are prepared to believe in magic, wouldn't it? What I recited was in fact a rather delicious recipe for Bajaxx Stew.' The Doctor lifted the book from the console and opened it, showing Ben a list of ingredients written in an indecipherable script. 'I had been intending to make us some for supper tomorrow evening.'

He beamed at his companions.

'Now, I think that Jamie could do with a good, hot meal to help him recover, so shall we see if this book has a breakfast recipe that would appeal to a hungry Scot?'

3

THE THIRD DOCTOR

THE MONSTER
IN THE WOODS

Written by Paul Magrs

'You're not to go knocking on all the neighbours' doors asking for sweets!' Mum yelled up the stairs before going to watch the end of *Crossroads*.

Ange was upstairs in her bedroom painting her younger brother's face for Hallowe'en. Terry was ten and amazingly patient as she finished off his David Bowie lightning flash.

'I want one as well!' said Ian, who was six and desperate to be just like his big brother.

'You're Frankenstein's monster, remember?' Ange told him.

Ian looked sulky, his face already painted a noxious green.

Ange, meanwhile, was a vampire lady and, at thirteen, felt like she was lumbered with babysitting her brothers when she could have been down at the precinct with her mates. But she'd promised Mum she'd take them round the streets to show off their Hallowe'en costumes.

'A quick walk round the estate, but no banging on doors, mind!' their mum had said earlier.

'Yeah, yeah . . .'

Mum was distracted, dashing back and forth to the kitchen, getting things ready for Dad's tea. The chip pan was sizzling. The kids' teatime had been straight after school, as usual. Dad got home much later, after his factory shift and a pint or two at the club. He'd probably be in a stinking mood again tonight, and that was why Mum was distracted.

'I hate you lot going round the streets in the dark,' she said.

'It's okay,' said Ange. 'All the kids are out tonight.'

'Just make sure you look after your brothers,' said Mum.

Eventually the three of them were set loose on the streets, bearing their lantern carefully so as not to put out the candle. Ian's eyes were wide with astonishment at being allowed out so late. Hallowe'en was like kids had taken over the world.

Of course, the Barnes kids weren't doing the same thing as all the other kids; they had another plan. A *secret* one. They were going where their mother had strictly forbidden them to go. They were doing something even worse than knocking on doors. They were going down to the woods.

The woods were a scrubby, neglected copse by the stream that chugged round the edge of town. Decades ago the woods had been much wilder, but the council estates were growing larger each year and even now diggers and chainsaws were poised to rip up yet more of the remaining gnarled and ancient trees. Soon there mightn't even be any more wilderness left in their town at all.

Ange warned her brothers to move quietly through the undergrowth. She was the vampiric mistress of the dark, leading the way under the swaying canopy of leaves. 'Keep as quiet as you can. We don't want Mum or anyone else knowing where we're going.'

She had made the two of them swear solemnly to stay quiet as they slipped into the shadows. Terry nodded and Ian was mute with excitement. The tiny flame in the lantern guttered and blew out in the chill breeze. Ange turned on her torch and led them into the very heart of the dark woods. To the exact spot where their friend was waiting for them.

Starman.

Even though he wasn't really a man, and he wouldn't tell them exactly which star he had come from, that was their name for him.

The three children stood on the damp mulchy earth and

Ange banged on the outer shell of the den.

There was a pause, then Starman summoned them inside.

The rank smell of battery acid made Ian wrinkle his nose as he entered the den. He had never been to see Starman before and all of this was new to him. He gripped his older brother's hand, determined not to cry or say anything wrong. As his eyes adjusted to the dim light, Ian saw the metal monster his brother and sister called Starman. He was roughly conical in shape, made of machine parts, and with two thin arms protruding from his battered body. There was a large, jagged hole in his side and Ian could see something dark and wet glimmering inside.

On the way there, Terry had explained to Ian that many years ago Starman had built the small den for himself out of strange bits and pieces, and he was trapped inside it. The den looked like a pile of junk, really. Starman was old. He didn't see so well and he found it hard to move around.

Starman seemed excited. His head swivelled about and his one eye lit up at the sight of them. He had news. 'The sig-nal has been sent!'

His harsh, grating voice came as a shock to Ian. It didn't sound like anyone he had ever heard before.

'You got the transmitter working?' Ange grinned. For

weeks she had been bringing him bits and pieces from her
dad's toolbox and shed. She had even nicked one or two
electrical parts from her technology class.

'It is sent. This night. It will be heard!' Starman said. 'It
must be!'

'This is our younger brother,' Terry told him, pushing
Ian closer to the bumps on Starman's shell that he had
said were sensors. Terry was having second thoughts about
having brought Ian along. He was only a little kid. What if he
blabbed to Mum?

Ian stared and said, 'It's the monster! The monster in
the woods!'

'Ex-plain,' demanded Starman.

'It's just a story,' Ange added hurriedly. 'That's what
some people say round here. Mum says we should stay away
from the woods, because there's a monster.'

Starman extended his electronic arms – one was a car
aerial with a claw and the other was a sink plunger – and the
children saw that he was making minute adjustments to an
extraordinary machine in the corner of his den. Part of it
was an old-fashioned radiogram that the children had found
at the town dump. Its wires and circuitry had been yanked
out and welded together in a bizarre new arrangement
incorporating all sorts of household objects. Now it was

blinking and humming and changing its tune slightly as Starman delicately turned dials.

'Soon there will no lon-ger be a mon-ster in the woods,' he said, grinding out the words. 'You will fetch one more item. To en-sure the mes-sage re-peats and re-peats.'

'If we can help, of course,' said Ange. 'We can come back tomorrow, perhaps. After school?'

'Now! You will bring it *now*!' Starman ordered angrily. His aerial arm lashed out and its claw grasped hold of Ian, who cried out in alarm. Starman dragged the small child towards him abruptly. 'The in-fant will stay with me here un-til you do.'

'Look, Jo, fond as I am of Miss Hawthorne and her fellow villagers at Devil's End, I'm afraid I won't be traipsing halfway across the country for a Hallowe'en shindig tonight.'

Jo Grant was already dressed up as a black cat, with whiskers, ears and a furry tail. She had brought the Doctor his tea in the UNIT laboratory, expecting to find him ready to race off in Bessie to enjoy the festivities. 'Olive will be so disappointed,' she said glumly. Jo had been looking forward to catching up with the friendly White Witch and reminiscing about their adventures.

The Doctor was deep in contemplation of a

sophisticated lash-up that was presumably all to do with
his endless efforts to get the TARDIS working again. 'You
humans really do have the silliest festivals,' he said, staring
intently at the machine.

'What is that thing, anyway?' Jo asked.

'It's what ensures that the temporal circuits never
overheat when the TARDIS moves between dimensions. It's
like a very tiny –'

'Time fridge?'

He pulled a face at her. 'Oh, really, Jo.' He blinked. 'Why
have you got cat ears and whiskers on?'

They were interrupted by an alarm bell from the
TARDIS. Jo followed the Doctor into the cavernous, glowing
interior, where the noise was ear-splitting.

'It's bound to be something annoyingly urgent.' The
Doctor sighed.

Jo covered her ears. 'Switch it off!'

'I set up this alarm to detect erroneous time technology,'
said the Doctor, his hands roving over the control panels. 'In
case anyone's up to something they ought not to be, or using
something I might find useful for my own experiments . . .
Aha! It's a kind of transmitter. It's operating from a town
not seventy miles from here . . . and it's broadcasting straight
into the Time Vortex.' He looked up with a smile. 'You were

wanting a run out in the car, weren't you?'

'To a *party*.' Jo tapped her cat's tail wistfully against the console. 'Not an investigation.'

But already the Doctor was dashing back into the lab and yanking his black velvet opera cloak off the hatstand. He grinned at her as they exited the TARDIS. 'It's a trip out, isn't it?'

Ange and Terry made their way back home from the woods, emerging from the undergrowth dishevelled and worried. They wouldn't admit it to one another, but they were terrified of what Starman would do to their little brother if they couldn't find the object he needed.

How could we just leave him? Ange thought frantically. *Even for a minute? He's only just started infants' school and we left him there in the woods with . . . with Starman.*

She and Terry had tried to look as if they were just pretending and playing a game. Ian had been so brave, but the electronic arm that held him was clearly nipping his skin. Ange had seen the tears welling up in his eyes. 'We'll be back as soon as we can,' she had promised.

They took a shortcut through the building site, where rows of new houses stood half built, ringed with moats of deep, muddy puddles, and surrounded by machinery that looked like frozen prehistoric monsters.

'He'll be okay,' Ange said, trying to reassure herself as much as Terry.

'Mum is going to kill us . . .' Terry whispered.

They slipped back into the quiet streets of their estate. By now, most of the kids had gone home for the night. The street lamps cast a sickly yellow glow over everything and the tarmac glistened.

'Starman's our friend,' Ange continued. 'He won't hurt Ian.'

'What do we really know about him, Ange?' Terry replied angrily. 'He's a monster! Did you see the way he grabbed hold of him? Our Ian's a . . . *hostage.*'

Ange gulped. Terry was right. 'Then we just have to do exactly what he told us, don't we?'

As they let themselves into their garden, Ange was thinking about the first time they'd found Starman, weeks ago, down in that wooded dell. They'd seen ice-blue lights flickering through the trees and had steeled themselves to approach. They found him in his den, where he had lived secretly for so many years. Tinkering with his machines. Repairing his own body. Talking about escape.

He'd been frightening, but friendly enough. He talked a bit funny and shouted sometimes, but Ange and Terry had been entranced by him. 'A talking robot!' Terry had gasped.

That hadn't pleased Starman at all. 'I am not a ro-bot!' he'd shrieked. 'I am a su-per-i-or be-ing!'

When they finally got home, they could hear their parents rowing before they even opened the door.

'They're at it again,' said Terry with a sigh.

Judging by the broken crockery and smeared food on the kitchen lino, their parents must have started fighting shortly after Dad had got home. The ruckus now blared from the living room, louder than the telly.

'Look at it this way,' Ange said. 'They won't notice us creeping in and out again.' Her heart was beating like crazy. What if they came face-to-face with Mum? How would they explain that a robot was holding Ian prisoner?

But the adults were too absorbed in their fighting to notice.

'Come on,' Terry said, heading upstairs. 'It's in my room.'

They had come to fetch the old 1960s tape recorder Granny Barnes had given them. It had spools of magnetic tape the size of dinner plates – just the thing Starman needed for looping and repeating his message to outer space. It was in a leatherette carry-case. A family heirloom. The kids were loath to hand it over, as the tape held recordings of long-gone family members, aunts, Granny Barnes herself, and even Dad when he was little, singing at Christmas. All these recordings would be lost if they took the recorder into the woods.

'We have to,' insisted Ange, seeing a moment of doubt flicker across Terry's face. 'He's got Ian. We must do *exactly* as he says.'

'I wish we'd never met Starman,' Terry said.

The Doctor's mouth was set in a determined line as he gripped the steering wheel of his vintage yellow roadster, Bessie.

'You've hardly said a word all the way down the motorway,' Jo shouted over the shrieking of the wind.

Glancing at her, the Doctor's expression softened. 'I'm sorry, Jo. It's just that for a moment I was alarmed by the energy signature of that transmission. It could be the most ghastly news.'

'Oh,' she said, trying to look confident. 'Well, I'm sure we'll be able to deal with it, whatever it is.'

She had absolute faith in the Doctor and her smile cheered him up as he veered abruptly off the motorway at the turn-off for New Alverton, a modern and obscure little town that appeared to be the epicentre of the cosmic transmission.

'It's such an ordinary place,' Jo said minutes later, as

they surveyed the housing estates and rows of identical, boxy houses. But by now she knew – after a couple of years with UNIT and the Doctor – that looks could be deceiving and there was no such thing as a completely ordinary place.

The Doctor produced a sophisticated-looking homing device that pulsed with green light. 'We're very close.'

The kids knew it was much too late for them to be out, but what could they do? Starman kept a tight grip on Ian as he worked on the tape recorder. He displayed little gratitude and hardly said a word as he picked apart the device, tugging the shiny tape from its spools.

Eventually Ange spoke up. 'Can we take our little brother home, please? Mum will be frantic.'

Starman wheezed mechanically as he went about his work.

'It'll be worse for you,' Terry said bravely, 'if she phones the police and everyone comes looking for us. They'll search everywhere, especially the woods. They'll find you.'

'I will de-fend my-self as I have done be-fore.'

Neither Ange nor Terry knew what that meant, but there were many horrible tales of people disappearing forever in these woods. Hence the local legend to do with the monster.

Now the machine was rattling and hissing as the tape

ran round. Starman was speaking in an unknown tongue, repeating phrases. The children imagined his message spiralling into the stars.

'Will they come to get you?' asked Ange.

'I do not know.'

'Don't you have family?' Terry said. 'Others like you who'll be worried about you? Who'll want to see you again?'

Starman said, 'I have no fam-i-ly. If it proves ad-van-tage-ous to them, the Da-leks will come here. Per-haps.' His eyestalk flashed cobalt blue. 'And if they come they will con-quer this –' he stopped abruptly. His machine was emitting a high-pitched noise. 'My mes-sage has been in-ter-cept-ed.'

A green light was blinking busily.

'By your kind?' Terry asked.

Starman swivelled round to shout at the children. 'No! By our enemy. He is app-roach-ing! You must bring him here to me! At once!'

'W-who?' asked Ange. 'Who must we bring?'

'The one they call Doc-tor!" shrieked Starman. 'At once!'

Jo and the Doctor had spent almost an hour wandering the labyrinthine streets of the estate. Jo was becoming uneasy about what they were supposed to be on the look-out for. When they reached a small playground she sat on a swing and asked him straight out.

The Doctor rubbed the back of his neck and told her.

'There's a *Dalek* ship somewhere in this town?' she gasped.

'A small one. Clearly lost and out of phase. Probably it was travelling back from the twenty-second century and all the mischief they caused there . . .'

'I remember,' said Jo, reflecting that she'd hardly describe the mayhem she'd witnessed in the future as simple mischief. 'Look, shouldn't we have told the brig straight away?'

The Doctor pulled a face. 'I'm not having the brigadier swarming down here mob-handed with tanks and helicopters. I want to see what's going on first.'

At that moment Jo became aware of a movement in the mist at the other side of the playground. Two figures came to stand underneath the yellow lamp. 'Look!' she said, pointing at them.

The Doctor's head jerked round. 'Who is that?' he asked sharply.

Jo got to her feet. 'They're only children, Doctor. Don't scare them.'

She hurried past the slide and came face-to-face with Ange and Terry. Straight away she could tell there was something terribly wrong. 'It's nearly midnight. What are you doing out so late?'

'H-he's got our kid brother, miss,' Terry burst out. 'And he won't let him go.'

'Who has? Who's got your brother?'

'He has,' Ange said. 'The monster. He's been getting us to help with his machine and it's been okay, but tonight he's finished it and the thing's working and he's gone nasty and taken our kid brother.'

'Where is this person?' Jo asked.

The Doctor crossed the playground in two strides, his cloak billowing behind him. His white hair glowed in the harsh streetlight and the two children shrank back. 'You'd better tell us at once. If I'm right, we're all in the most terrible danger.'

'We can take you to him,' said Terry, reaching out to grab Jo's hand.

Over the years there had been other children – and some adults – who had strayed into the woods and made the monster's acquaintance. Some had been almost as useful as the Barnes children. Starman remembered one child in particular, perhaps as many as twenty Earth years ago, who had brought him a box full of lead soldiers when the Dalek had demanded a supply of metal. The little boy had brought his most treasured possessions quite willingly and watched as the Dalek had heated them up and melted them into a brilliant, shining soup, which he then used to fix the shielding around his interior shell. Almost too late, for the cracks in his interior caused by the crash-landing had partly exposed his vulnerable innermost self to the noxious pollutants of the Terran atmosphere – but the molten soldiers had done their work and saved him. Yes, that boy twenty years ago had saved his life. It had almost been a pity when the time had come to exterminate him.

Pity? The Dalek checked himself. Why was that word even in his vocabulary? Let alone in his thoughts and memories. He was more polluted than he had realised. If only his laser weapon still worked as it had sixty years ago.

'Please,' the human creature they called Ian was whimpering. 'What if they can't find this man? What will you do, Starman?'

The Dalek ignored him. He was feeling annoyed by this present generation of helpers. He noticed that the green light was flashing more frenetically. 'They have lo-ca-ted him. They have brought him in-to the woods.'

'Who is it?' Ian asked.

'He is our great-est –'

They were interrupted by a great burst of laughter. 'You're hardly the scourge of the galaxy, are you?' came a voice that sounded both young and old, loud and soft, confident and yet filled with wonder.

Ian stared as the stranger crouched to enter the tiny den. He was followed by a lady with blonde hair, then Ian's brother and sister.

'Doc-tor.'

'Oh, dear, dear. You *are* in a bad way. Separated from your fleet. Away from your bombs and armies.'

'You will o-bey me!' the Dalek cried.

'I'll do nothing of the sort, old chap.'

'What's the matter with it?' asked Jo.

'You're far from the time and place you're meant to be. You're stuck here,' the Doctor continued. 'Rather like myself.'

'Ex-act-ly,' Starman said. 'We know a-bout your ex-ile to this time zone.'

'You do?' The Doctor frowned.

'News of your shame tra-velled far and wide. Your en-em-ies re-joiced.'

The man in the cloak looked briefly annoyed. 'Why are you involving these children in your undoubtedly wicked schemes?'

'They are help-ing me, as oth-ers have in the past.'

'Yes,' mused the Doctor. 'It looks like you've patched yourself up with all kinds of bits and pieces of junk. It's like a scrapyard in here. I congratulate you on your ingenuity, but this can't go on.'

All at once an ice-blue glare surrounded the Dalek, rippling along his outer shell. Ian felt it creeping coldly up his arm and all over his own body.

'What's he doing to Ian?' shouted Ange. 'Make him stop!'

'Doctor, do something,' gasped Jo.

'Dalek!' said the Doctor in a very calm voice. 'These are hatchlings you are threatening. Juveniles. You will *not* hurt them.'

'You will do as I com-mand, Doc-tor, or they will die.'

'Very well.'

'My mess-age has been sent in-to the Vor-tex to sum-mon the Da-lek fleet.'

'No!' cried Jo.

'If you help me, I will stop them in-vad-ing this planet.'

'Ha!' said the Doctor. 'Who'd want to invade 1973? Your lot are much more interested in the future.'

'They would come here for *you*.'

The Doctor narrowed his eyes. 'Your years of seclusion have sharpened your cunning.' He stepped closer and the crackling intensified. 'Let the boy go and I will help you.'

The clawed arm relinquished Ian, who jumped with surprise. He rubbed the marks on his skin and flew straight into his big sister's arms.

The Doctor was examining his enemy. 'Yes, I can see that you *do* need help, don't you? You're blind, aren't you? And you've no weapon. Your arms are actually kitchen implements. Oh dear . . .' His voice became hushed, betraying his scientific curiosity. Now he was close enough to see that the Dalek's metallic chest cavity was badly smashed. Inside there was a glint of silvery material. It looked rather like a large, primitive tooth filling. There was even, in the darkness, a shimmer of topaz and green flesh belonging to the Dalek mutant deep within the shell. It was a wonder this creature was still alive.

'Jo, would you help me? And you others, too. He won't hurt you now. We must carry him and his strange machine to my car.'

'Where are we taking him?' asked Jo.

'Back to UNIT Headquarters,' said the Time Lord. 'We're going to help him as best we can.'

Jo and the children exchanged worried glances.

'Thank you, Doc-tor,' Starman said painfully.

It was a hellish journey back through the dark woods. The gaps between the trees were narrow and the branches seemed to lash out purposefully, snagging their clothes and trying to drag them back.

Among the junk in the den they had found a set of pram wheels the Dalek had once tried to make use of, and now his middle section sat lopsidedly on top, with the Doctor and Jo pushing from behind. The three children carried the heavy, mutilated radiogram between them.

'If you att-empt to stop the mess-age my mach-ine will self-des-truct and des-troy you,' the Dalek warned.

'Yes, I thought it might.' The Doctor smiled. 'Come on, Jo! Push!'

Only a few lights were on this late in the houses near the car-park. The mist was thicker than ever as they wheeled closer to Bessie. It took some time to manoeuvre the Dalek on to the back seat, with his machine squashed beside him, still bleeping and blinking away.

'Say your goodbyes,' the Doctor told the children.

'We'll never see him again?' asked Ian.

'You are free of your bond,' Starman told them.

'You should thank them for helping you,' Jo said.

'Be grate-ful you have sur-vived our time to-geth-er,' was the best the Dalek could do.

'All right, old chap, that's enough of the sentimental farewells.' The Doctor chuckled. He took off his cloak and laid it like a tarpaulin over the Dalek's head. Then he looked at the children. 'You lot had best get back to your parents.'

'They'll be out of their minds with worry,' said Jo. 'It's gone midnight!'

Ange, Terry and Ian were much more interested in finding out what was going to happen next, but they stood back as the funny old-fashioned car revved its powerful engines and roared off much faster than might have been expected.

'Well, that's the children out of harm's way,' said the Doctor. 'Now to deal with the rest of it.'

'The Dalek's blind and unarmed, isn't it? Why are you still doing what it wants?'

The Doctor tapped his nose. 'There's a lot I can learn from a helpless Dalek. Even a mad and injured one. Its mind is a vast storehouse of future technology.'

Jo suddenly realised. *He's after the Dalek version of the time-travel codes. He's doing this all for himself . . .*

The Doctor put his foot on the accelerator and Jo spent the journey back to UNIT HQ fretting about the ominously quiet Dalek in the back of the car.

In the small hours of the morning, they arrived back at the stately home where UNIT had its British Headquarters. The guards were quite used to the Doctor coming and going at strange times, often bringing with him bizarre equipment, so they waved him sleepily through the main gates.

'We don't want them taking too close a look at what we're carrying,' he muttered, swerving round to the mews buildings at the back of the complex.

Jo questioned the wisdom of what he was attempting. They were smuggling a Dalek into the very heart of UNIT HQ. *Are we getting out of our depth here?* she wondered.

'All right there, old chap?' the Doctor asked, as they manhandled the bulky alien out of the car.

'Are you sure you don't want me to fetch Mike or Sergeant Benton to help?'

The Doctor shot her a severe look.

Keeping the Doctor's cloak draped over their enemy, they pushed him on his improvised wheels into the shrouded corridors of the main building.

'Your TAR-DIS is here some-where,' said the Dalek. Its voice made Jo jump. 'I can sense its pow-er.'

'That's right,' said the Doctor, patting the alien's dome with mock fondness. 'Now, shush. We're going to take you and your marvellous space-telegraph machine to my laboratory and then we can have a little chat.'

After what seemed a horribly long and tense interval they were installed in the lab and Jo watched as the Doctor examined the ruined Dalek. Their captive stared, meanwhile, with rapt attention at the police-box shell of the TARDIS. 'This is the ship that has tak-en you all over the gal-ax-y, war-ring with my race for count-less mill-enn-i-a.'

'I suppose it is, yes.' The Doctor smiled modestly. 'Though I do other things besides fight the Daleks, you know. You *are* a conceited lot, aren't you? Now, don't over-excite yourself, my dear fellow . . .' He peered into the cankered and mildewed interior of the Dalek's casing, astonished once more that the creature was still alive.

A single purple eye stared back from deep within the Dalek shell. It blinked sadly at the Doctor.

'Now, this message of yours to your people. I want you to stop it. Tell them there is nothing for them here in 1973.'

The Dalek laughed croakily, a sound that made Jo's skin crawl. She had never heard a Dalek laugh before.

The Doctor became annoyed. 'I'll turn it off myself. How do I work this?' He hovered over the primitive radiogram. 'Tell me.'

More gurgling laughter.

'You know,' said the Doctor crossly, 'if the Daleks actually respond and come here they won't want anything to do with you. What do your lot want? Purity. Perfection. You're far from that. You're patched together. Falling apart. How long have you lived here?'

'O-ver six-ty Ter-ran years. I crash-lan-ded be-fore that hu-man town was e-ver built. When it was all woods.'

The Doctor stared at him calmly. 'And in that time you have been terribly injured and slowly going half mad.'

'On-ly half mad?' The laughter stopped.

'They'll want nothing to do with you.' The Doctor shook his head. 'They will exterminate *you*.'

'No,' said the monster from the woods. 'They will see that I have brought them to you, Doc-tor. You will be a prize for them. They will be grate-ful to me.'

'They will destroy you. As a result of living sixty years on Earth, you have mutated. You have lived among humans. Depended upon them. Look how you let that smallest child go free. You even regretted holding him hostage. I could hear it in your voice. You're developing a conscience, aren't you?'

'No!' the Dalek cried.

Jo glanced sharply at the Doctor. The conversation was becoming noisy. A part of her wished they'd be heard so that soldiers would come rushing to their rescue.

'Halt that message,' said the Doctor, 'and I will save your life.' He held aloft the elegant wand of his sonic screwdriver, plus another device Jo recognised. 'I can fix your shielding permanently. You're dying, aren't you? That's why everything's become so urgent for you lately. You know you have little time left.'

The Dalek's eye dimmed slightly. 'Ve-ry well. Help me. The mess-age I trans-mit-ted . . . it would ne-ver reach my kind an-y-way. It was de-signed on-ly to capture your att-en-tion, Doc-tor.'

The Doctor raised an eyebrow. 'Well, that's something. Now you can tell me something else: the time codes. Give me access to the Dalek time-travel codes. Then I will help you.'

The creature was puzzled. 'Is that why you brought me here? Not out of fear for the hu-mans, but so that I would help you fix your TAR-DIS?' It laughed raspingly again. 'Fool-ish Doc-tor. To stake so much, to take such a risk, on such a stu-pid hope.'

'What do you mean?'

'I am a low-ly troo-per. I know no-thing of time trav-el. I know so lit-tle.'

'I don't believe you,' said the Doctor.

'If I am be-yond re-pair, my on-ly log-i-cal re-main-ing func-tion is to des-troy you.'

'What?'

Jo jumped in alarm. 'Doctor, he's glowing! What's happening?'

'Oh!' The Doctor looked worried as a strange golden glow suffused the Dalek. 'Er . . . I may have miscalculated.'

'What?'

'I believe he's planning to blow himself up.'

Jo was rooted to the spot in shock.

The Doctor added, 'He'll take the whole of UNIT HQ with him if he puts his mind to it.'

'Do something, Doctor!'

Waves of scarlet energy were now rippling over the cracked hull of the Dalek. His maniacal laughter seemed to fill Jo's whole mind.

'I was rather hoping not to have to do this,' said the Doctor. He held up the device Jo had seen him working on yesterday evening. He shot his cuffs like a stage magician and gained the Dalek's attention. He was holding up the thing Jo had dubbed the 'time fridge'.

'I'm reversing the polarity of this handy implement's neutron flow,' said the Doctor, buzzing it with his sonic screwdriver. Then he tossed it into the cavity in the Dalek's shell.

'Will that help?' Jo shouted into the rapidly worsening din.

'Hopefully it'll make things better rather than worse.'

'But will it stop him from blowing us all sky-high?'

The Doctor looked sorrowful. Almost ashamed. He said, 'It will melt his heart.'

'What?'

'The device will heat up rather than cool, and it will boil the lead that he shielded his mutant self with. The effect will be, I'm afraid, quite deadly.'

The Dalek's pulsating light show ended abruptly. He was no longer capable of building up the energy required to self-destruct. 'What have you done to me?' he shrieked. 'Doc-tor, what is this burn-ing? This heat . . . What have you . . . put in-side . . . my heart?'

Jo looked away as the Doctor stepped up to address his enemy. 'I'm so sorry about this.'

'You were go-ing to help me . . . You said you were go-ing to help!'

'I've killed you,' said the Doctor. 'I'm sorry. I had no other choice.'

Jo tried to close her ears to the Dalek's dying cries. They became so loud that they attracted military attention at last.

It didn't take long for the Dalek to die, or for Brigadier Lethbridge-Stewart to come and marvel at the remains. He stared in amazement at the Doctor. 'Well done for stopping him, Doctor!' the brigadier said.

'No, old chap. Save your congratulations. This was a failure on my part. We might have learned so much from him,' the Doctor said ruefully.

'He would have blown us all into tomorrow,' said Jo.

'Such ingenuity,' said the Doctor. 'Such cunning. What a terrible waste.'

The brigadier slapped his back. 'It was a monster. They're all monsters.'

Jo saw that this night had cost the Doctor greatly.

'He was developing a conscience, wasn't he? He let that child Ian go. But he forced me to destroy him; he forced me to do it.'

Jo knew the Doctor would never forget what he had learned this Hallowe'en.

THE FOURTH DOCTOR

TOIL AND TROUBLE

Written by Richard Dungworth

Fight as she might, Sarah Jane was drowning. She was submerged in a dark, suffocating nightmare of thick, blood-warm liquid. Her lungs screamed to be allowed to inhale. Her oxygen-starved brain was already beginning to cloud with confusion. Tiny stars pricked her blurring vision.

Refusing to surrender, she made one last, desperate bid for survival. She fought to move her leaden limbs, striving to propel herself to the surface – though she could only guess in which direction it lay.

It was no use. Her lungs would surely burst. She *had* to breathe.

Something touched her outstretched arm. A hand. It clamped round her wrist and began to pull. Bony fingers clawed at her shoulder. The pain of their biting grip brought her back from the brink of unconsciousness. More hands grasped at her, tugging her by her hair, her clothing, her other arm. They dragged her limp, energy-sapped body through the murky ooze . . .

As she broke the surface, Sarah Jane sucked in a great, shuddering breath. A violent fit of coughing and spluttering seized her. She was drunkenly aware of being hauled on to dry land, of sharp fingers digging into her flesh. Dumped on her back, she managed to roll feebly on to one side to retch up the bitter, dark fluid she had swallowed. She lay with her chest heaving, too weak and dazed to move. As her breathing gradually calmed, she vaguely registered a voice close by.

'Shall I stop its heart, sister?'

'No, Doomfinger!' The second speaker's voice, like the first, was a rasping croak, cracked with age. 'I have an appetite for living flesh!'

'Patience, Mother Bloodtide!' The third sounded less ancient, but no less harsh. 'We will feast soon enough. But first –'

Sarah Jane winced as something tugged sharply at her wet hair, making her scalp sting.

'Let us learn what we can of our pretty little catch.'

With difficulty, Sarah Jane rose on to all fours. Her head

swam. The surface beneath her crackled under the pressure of her knees and palms. It appeared to be covered in a layer of pale, brittle twigs. It was certainly *not* the floor of the TARDIS attic, as it ought to be.

Only moments earlier, she had been safely aboard the Doctor's remarkable vessel, happily exploring one of the cluttered chambers in which he stashed the souvenirs of his adventures in time and space. She had no idea why she wasn't there still.

Sarah Jane gave a sudden shiver. She had just realised what she was kneeling on. They weren't twigs at all; they were tiny bones.

'Be swift, Mother Bloodtide! It revives!'

'Complete the binding!'

Sarah Jane got unsteadily to her feet. She turned towards the voices . . . and recoiled at the sight of the three hideous hags to whom they belonged. They bore an alarming resemblance to the wicked witches of classic fairy tales: repulsively ugly with straggly grey hair, warts, wrinkled skin, hooked noses, jutting chins and jagged yellow teeth. The scrawny frame of each, bent with age, was wrapped in a ragged, drab cloak and a tattered black shawl. Two had their bloodshot eyes fixed on Sarah Jane. The third, muttering under her breath, seemed preoccupied with something clutched in her gnarled, taloned fingers.

The frightful trio even appeared to have a witch's cauldron of sorts. An area of ground behind them was largely clear of the bone-litter that lay elsewhere. At its centre bubbled a dark circular pool edged by a mud-sculpted rim. The steaming liquid it held was the colour of dried blood. It was from this, Sarah Jane realised, that she had been dragged moments ago. Glistening ooze still clung to her clothes and hair. It had a foul, sulphurous stench.

The muttering hag – one of the two elders – looked up with a gleeful cackle.

'It is done, Lilith!' she croaked. 'The words have been spoken!'

She passed the thing in her grasp to her younger companion, who received it with an unpleasant yellow-toothed grin.

Sarah Jane tried to pull herself together. Witches were the stuff of story-land. She had no idea who these three old crones were, but she shouldn't assume that just because they were ugly they were dangerous. Appearances, as the Doctor had impressed upon her, could be deceptive. She must talk to them. Find out who they were. Communication was key.

Nervously, she tried to make a start . . . but found to her dismay that she was unable to do so. Her mouth refused to

open. Her lips were tightly sealed, as if stitched together. As
Sarah Jane's eyes widened with alarm, the grotesque faces of
the watching hags filled with cruel amusement.

'Hark, mothers!' mocked the one called Lilith. 'It wishes
to speak!'

As her elders cackled nastily, Lilith held out a gnarled
hand to display the object Mother Bloodtide had passed her.
Her eyes narrowed. 'I think *not*, human!'

Her bony fingers were clasped round a crudely made
doll. A lock of brown hair was attached to its wooden head.
Sarah Jane recalled the sharp, painful tug at her scalp. Her
blood ran cold as she saw that the doll's mouth was gagged
with a strip of filthy cloth.

Lilith advanced. Sarah Jane tried to raise her arms to
fend her off, but they also seemed invisibly bound. The hag
brought her hook-nosed face close to Sarah Jane's.

'We shall let you utter no words,' she rasped, eyes full
of malice. Her fetid breath made Sarah Jane's stomach turn.
'For we, more than any, know the power they hold!'

Harry staggered as the floor lurched beneath his feet. 'I say,
Doctor – *what* was *that?*'

The Doctor shooed him back from the control console,
scowling. Harry had grabbed hold of its edge to steady

himself. There wasn't much else to grab in the clinical white console room. Apart from the out-of-place antique hatstand on which the Doctor's battered brown fedora and absurdly long scarf hung, it was all smooth, gleaming surfaces.

'Nothing of consequence,' rumbled the Doctor. 'Just a little temporal turbulence.' He gave Harry a sarcastic smile. 'You didn't expect riding the Time Vortex to be smooth sailing the entire while, did you?'

Harry wasn't sure what to expect any more. Since meeting the Doctor, expectations had quickly come to seem pointless. In the Time Lord's company, it appeared, anything was possible. Harry's mind was still reeling from his previous TARDIS trip – also his first. It hadn't gone terribly well. His accidental interference with something called a 'helmic regulator' had resulted in a drastic change to their course. This explained the Doctor's eagerness to keep him clear of the controls, Harry supposed.

'I expect we crossed a particularly tempestuous time node,' said the Doctor, as much to himself as to Harry. 'An intersection of multiple galactic wars or some such. Unless another TARDIS passed close enough for us to catch a little backwash.'

'I see,' said Harry, which was something of an exaggeration. 'Not to worry,' he continued gamely. 'I'm sure

I'll find my sea legs soon.'

An instant later he went reeling sideways into the nearest wall, as the TARDIS lurched again with considerably more violence.

This time it was the Doctor who clung to the console for support.

'Now *that*,' he growled, 'was rather more interesting.' He hastily studied the console's complex instrumentation. 'Fascinating, in fact. Analysis of the deflection data suggests a definite impact.' He consulted another set of dials. 'The shield readings, too. A collision. Possibly an assault by an active agent.'

Harry rubbed his bruised shoulder. 'What sort of agent?'

'Difficult to say. Whatever it was, it's knocked us way off course. I'll have to recalculate the space–time vectors to get us back on track.' The Doctor threw Harry a wry smile. 'It wouldn't do to keep the brigadier waiting now, would it?'

Judging by the Doctor's tetchy mood since their departure from the Nerva Beacon space station, Harry had the distinct sense that the Time Lord didn't appreciate being at the brigadier's beck and call. It had been the Doctor's own idea to provide the UNIT commander back on Earth with a means to contact him in an emergency: a dedicated Space–Time Telegraph. He seemed less than delighted, however, that the brigadier had seen fit to use it quite so soon.

Another sudden pitch in the TARDIS's flight drove thoughts of the brigadier from Harry's mind. 'Doctor? What's going on?'

As the Doctor pored over the console, his expression darkened. 'Perhaps if you could manage to keep quiet for a moment . . .' He brooded over the read-outs for several seconds. 'Ah-haa!' His shining eyes grew wide. 'We have company, Harry Sullivan!' he declared. '*Reapers*. Several of them, by the looks of it.'

'Reapers?'

'One of the few lifeforms native to the Vortex.'

'And . . . they're mobbing us?'

The floor lurched violently again.

'So it appears!' The Doctor had begun hastily punching buttons and throwing levers – taking evasive action, Harry assumed.

'Judging by the intensity of their attack, I'd say they're trying to force us into an emergency landing.' The Doctor darted round to an adjacent side of the hexagonal console. 'They can't board us while we're in flight. But if the old girl rematerialises, they'll be able to enter at will.'

Harry narrowly managed to keep his feet as another tremor struck. 'What for? What are they after?'

'There's only one thing guaranteed to bring Reapers flocking: a time paradox. Or even the *scent* of one – an anachronism with the potential to create a significant history shift.'

'An anachronism?'

'A temporal anomaly. A thing-out-of-its-time,' snapped the Doctor impatiently. 'Hovercraft in the Middle Ages. Einstein in the Mesozoic. An *anachronism*, man!'

Another jolt shook the TARDIS.

'At the first sniff of temporal corruption, Reapers swarm to its source, like white blood cells to an infection. They materialise in normal space to devour the offending anachronism – and all resulting anomalies. Their action heals any timelines that may have been corrupted.'

'They sort of put history back on track, you mean?' As a medical man, Harry felt a certain empathy with the Reapers' corrective role. 'They sound rather a decent sort.'

Another violent shudder seemed to contradict him. The Doctor made more frantic adjustments to the flight controls.

'Decency has nothing to do with it,' he growled. 'Reapers have no moral or ethical goal. Only an insatiable hunger for temporal anomalies.' He glanced up to give Harry a dark look. 'Such as two twentieth-century humans existing outside their own timeframe.'

Harry processed this, as another Reaper strike hit. 'You think they've come for Sarah Jane and me?'

'No, my dear fellow. I doubt that either of you are significant enough to draw their full attention.'

Harry couldn't help wondering how the feisty Sarah Jane would like being deemed insignificant. It was perhaps a good thing she was off elsewhere, exploring the TARDIS's attic.

'No . . .' mused the Doctor, frowning. 'They must be seeking something we've taken on board – though the what, the how and the when elude me at present.' He gave Harry another grave look. 'Nonetheless, you *will* be in mortal danger if we're forced to rematerialise. We could land anywhere and anywhen. Whatever has attracted them, the Reapers are all too likely to carry out a clean sweep.'

A flashing alert called the Doctor's full attention back to the controls.

'Can't you stop us from landing?' asked Harry.

'For a short while, perhaps. *If* I'm allowed to concentrate,' replied the Doctor testily. 'Why don't you run along and inform Sarah Jane we have guests?'

The Doctor was right, of course, Harry knew. He should find Sarah Jane. If the Reapers were to get in, she shouldn't face them alone.

Harry hurried for the corridor. As another tremor sent

him staggering, he heard the Doctor's booming voice call
after him.

'And don't touch anything!'

Sarah Jane was already facing deadly creatures alone, and
with the horrid doll still in the bony grip of the hag called
Lilith she was powerless to resist them.

All three hags had pressed in around her. Mother
Doomfinger had the palm of one warty hand spread against
Sarah Jane's forehead. Her touch was ice-cold. Doomfinger's
eyes were closed, and she was muttering to herself – strange
rhythmic words that Sarah Jane could not understand.

'Well, sister? Does it know it?' demanded Mother
Bloodtide. 'The Time Lord's true name?'

Lilith's eyes, too, burned with evil anticipation. 'You *will*
yield it to us!' she rasped in Sarah Jane's face. 'He *must* be
named – and die! Were it not for him, our kind would be free
of the Eternals' curse!'

'It is because of his meddling that our Carrionite sisters
still languish in the Deep Darkness!' croaked Bloodtide. She
turned and took a few hobbling steps, until her path was
barred by an arching wall of clouded crystal – part of the
smooth, spherical shell that encapsulated the hags' entire tiny
domain. She dragged her foul fingernails across it, creating

an ear-splitting screech. 'It is he who confined us to this loathsome dimension!'

Sarah Jane tried to make sense of the strange, crystal-bordered space. An image flashed across her mind's eye: the orb of dark crystal, clasped in a macabre metal mounting, that had drawn her attention back in the TARDIS's attic. The last thing she remembered before her near-drowning was reaching for this crystal ball, to take a closer look.

'Gargh!' snarled Doomfinger, snatching her hand away from Sarah Jane's brow. 'The creature's mind swims with words, but our foe's true name is not among them!'

'The Darkness take her!' spat Lilith. 'No matter. There are other ways to end him.'

There was a sudden cracking, splintering sound.

Bloodtide let out a triumphant shriek. 'It begins! Behold!' Her shining eyes were fixed on a thin fracture that had appeared in the wall of crystal before her. 'Our words do their work!' she crowed.

'Words we learned from the Doctor's own lips!' Lilith told Sarah Jane gloatingly.

Doomfinger leered at her. 'We have waited three cycles of his life . . .'

'Listened to three slippery shades of him . . .' hissed Lilith.

'It was *his* knowledge that revealed the words of power we craved.'

'So many shining words – of time, and space, and matter.'

'It was *his* fathomless grief upon which we drew to wield them!'

There was another cracking sound and a second hairline fracture appeared in the crystal shell.

'By translating our prison dimension from the Doctor's time-vessel to its own past shadow as the two crossed in the Vortex, we have rendered it unstable,' Lilith explained gleefully. 'Its boundary has already weakened enough for us to draw you across, pretty one! Soon it will fail entirely!'

'And once we are free,' sneered Doomfinger, 'a mere finger-touch will serve to stop your precious Doctor's heart!'

'*Two* touches, mother, remember?' corrected Lilith. 'To still *two* Time Lord hearts.'

'Yesss, yesss.'

At the sound of more cracks forming, the three hags could barely contain their evil delight.

'When this Doctor of the past is slain, his future selves will turn to dust!'

'No longer to oppose us at the Hour of Woven Words!'

'Our Carrionite kin will be released from the Darkness . . .'

'And the universe will once again know rule by blood and magic!'

Lilith looked to her mothers, rubbing her bony hands together. 'We need wait only a little longer for our freedom – and our vengeance!' She turned her gaze back to Sarah Jane. 'And, while we do, we shall not go hungry.'

Bending, she scooped a handful of tiny bones from the ground. She crushed them, letting their powder run through her gnarled fingers. 'We have fed on dead things fished from the Void for long enough.'

'Eurgh!' spat Bloodtide. 'Cold, lifeless, bloodless things!'

'Since your mind contains no words to aid us . . .' hissed Lilith.

All three hags began to shuffle closer, hunger in their eyes.

'Your flesh will nourish us instead!'

Sarah Jane had never been more desperate to cry out for help, but she had no voice to scream with.

This has to be the place, thought Harry, as the door sliced shut behind him.

'Keep going straight until you cross a bridge,' Sarah Jane had told him, 'then it's the second room on the left. Just in case you need me.'

Harry was glad the directions had been so simple. Even

his brief trek through the TARDIS's interior had left his mind aching. Getting hopelessly lost in its logic-defying space would be all too easy. The bridge, and the deep canyon it spanned, had been quite something. *A canyon inside a police box*, thought Harry, shaking his head. He had seen his share of remarkable technology during his time with UNIT, but the Doctor's dimensionally transcendental craft was off the scale.

Harry cast his gaze around the attic.

'You'll know it when you see it,' Sarah Jane had said. 'It's packed with weird and wonderful junk.'

She hadn't been exaggerating. Harry had never seen such a collection. There were *some* identifiable items among the muddle: a golf caddy crammed with hockey sticks; a section of brightly painted totem pole; a penny-farthing fitted with stabilisers. A nearby crate appeared to be full of assorted toasters. The greater proportion of the hoard, however, was distinctly alien-looking.

A sudden violent lurch made Harry stagger, and brought his mind back to the reason he'd come: the Reapers. He must warn Sarah Jane. Unfortunately, Sarah Jane seemed to be one of the few things the attic did *not* contain. There was no sign of her.

'Sarah Jane?'

No reply. It occurred to Harry that the fierce turbulence

might already have prompted her to return to the console room. But surely he would have run into her? Was there another route back, perhaps?

'Sarah Jane?' He tried a little louder, picking his way through the junk as he moved further into the room. 'Where are you, old girl?'

Sarah Jane was in an evil place, in evil company. Thanks to Harry, however, she was no longer in imminent danger of becoming hag-food. His cries had carried into the crystal-walled space of the Carrionites' prison dimension. On hearing his voice calling for her, Sarah Jane's captors had – to her great relief – swiftly turned their malevolent attention to him.

The three repulsive hags stooped over their mud-sculpted cauldron, scowling at Harry's image in the dark surface of the foul-smelling pool.

'Another meddling human!' croaked Lilith, flexing her gnarled fingers in agitation. 'He must not discover us! The Doctor must not learn of our presence before we are free!'

'Shall I name the wretch?' suggested Mother Bloodtide.

Lilith shook her wrinkled brow. 'A naming may not end him. He is out of his own time. Remember the Dark Lady, mothers. The human Martha Jones.' She spoke the name with loathing.

'What, then?' croaked Doomfinger. 'How shall we silence him?'

Lilith's eyes flashed. Baring her frightful teeth in a wicked grin, she fixed her gaze on Sarah Jane. 'The pretty one can deliver his doom!'

Lilith reached beneath her filthy cloak, and drew out a long, curving dagger. Its hilt was black, its blade a cruel hook of razor-edged bone. She then raised the gagged doll in her other hand, dangling it by its lock of human hair. With a slash of the dagger, she sliced through the hair. As the doll fell to the ground, Sarah Jane felt her invisible bonds release. She found she could open her mouth.

'You're mad!' she told Lilith defiantly, backing away. Her eyes darted around for something with which to defend herself. 'Why would I hurt Harry?' It was such a relief to be able to speak, to move. 'There's nothing you can say or do that would make me!'

Lilith cackled nastily. She had produced something else from under her cloak. It was a primitive string puppet. An ugly marionette.

'Oh, but there is!'

With a twist of her bony fingers, Lilith attached the lock of hair to the puppet's head, muttering as she did so. Then, leering at Sarah Jane, she let the puppet dangle by its strings.

She tugged on the string attached to its right hand.

To her horror, Sarah Jane felt her own right hand jerk upwards.

Lilith jiggled the puppet's strings again – and Sarah Jane found herself walking, against her will, straight towards the cauldron. The jerky movements of her limbs were awkward and clumsy.

'What are you doing? Stop it!' she shrieked at Lilith.

Lilith only pressed the hilt of the bone dagger into Sarah Jane's unresisting grip.

Bloodtide and Doomfinger were watching with wicked delight.

'A few words, I think, before we send her back,' croaked Bloodtide. 'Dark deeds are best accomplished under cover of darkness!' Turning to the cauldron, she extended a hand over it and began to chant.

'*By fourteen sister-worlds aligned . . .*'

As Lilith's puppetry made her stagger to the cauldron's edge, Sarah Jane tried desperately to resist.

'I won't do it! I'll . . . I'll tell him to run!'

Mother Doomfinger descended upon her, holding a tiny glass vial from which wisps of green vapour were rising. With a puff of stinking breath, Doomfinger blew a cloud of the vapour straight into Sarah Jane's face.

'You will tell *nothing*!' she sneered.

The potion took immediate effect. The last thing Sarah Jane heard, before her eyes rolled back and her mind slipped into oblivion, was Mother Bloodtide's continuing incantation.

'*We quench the light, our prey to blind!*'

'Terrific!' muttered Harry bitterly. '*Not* what the doctor ordered.'

A black-out was the last thing he needed. As yet another tremor shook the TARDIS, he staggered awkwardly in the gloom.

Thankfully, the sudden failure of the lighting had not plunged the attic into total darkness. As Harry's eyes adjusted, he realised that a faint greenish glow was coming from something luminescent somewhere among the Doctor's muddle of memorabilia. The eerie green light enabled him to get his bearings. He shuffled cautiously back towards the sealed door, hoping that when it opened he would find the corridor beyond still fully lit. The Reaper onslaught had presumably caused the black-out. If it was more widespread, finding his way back to the console room would be tricky.

Harry froze. He had heard something behind him.

He turned to find nothing but shadows.

'Sarah Jane? Is that you, old girl?'

He heard the apprehension in his own voice, felt it grip his heart. His sudden sense of dread was irrational, he knew, but compelling. *Buck up, old boy*, he told himself firmly. *You're too old to be afraid of the dark.*

'Sarah Jane?'

Silence and stillness. He was imagining things.

He turned back towards the door . . . and found himself face-to-face with a nightmarish ghoul.

Raw shock robbed Harry of the ability to react. To his horror and confusion, he recognised the creature that came looming from the murk. It was Sarah Jane – but not the Sarah Jane that Harry knew. Her eyes were horribly wrong. Only the whites of her eyeballs showed. Her sodden clothes and hair clung to her, slimed with a dark, glistening ooze. She had a pale, curved blade grasped in one hand, raised to strike. As she lunged at him, her body moved in an awkward, jerking fashion.

Harry had no time to save himself. The dagger was already slicing down towards his chest when the floor shook violently once more.

Sarah Jane's blade slashed harmlessly through thin air, as both she and Harry went sprawling. Harry crashed down into a pile of junk, sending it tumbling and clattering in all directions. He scrambled back to his feet, desperate to defend himself against the next attack, but none came.

Sarah Jane had fared rather worse in her fall. She lay unmoving on the floor beside the sturdy metal trunk with which she had collided. Harry could see the pale dagger lying not far from her side.

He approached her warily, kicking the blade away. As he crouched over her, she gave a feeble groan, then let out a sigh. Harry was baffled to see twin wisps of green vapour escape her nostrils, then dissolve away.

Sarah Jane's eyelids flickered open. To Harry's great relief, her eyes had returned to their normal state.

'Harry?' Her voice was weak.

'Take it easy, old girl. You're in a bad way. Whatever happened to you?'

Sarah Jane didn't reply – only twisted her neck feebly to look over to her right. Harry sensed that she was trying to direct his attention to something. He followed her gaze.

Nestled amid one of the heaps of assorted junk was a glowing, glassy orb. It closely resembled a fortune-teller's crystal ball, but for the fact that its dark surface was veined with luminous hairline cracks. It was from these cracks that the eerie green light that dimly lit the attic was escaping.

Sarah Jane turned her bleary eyes back to Harry.

'Witches . . .' she murmured. 'From . . . the future.'

Harry could see that she was fighting her confusion to convey something urgent.

'Mustn't . . . touch!' With another sigh, she slipped into unconsciousness.

Harry anxiously checked her over. There was no sign of serious injury; her breathing was regular and her pulse strong. Her body was evidently demanding that she sleep off whatever trauma had left her in her present sorry state. He carefully moved her into the recovery position, then took stock.

What had Sarah Jane been trying to tell him? He turned her words over in his mind. *Witches?* That made no sense. And that reference to something from the future? He recalled the Doctor's talk of 'a-thing-out-of-its-time'.

Harry turned his gaze back to the glowing crystal sphere – and half thought he glimpsed a hideous face glowering back at him. But it was hard to look directly at the thing now. The veins of green light in its glassy surface had increased in number and intensity. Peering at it through screwed-up eyes, Harry suddenly knew, beyond a doubt, that it was *this*, whatever it was, that had brought the Reapers down upon them.

The Doctor had a plan. He knew just what he had to do in order to save his human companions. Finding a way to do it, however, was proving far from easy. And he was rapidly running out of time.

'*Think*, you addle-brained old fool!' he scolded himself, reaching urgently for the switches beside a twitching shield-meter.

He had tried every evasive trick up his sleeve to shake off the Reapers, but the TARDIS was being buffeted more fiercely than ever. Tough as she was, she wouldn't take much more. It was only a matter of time before her self-preservation reflex triggered an emergency rematerialisation.

That needn't spell doom, the Doctor knew. If he could only ensure that the forced landing took place on Earth, in the last third of the twentieth century, Sarah Jane and Harry should be spared. That was the plan. That way, neither of his companions would represent an anachronism at the moment of the Reapers' purge. They'd be in their own timeframe. The Reapers ought to leave them be. He had little fear of them taking him. A Time Lord could hardly be out of his proper temporal place. He belonged anywhere and anywhen.

Which is to say nowhere, thought the Doctor darkly.

The problem lay in securing the targeted landing. He had already made several attempts to program the necessary vectors. Each time, before he could complete the task, a

violent Reaper strike had caused a major course deflection –
rendering his calculations useless.

'Gaaargh!'

He let out a bellow of frustration as another wild jolt
scuppered his fifth attempt to attain the crucial destination
lock. This latest jolt, however, brought inspiration. It
dislodged something on the console. The Doctor watched
it skitter across the control panel. He snatched it up, eyes
shining. A manic smile lit his face.

'The Space–Time Telegraph! By the Seven Systems!
Of course!'

Since their hurried departure from the Nerva Beacon,
the Doctor hadn't given the device another thought. He had
used the source coordinates of the brigadier's mayday signal
to set a course, then put the telegraph aside. Now he saw it
held the answer.

The brigadier's transmission – a psionic beam – would
have left a residual charge trail across the Vortex. Faint and
only short-lived, yes . . .

'But if the old girl's sensors can trace it before it fades . . .'

The Doctor hastily inputted the necessary algorithms.
If the TARDIS's navigational systems could lock on to
the psionic beam's trail, they could auto-adjust after any
deflection. She could follow it home.

As the Doctor launched the tracer program, another Reaper strike rocked the TARDIS. Warning lights blinked urgently at him from the console. Every read-out screamed at him that his faithful craft was in a critical state, desperate to exit the Vortex, desperate to prevent herself and her crew from terminally disintegrating within it. He fought to override her emergency abort procedures for a few more seconds – precious seconds the tracer program needed.

'Come on! *Come on!*' he urged, his wide-eyed stare fixed on the console viewscreen.

Another tremor struck.

The Doctor threw back his head to rage at his craft's unseen assailants. 'Confound you, you devils! What is it you *want?*'

'Doctor!'

Harry burst into the console room. He was in his shirtsleeves, having used his sports jacket to bundle up something he was carrying at arm's length. The something was emitting a powerful green glow that penetrated its jacket wrap. There was a mixture of triumph and panic in Harry's eyes. 'I've found it!'

The green glow suddenly flared to a dazzling glare. With a look of dismay, Harry released his incandescent burden. The crystal ball he had carried from the TARDIS's attic spilled from its wrap, then fell and disintegrated in a blinding explosion of energy before it could hit the floor.

Three dark forms came swooping from the epicentre of the blast. Each split the air with a bloodcurdling screech as it grew and mutated into a huge wraith-like creature.

In this, their natural form, Lilith and her mothers were infinitely more terrifying than in their guise as hags. As they swooped and circled, the billowing of their cowled cloaks revealed a hideous alien anatomy beneath. Their faces were a fleshless nightmare of raven-like beak, lipless mouth and protruding jaw. Their grotesquely outsize hands had long, thin, clawing fingers.

Harry, wide-eyed with horror, pressed himself back against the wall.

But the Carrionites had no interest in Harry.

Eyes burning with vengeance, they circled the Doctor menacingly, as he gaped at them, for once tongue-tied with surprise.

'We have him, mothers!' screeched the vile creature that had tormented Sarah Jane as Lilith.

'No silken words, Doctor?' mocked Doomfinger. She let out a crowing cackle. ''Tis well. None can save you now!'

'Your doom,' screamed Bloodtide, preparing to strike, 'has come!'

With a cheerful bleep, a green indicator lit on the console. Its viewscreen flashed up an alert. The tracer had locked on.

'Hold tight, Harry!' With a yell, the Doctor lunged for the controls. He threw a lever, and all hell broke loose.

An emergency landing meant an accelerated, no-frills rematerialisation: no spatial dampeners, no temporal stabilisers, just several seconds of whirling, whooshing, juddering mayhem, ending in an almighty, bone-shaking thud.

Even before the time-rotor column had stopped moving, the Reapers too burst from the Vortex. They materialised through the TARDIS's walls like three vast, grey, bat-winged phantoms. They were formidable creatures, each with a long scythe-tipped tail and six barbed limbs, the strongest of which were stretched with a leathery membrane to serve as wings. Red eyes burned in a bizarrely angular head with no mouth. Instead, each Reaper had a gaping chest-maw: a hideous, fang-lined opening in its thorax.

They fell upon the Carrionites with awesome swiftness.

For Harry's instinct had been right: it *was* the time-shifted crystal ball and the beings within it that had brought the Reapers rushing. It was the Carrionites' attempt to change their fate by erasing their nemesis – the Doctor – from the past that had created the time paradox the Reapers had scented.

The three Carrionites would have been a match for

all but the most deadly of foes. Reapers, however, were predators of a different order. The first to attack plucked Bloodtide from the air and drove her, screeching, down on to the console-room floor, where it enveloped her in its mighty, smothering wings. Within moments, Lilith and Doomfinger had been brought down and pinioned in similar fashion.

The Reapers' limbs and wings stifled the screeching, thrashing resistance of their victims as their chest-maws went about their gruesome business, tearing and swallowing ravenously.

Then suddenly the horror was over.

Their prey consumed, the Reapers dematerialised as quickly as they had come, dissolving back into the Time Vortex in the blink of an eye. As they withdrew, history restored itself, timelines realigned, healed, resumed their uncorrupted paths . . .

Harry staggered as the floor lurched beneath his feet. 'I say, Doctor – *what* was *that?*'

As the time rotor eased to a standstill, the Doctor glowered at him.

'A perfectly good landing is what that was,' he growled. 'As anyone who knew one end of a helmic regulator from the other would appreciate.'

Sarah Jane came hurrying into the console room.

'Are we there?' she said eagerly. 'And where *is* there, by the way?'

'Exactly where it should be,' replied the Doctor, with a pointed look at Harry. He grabbed his scarf and led the way out through the TARDIS's open door into a rugged, rolling landscape of gorse bushes and heather.

'Scotland, 1975,' rumbled the Doctor. 'Or thereabouts. Certainly within striking distance of the brigadier –' with a flourish, he produced a tartan-rimmed, feather-plumed tam-o'-shanter from behind his back and tugged it down over his wild curls – 'or I'll eat my hat!' He grinned broadly.

Sarah Jane was still admiring the view. 'I *adore* the Scottish moors!' she declared, beaming. 'They make me think of Shakespeare's *Macbeth*.'

'The Scottish play?' said Harry. 'We did that at school.'

'Murder, intrigue and witchcraft!' said Sarah Jane with relish.

'Witchcraft?' The Doctor pulled a sceptical face. 'Poppycock!' He made a final adjustment to his unique hat. 'Come along, then. This way!'

And he set off purposefully through the moorland heather, his two human companions following dutifully in his wake.

5

THE FIFTH DOCTOR

MARK OF THE
MEDUSA

Written by Mike Tucker

'Doctor! It is so good to see you once more. *Bene!*' Tegan and Turlough watched in amusement as a large man with an expensive-looking suit and a broad Italian accent engulfed the Doctor in a bear-hug that practically lifted him off his feet.

The Doctor struggled to free himself from the man's grip, obviously embarrassed by this show of affection. 'It's good to see you too, Vittorio. You're looking well.'

Releasing the Doctor, the man patted his ample stomach. 'A little *too* well, eh, my friend? Perhaps I need to take a few trips with you in your TARDIS. Travelling with you is always a good way of keeping fit, yes?'

'You're not wrong there,' said Tegan with a laugh.

As the man turned his attention to Tegan and Turlough, the Doctor hurried to make introductions. 'Tegan, Turlough, this is my good friend Professor Vittorio Levi.'

The man gave a short bow, then took Tegan's hand and kissed it theatrically. 'Friends of the Doctor are certain to be friends of mine.'

He then took Turlough's hand in a crushing grip. 'Although the Doctor seems to change his travelling companions as often as he changes his face, yes?' He laughed uproariously at his own joke. 'Still, you are all welcome. *Benvenuti!*'

'Vittorio.' The Doctor caught hold of the professor's arm. 'You sent a message asking me to come at once. What seems to be the trouble?'

'Trouble? There is no trouble, my friend! I invite you to my party!'

'A party?' Tegan's ears pricked up at that.

'Si, signorina Tegan. Does the Doctor never take you to any parties?'

'No, he does not!' Tegan glared pointedly at the Doctor. 'His idea of a good time is finding something appallingly dangerous.'

'And then making sure that we are right in the middle of it,' agreed Turlough.

'That's hardly fair.' The Doctor looked hurt. 'I always do my best to find things that are interesting, stimulating . . . It's not my fault if those situations also turn out to be dangerous.'

Levi gave another enormous belly-laugh and clapped the Doctor on the back. 'Well, I can assure you that you will find no danger here.'

'And where exactly is here, Vittorio?' asked the Doctor hesitantly. 'I mean, I'm aware that we are in a space station orbiting Earth, but –'

'Ah, but this is no ordinary space station,' Levi interrupted.

'Then what is it?' asked Turlough.

'Come, let me show you.'

Linking arms with a surprised Tegan, Professor Levi led the three time travellers from his office (which was large enough to contain not only his huge desk, but the TARDIS as well) and ushered them along a short corridor towards an impressive set of double doors.

'This –' Levi opened the doors with a flourish – 'is the greatest museum the human race has ever seen!'

Tegan stared in astonishment at the huge atrium in front of her: a grand circular space with twelve pillared galleries radiating from it like the spokes of a wheel. Every inch of floor and wall space was lined with sculptures, paintings, and display cases crammed with treasures from antiquity.

The Doctor scurried forward, gazing up in delight at a large marble statue of a bearded man. 'But isn't this Ammannati's statue of Neptune from the fountain in Florence?'

'Quite correct, Doctor.' Levi stood in the centre of the atrium, pointing at each of the radiating galleries in turn. 'Greece, Italy, Syria, Egypt . . . The antiquities of all the Earth are gathered here in this museum.'

'But why?' asked Tegan. 'Why remove them from Earth in the first place?'

Levi regarded her sadly. 'You are from the twentieth century, yes? Even in your time, the damage being caused by pollution to these priceless artefacts was of concern to scholars like me. A hundred years later . . .' He shrugged. 'Well, in order to preserve what was left of our past, we needed to look to the technology of the future.'

'But this must have cost a fortune!' Tegan said.

'Several fortunes,' agreed Levi. 'Luckily there are still enough people on the Earth willing to use their wealth and influence for the greater good.'

'It's magnificent,' said the Doctor, staring around in obvious approval.

'It is indeed. And tonight, my friends, you shall be my guests at the grand opening gala!'

■

'Tegan. We're going to be late.' The Doctor rapped impatiently at the door of Tegan's room.

'Just hold on a minute, will you?' came the irritated voice from inside. 'I'm not ready yet.'

Turlough rolled his eyes at the Doctor. 'Earthlings . . .'

After Professor Levi had finished showing them around the museum, the Doctor, Tegan and Turlough had returned to the TARDIS to get ready for the evening reception. Fortunately, the time machine contained an extensive wardrobe, and the Doctor and Turlough had already changed into smart dinner suits.

The door to Tegan's room opened at last, and she emerged into the corridor wearing a chic, brightly-patterned cocktail dress.

'How do I look?' she asked.

'You look fine!' said the Doctor, oblivious to how beautiful she was. 'Now hurry up or we'll miss the start of Vittorio's speech.'

The Doctor strode off along the corridor, and Tegan and Turlough hurried after him. As they entered the console room, a tall silver robot looked up from the controls.

'Ah, Kamelion, there you are,' said the Doctor. 'I'd wondered where you had got to.'

'Merely recharging, Doctor.' The robot cocked his head to one side. 'You have changed your appearance?'

'Only superficially.' The Doctor grinned. 'Although having your shape-shifting abilities would have certainly been a benefit in speeding things along.'

'Hey!' Tegan glared at him. 'An evening gown takes a little more preparation than a dinner suit, you know.'

Kamelion regarded their outfits. 'You are going to a formal event of some kind?'

'Ah, yes,' said the Doctor. 'A reception. A party.'

'May I come too?'

'Er, I'm not sure that's a good idea. You might attract rather too much attention.'

If a robot could look disappointed, then Kamelion managed it.

The Doctor patted him consolingly on the shoulder. 'I'll bring you back a vol-au-vent,' he joked.

The Doctor then turned to the console, operating the door control and ushering his companions out of the control room.

'Don't wait up,' Tegan called back over her shoulder.

Kamelion watched them go in silence.

The party was in full swing by the time the Doctor and his companions arrived. As soon as they stepped through the doors, several smartly dressed waiters hurried forward to greet them, thrusting glasses of champagne into their hands.

They were in one of the huge observation galleries situated on the rim of the space station, and the huge glass windows offered spectacular views of Earth below. Tegan would have been quite happy to stand and gawp at the view, but the Doctor was insistent that they listen to the speeches, and pushed them forward through the elegant crowd towards the small podium that had been set up at the far end of the room.

What followed was a long (and, as far as Tegan was concerned, extremely boring) half hour, during which a series of elderly men and women of differing nationalities took to the stage and spoke in sombre and ponderous tones about the importance of the museum and of the preservation of history. Tegan could only stare longingly at the buffet table on the far side of the room, which was covered in delicious-looking food that sat untouched.

Finally, and to tumultuous applause, Professor Levi took to the stage. His rich Italian accent was a welcome contrast to the previous speakers, but when he too started to speak about the vital role the museum played for the culture of Earth, Tegan found her mind wandering once more. She was only half listening when one phrase caught her attention, causing her to look up in alarm.

Levi had his arms wide and was gesturing expansively at the panoramic windows. 'Yes, my friends,' he was saying, 'you should all be proud of the part you have played in the creation of this great wheel in space.'

A great wheel . . . wondered Tegan. Why did that sound so familiar?

'This space station will now become part of human history itself,' continued Levi. 'As the wheel turns, civilisations will rise. As the wheel turns, civilisations will fall.'

Wheel turns, civilisations rise. Wheel turns, civilisations fall. Something about the phrase echoed in Tegan's mind. It was making her dizzy. She needed to get some air, to go and sit somewhere quiet.

Ignoring the puzzled looks of several other partygoers, Tegan pushed her way through the crowd, and made her way out of the observation gallery and back to the museum atrium. The huge space was cool and calm, and she tried to clear her head, but Levi's words kept swirling in her mind, over and over. The dizziness overwhelmed her, and she looked around for somewhere to sit down, but the atrium offered nothing as far as she could see. Choosing one of the radiating galleries at random, Tegan set off in search of a quiet seat, but it soon became clear that the architects of the museum had not designed it with the comfort of its visitors in mind.

'Typical,' muttered Tegan groggily.

Her head was pounding now, her eyelids becoming impossibly heavy. The statues around her seemed to loom from the shadows, creatures from myth and legend, their eyes following her as she staggered almost drunkenly through their midst.

Finally, it all became too much for her.

She dropped to the floor in a dead faint.

Elsewhere in the museum, the door of Professor Levi's office creaked open and the long, empty corridor echoed with a low, drawn-out hiss. Slowly, cautiously, something started to move along the corridor, slithering over the marble floors.

Triggered by the movement, lights in the ceiling snapped on. The thing gave a hiss of displeasure, recoiling against the wall as the corridor was bathed in warm amber light.

Shielding its eyes from the glare, the thing slid forward, finally locating a lighting control panel next to the far door. Clawed fingers scrabbled at the controls, and razor-sharp nails raked across the metal, sending long, curling ribbons of paint coiling to the floor. With a shriek of metal, the thing tore the panel from the wall. There was a shower of sparks as the knife-like claws slashed and tore at the wiring inside.

The corridor was plunged once more into blackness.

With a rattling cry of satisfaction, the thing slipped through the door and out into the darkened museum.

Levi was making his closing remarks when the lights suddenly went out. Someone let out a shrill scream, and an uneasy muttering flickered through the crowd.

'Please, my friends, there is no reason to be alarmed.' Levi did his best to keep the situation calm. 'I am sure this is merely a small technical error and the lights will be restored momentarily.'

The Doctor peered around the room. Everything was now bathed in the cool blue light from Earth, which cast long shadows across the floor.

'Where's Tegan?' he asked.

Turlough glanced at the people around him, then shrugged. 'She was here a moment ago.'

'Of all the times for her to wander off . . .' The Doctor sighed. 'Come on, we'd better go and find her.'

Harry Gordon was on his way back from the kitchen with more champagne when everything was plunged into darkness. He stopped, heart pounding, waiting for the emergency lights to kick in, but for some reason they didn't.

After a few moments, his eyes began to grow used to the dark and he started to calm down. If this had been some kind of emergency, there would have been alarms; the fact that the station was so silent meant it was more likely to be a simple technical malfunction or something similar.

Except that the station wasn't *totally* silent.

From the far side of the atrium, Harry heard something: a strange, wet, slithering noise.

'Who's there?' he called.

The slithering noise came again, and Harry started to edge forwards, trying to see if he might be able to get a glimpse of whatever was causing it.

He gave a yell of pain as his shins cracked against something hard, and he threw out an arm to stop himself from falling. As he did so, one of the bottles of champagne slipped from his grasp and shattered on the floor. He reached his free hand out in front of him to feel for whatever it was that he had collided with. His fingers touched cold marble. He'd walked right into the statue of Neptune that stood in the centre of the atrium.

Glass crunching underfoot, he leaned forward to place the unbroken bottle of champagne on the plinth at the base of the statue. As he straightened up again, he was suddenly aware that a new noise – a hissing, wheezing breathing – had joined that awful wet, sliding sound. It sounded close. Very close.

Just as Harry turned around, the emergency lighting finally came on.

Harry found himself face-to-face with a creature that he could never have imagined in his worst nightmares.

Even as he drew in the breath to scream, Harry felt the most unpleasant sensation start to grow within him. A numbness spread out from his body and along his arms and legs, making him feel slow, heavy and oh so cold.

As the dying scream burst from his lips, Harry realised that he recognised the face of the creature.

It was someone he had served champagne to at the party.

'There,' said the Doctor, looking up in satisfaction as the dull red emergency lighting flickered to life.

He replaced the cover on the lighting control panel and scrambled to his feet. He had intended to keep well out of the way and let the space station's technical crew do their job, but after several minutes of searching for Tegan in the dark the Doctor had decided to take matters into his own hands.

'Do you know what caused the black-out?' asked Turlough.

'No.' The Doctor shook his head. 'But that little lash-up should give us some light while we find the trouble.'

A terrified scream echoed through the gallery.

'What was that about finding the trouble?' said Turlough.

'That came from the atrium.' The Doctor raced off towards the source of the noise.

Turlough caught up with the Doctor at the base of the statue of Neptune that had caught his attention when they had first arrived. He frowned. The Doctor was busy examining another, smaller statue alongside it that Turlough didn't recognise.

'That wasn't there before,' he pointed out.

'Quiet a moment, Turlough.' The Doctor's face was grim. 'This could be serious.'

The Doctor stooped down and picked up what looked like the neck of a broken champagne bottle. He examined it, then placed it on the plinth at the base of the Neptune statue, alongside an intact bottle of champagne.

As Turlough looked more closely at the new statue, he realised with a start that he recognised the stone figure in front of him. It was one of the waiters who had been serving at the party. 'Doctor –' he started.

'Shhh!' the Doctor interrupted urgently, holding up a warning finger. 'Did you hear that?'

A horrible slithering noise was echoing around the atrium. Turlough and the Doctor looked at each other, then turned in tandem away from the statue of Neptune.

Emerging from the door to one of the galleries behind them was a terrifying creature.

The creature appeared to be female – or at least half of it looked like a female human. From the waist up, it had the shape of a woman – slim, bare-shouldered and with serpentine tattoos winding down each arm – but in place of legs a long snake-like body coiled and twisted, green scales sliding across each other, the thin tail twitching and quivering. Its face could almost have been described as beautiful if not for the way that the mouth curled into a leering snarl, and for the hate that glared from the dark eyes set beneath the creased and angry brow.

Worst of all, though, were the snakes that writhed and twisted in a ghastly parody of hair. As Turlough took a stumbling step backwards, the snakes turned as one, fixed him with the same blazing glare and bared their fangs.

At that moment Turlough recognised the creature's face. 'Doctor . . .' he stammered. 'It's . . . it's Tegan!'

'Not possible.' The Doctor was staring in disbelief. 'It's just not possible.'

With a hiss of anger, the creature raised its arms and a

fiery red glow started to burn within its eyes.

The Doctor grabbed Turlough's arm. 'Quickly, Turlough, turn away from it!'

Turlough did as he was instructed. 'But what's happened to her?'

'I don't know,' the Doctor confessed. 'What I *do* know is that if we want to avoid the fate of that waiter over there, then we must not look into her eyes.'

Turlough could hear the thing slithering closer to them, its hissing breath getting louder and louder.

'Ah, Doctor. There you are!' A familiar voice boomed across the atrium, and Turlough glanced over his shoulder to see Professor Levi and a small group of partygoers making their way towards them. With a startling turn of speed, the creature whipped round to face the newcomers.

'Don't look at her eyes, Vittorio!' yelled the Doctor. 'Run! All of you!'

There were screams of terror as most of the group turned to flee, Levi among them. One unfortunate woman was too late though, staring at the creature in disbelief as it bore down on her. There was a horrible, brittle cracking noise, and the woman's skin instantly started to harden, her body stiffening as all the soft tissue was turned to cold, grey stone.

Its grisly task complete, the creature slithered off in pursuit of Levi and the others, who had by now disappeared from the atrium.

Turlough could only gaze on in horror. 'Why is she doing this?'

'More to the point, *how* is she doing this?' The Doctor's face was a mask of confusion. 'Transmutation of matter like that is not possible for any organic creature to –' He broke off, eyes widening. 'It's not Tegan,' he gasped. 'It's Kamelion.'

'Kamelion?'

'Yes. Using the same transformative energies that he uses for his own shape-shifting.' Another insight struck the Doctor. 'He's being controlled by Tegan's subconscious!'

He turned to face Turlough, his voice urgent. 'Turlough, go after the others. Warn them of the danger. And, whatever you do, don't look into her eyes once they start to glow.'

'Where are you going?'

'I must find Tegan. The *real* Tegan.'

Before Turlough could argue, the Doctor had set off into the bowels of the museum, yelling back over his shoulder as he went. 'Remember Perseus!'

As the Doctor made his way through the gloomy museum galleries, his mind was racing. The tattoos on the snake creature's arms flashed up in his memory. Far from being purely decorative, they were all too familiar to the Doctor. He had seen those marks before. The mark of the Mara.

He had encountered the Mara twice before. It was a dark force that hid in the mind, in dreams – in the Dark Places of the Inside. The Mara desperately wanted a physical form, and used fear as its weapon. The image of the snake was almost like its calling card.

It would seem that, in their last encounter, the Doctor had failed to destroy the dark force entirely, and it had lain dormant somewhere, waiting for another opportunity to achieve its goal of existence in the real world. Kamelion had been perfect for its needs. Now its objective was to create fear – fear that would feed its power.

The Doctor had to move quickly if there was to be any hope of defeating it this time around.

He stopped at a map of the museum that was affixed to one of the walls.

Somewhere in this museum, Tegan was sleeping, her dreams helping to shape the creature that had been created. Given the form that it had taken . . .

The Doctor tapped his finger on the map. 'The Greek gallery.'

■

'No, please, signor Turlough. Those are priceless.'

Vittorio Levi watched in despair as Turlough forced open more and more display cabinets and began handing out swords and spears to the frightened guests.

'We have to have the means to defend ourselves, Professor.'

'But, if I can just reach my office, I can call for help, and there will be no need for this vandalism.'

'And reaching your office might have been an option if there wasn't something unpleasant slithering around out there trying to kill us, wouldn't it? You were lucky to make it this far.'

They really had been lucky. Turlough had followed the group of frightened partygoers as they had fled from the pursuing creature, only to lose them amongst the spectacular exhibits in the Egyptian gallery. As he had cautiously made his way through the towering columns and obelisks, he'd suddenly become aware of someone waving frantically at him from the shadows cast by a vast stone sphinx.

Hurrying over, he had found Levi and the others huddled in the space between the statue's outstretched paws. Any questions that he might have had were quickly silenced as Levi pointed towards the far side of the gallery.

The creature was there, writhing around the stone

remains of two more victims. That had stiffened Turlough's resolve; the Doctor had given him the task of warning these people of the danger, and now two more were dead. He had to do something.

As they had watched, the creature began to move slowly through the gallery, obviously searching for them. As the professor and the remaining partygoers had become more agitated, Turlough looked around desperately for a solution.

A sign above a doorway had caught his eye: ANCIENT ROMAN GALLERY. The endless history lessons from Brendon Public School popped into Turlough's head – in particular a textbook that had featured dozens of illustrations of gladiators.

'Weapons.'

Urging everyone to keep quiet, Turlough had led the frightened group through the endless lines of Egyptian statues and into the neighbouring gallery. Here there were fewer statues, but dozens of glass display cases; cases filled with swords, spears and, most importantly, polished shields.

Now, with a Roman short sword in one hand and one of those shields on his arm, Turlough was beginning to feel a little more confident. He held up the shield, using its polished surface to watch the door behind him for signs of movement. Levi watched him with interest.

'The legend of the Medusa? Snake-headed, turning people into stone with just a stare?' The doubt in the professor's voice was clear. 'Surely you don't believe . . .'

'Whether I believe it or not doesn't really matter, does it?' said Turlough bluntly. 'The fact is, that creature is *acting* like the Medusa, and so we must act like the ancient Greek hero who defeated her: Perseus.'

Professor Levi looked thoughtful. 'By only viewing her through reflections.'

Turlough nodded. 'Help me explain to the others. And quickly, before the creature finds us again.'

Locating Tegan proved even easier than the Doctor had anticipated: she was right at the centre of the Greek gallery, slumped at the feet of a huge bronze statue of Zeus, her dress crumpled around her and her head resting on her arms. As the Doctor hurried over, he could see that she was deep in a troubled sleep, her brow furrowed, her eyes flicking to and fro beneath her eyelids.

Gently he eased her off the floor, leaning her back against the marble plinth at the statue's base.

'Tegan.' He shook her gently by the arm. 'Tegan, it's the Doctor.'

Still asleep, she pulled away from him sharply, a hiss of

displeasure escaping her lips.

The Doctor shook her again, harder this time. He was aware that waking her so abruptly was dangerous – but not as dangerous as letting her sleep.

'Tegan, you must listen to me. You must wake up.'

From somewhere nearby came a series of terrified screams.

The Doctor was running out of time.

Turlough watched in horror as the Tegan-Medusa slithered through the doorway of the Roman gallery, the snakes on its head hissing venomously.

Gripping the sword tightly in his hand, Turlough started to back away, making sure to only view the creature through the reflection in his shield. To his relief, the others were all doing the same, using their highly polished swords or shields to ensure that they didn't stare into those blazing eyes.

Somehow aware that its plans were being thwarted, the Medusa lunged at one of the party guests, razor claws slashing at the man. With a cry of pain, the man dropped his shield. It clattered noisily to the floor. The Medusa slithered round the man, getting into his eyeline.

'No!' yelled Turlough, but it was too late.

The horrible cracking noise filled the air once more and

the man was frozen into cold, dead stone.

Panic rippled through the others, seemingly giving the creature strength. It reared up, hissing in triumph. Turlough took a deep breath and raised his sword. He would never have considered himself a hero, but unless someone tried to stop the thing it was going to kill everyone.

Before Turlough could move, the Doctor's voice rang out across the gallery. 'Mara!'

Turlough turned to see the Doctor and Tegan standing in the doorway. The Doctor had one hand across his eyes, but the other was on Tegan's shoulder, forcing her to look at her monstrous duplicate. Her face contorted with fear and revulsion as the creature swung round to face them.

With a jolt, Turlough realised that Tegan had no reflective surface in which to view the creature. She was facing it directly!

'Doctor, no, you can't let her!'

'Stay back, Turlough,' yelled the Doctor. 'She must confront it.'

'I'm not sure I can do this, Doctor,' said Tegan.

'Brave heart, Tegan.'

Turlough watched helplessly as the Medusa slithered across the floor towards Tegan, until the two of them were face-to-face. With a hiss of venomous anger, the Medusa's

eyes started to blaze, brighter and brighter until Turlough was forced to turn away.

When the glare faded, Tegan was standing in front of the familiar silver shape of Kamelion. The robot was lifeless, his head bowed, all power drained from him. There were gasps of relief from the party guests. Levi mumbled a heartfelt prayer.

The Doctor gave a great sigh, and patted Tegan reassuringly on the shoulder. 'Well done, Tegan.'

'What happened?' asked Turlough.

'The Mara is unable to face itself,' explained the Doctor. 'It's how I was able to defeat it on the Kinda world with mirrors. It has no choice; it must recoil from its true image.'

'And Tegan was its true image – not Kamelion.'

'Exactly! Kamelion was merely a projection of Tegan's subconscious, her mind forcing him to shape-shift into the image of the Medusa.'

'But where has the Mara been hiding?' asked Tegan. She was clearly exhausted. 'I thought that we had destroyed it on Manussa!'

'Yes, so did I,' said the Doctor thoughtfully. 'We certainly banished it from *your* subconscious. This time it was merely using you as a conduit, a transmitter.'

'So the Mara is still hiding somewhere?' asked Turlough.

'Waiting for another chance to strike?'

'Yes.' The Doctor was grim. 'I'm afraid I don't think we've seen the last of it.'

In the TARDIS, deep in the machinery, in the databanks and memory stores that were more like a living brain than a computer, the Mara coiled and twisted. Once again the Time Lord had outwitted it; once again it had been banished to the Dark Places of the Inside. But its patience was infinite. The wheel would turn once more, and one day, one day very soon, it would be free again.

THE SIXTH DOCTOR

TRICK OR TREAT

Written by Jacqueline Rayner

There was a knock on the door of the TARDIS.
This was unexpected. More than unexpected.
Practically unprecedented. Because the TARDIS was
currently in flight.

The Doctor, frowning, operated the scanner. He didn't
expect it to show anything. And it didn't, because there was
nothing to show. The TARDIS was in the Time Vortex, and
nothing – well, as near to nothing as made no difference –
existed there.

He'd obviously imagined it.

The knock came again.

All right, so it *was* real. Nevertheless, it was impossible –
or at the very least insanely dangerous – to open the TARDIS

doors while in flight. Even if some incredible being was out there, he couldn't do anything about it.

Another knock – harder. More of a series of thumps, an angry tattoo.

The Doctor glanced again at the scanner. He prided himself on reacting calmly to any situation, but couldn't prevent a slight start of alarm. A crowd of faces stared at him from the screen; the stuff of nightmares. Monstrous, fanged, warped, each one more grotesque than the last.

The knocking became even louder and then, with a crash, the doors were forced inwards. It shouldn't – *couldn't* – have happened. He braced himself behind the console, waiting to defend himself against whatever diabolic creatures had breached his sanctuary.

His first observation when they forced their way in was that the demonic hordes were considerably shorter than he was expecting. There were four of them: two came up to about his shoulder, with the other two shorter than that. They dragged a cart on which a fifth figure reclined. The monstrous faces he'd seen on the scanner screen were no more than masks, which were now removed to show four young faces.

All four boys stuck out a hand. 'Trick or treat!' they demanded.

The Doctor boggled. Rarely at a loss for words, he just stared at them. After a few moments of incredulity, the best he could manage was an indignant, 'No!'

'Come on, mister,' said one. 'You've got to give us a treat, or we'll play a trick on you.'

'I am not giving anyone a treat!' The Doctor's outrage was rising. 'Who are you, anyway?'

One of the boys shrugged. 'We're trick-or-treaters, ain't we?'

'Aren't we,' the Doctor corrected automatically. 'So what's that?' He pointed at the figure on the trolley, a mishmash of old clothes and stuffing and straw with a grimacing mask on top.

'Penny for the guy,' said another of the boys, the shortest, who had straight dark hair. (The boys' differing hairstyles and colours were the easiest way to distinguish them from each other at first glance. Two were dark and two were fair, with a curly-haired and a straight-haired boy for each shade.)

'Penny for the guy has nothing to do with trick or treating,' the Doctor told them, hardly able to believe that he was having this discussion under these circumstances. 'One's a Hallowe'en custom and the other's for Guy Fawkes Night.'

'Told you,' said the fair boy with curly hair to the shortest boy, who stuck his tongue out in reply.

'All right,' the shortest boy continued. 'So I got that wrong. But it doesn't change what we're here for.'

And in unison, all four chanted again, 'Trick or treat!'

'You've broken into my TARDIS in the middle of the Time Vortex and have the audacity to ask me for a treat? No! No treat!'

'Not even a jelly baby?' asked the boy with curly dark hair.

'Not even a jelly baby! Nothing!'

The boy with fair straight hair shook his head in disappointment. 'I'm sorry. We hoped you'd cooperate, but if not, well, we've got no alternative.' He turned to the other three. 'I'm afraid it's going to have to be *trick*.'

Before the Doctor quite knew what was happening, each of his arms had been grabbed by two boys and he was being dragged towards the still-open TARDIS doors.

'Let go! Going out there will kill me! I don't know why it didn't kill you!'

'It didn't kill us because it likes us,' said the shortest boy. 'Let's just hope it likes you too.'

They were outside of the TARDIS now, although the doors remained open, a tantalising glimpse of sanctuary. The boys' movements made no sense: a bouncing, soaring walk with nothing underfoot, both defying gravity and bound by it at the same time.

'This has got to be a dream,' the Doctor said.

The fair boy with curly hair pinched him. It hurt. 'Not dreaming,' the boy said. 'Sorry. I'm afraid this *is* real.' He paused, looking down at the Doctor's arm. 'Oh dear. Looks like it doesn't like you after all.'

The Doctor followed the boy's gaze. Where the boy had pinched him, the cloth of his multicoloured suit was crumpling away, the rot of a thousand years condensed into a few seconds. And below it, below the cloth . . .

The flesh of his arms was melting.

He put his hand to his face and felt nothing, then saw with horror that his fingers were dissolving in front of his – did he even still have eyes? He was surrounded by nothingness and didn't know if he could still see and nothing was all there was, or if this was what it was like when there was nothing left of you – not the blindness that came of closing your eyelids but an emptiness that was both internal and external.

It seemed like he was both floating and spinning, even though it felt like there was nothing left of him to spin. Then, as he spun, his bones re-formed, began to be clothed in flesh again. Was it over? Was he reborn? No. As soon as the renewal was complete, his substance once more melted away.

Five times this happened: five times he became nothing then was re-created, until finally the terrible sequence ended and he was real and solid again. The boys and the TARDIS reappeared – or had they been there all along?

'Have you changed your mind yet?' asked the short boy, suddenly right in front of the Doctor. 'Are you going to give us a treat? Or do you want another trick?'

'You mean you'll stop all this if I hand over a few gobstoppers?'

'Not quite,' said one of the taller boys. 'We want a bit more than that.'

'What? Like my TARDIS? Or my life?'

The boy with dark curly hair stamped his foot. 'Oh, you're an imbecile! We'll have to play another trick.'

And suddenly the Doctor was back inside the TARDIS. Alone, except for the sorry-looking guy, which was still lying in its wooden-crate-and-rope cart.

'I don't suppose *you* want to tell me what's going on?' he asked it, but its mask just stared back mockingly.

The Doctor sighed. He had no illusions about the ordeal being over. It was just a question of waiting to see what was going to happen to him next.

Everything went dark, and a shout rang out: 'Catch us if you can!'

The Doctor didn't hesitate for a second. If they hoped to find him off guard, they would fail. He launched himself towards the voice with his arms outstretched and found himself holding something cold and smooth. He felt it. A hatstand? There certainly hadn't been a hatstand there earlier . . .

A giggle from the other side of the room. He changed course, dived towards it. Again he grabbed, and this time found himself embracing the cold, hard bones of a skeleton. He leaped backwards and heard it clatter to the floor.

The nightmarish game continued. The Doctor pursued the laughing, mocking boys here, there and everywhere, occasionally catching one but more often finding himself grasping some strange object, many of which he couldn't identify and didn't particularly want to.

Finally, he had managed to catch all four of the boys, and to his relief the world became light again. 'All right,' he said. 'I've played your ridiculous game. Perhaps you would now care to tell me exactly what you're doing here.'

'We've told you,' said one. 'We're here for trick or treat. You've seen some of our tricks. Now, are you ready to give us our treat?'

'I don't think I'm likely to want to give you whatever it is you're after,' said the Doctor.

'He needs more convincing,' said the boy with straight blond hair.

'Hold on, at least tell me exactly what is it you wa–' the Doctor began, but something strange was happening. Something was welling up inside his throat, up into his mouth, and as he tried to speak it fell from his mouth. With horror, he saw that it was a toad. Once more he attempted to speak, but another lump was forming in his throat.

'There's a fairy tale,' said the tall boy with curly dark hair. 'The good daughter is generous to a fairy, and as a reward, whenever she speaks, diamonds and flowers fall from her mouth. But the bad daughter doesn't give the fairy what she asks for, and instead of jewels she produces toads and snakes. At the moment you're the bad doctor. Why not try being the good doctor instead?'

'Why don't you . . . at least tell me . . . what it is . . . you want!' the Doctor forced out, through a cluster of toads.

The shortest boy turned on him, and for a moment the Doctor was convinced he saw absolute despair in his eyes. 'Oh, why can't you see? It's because we can't!'

The other three hurriedly shushed him. 'Be careful!' the Doctor heard one of them hiss. 'If we don't play by the rules, we're done for!'

But that glimpse of despair had turned things upside-down for the Doctor. Suddenly these children were no longer villains out to taunt and torture him. They were . . .

victims? Perhaps. So what did they want from him? What so many people had wanted from him across the centuries: help. But in what way? They couldn't speak freely, it seemed, but perhaps there were clues. The fairy-tale toads from his mouth – could it be that they weren't just a punishment for not giving them what they wanted, but a clue to the *nature* of what they wanted? Something to do with words that needed to be spoken?

And the five times he'd disappeared – a representation of five deaths? No, five deaths and five rebirths; in effect, five regenerations. He had regenerated five times. It was something to do with that, with his six lives . . .

And the strange game of blind man's buff? Maybe he had to find something hidden, something unexpected, something out of place – like a guy at Hallowe'en . . .

'Ask me the question,' he demanded of the boys. 'Ask me now.'

They all held out their hands and in unison called, 'Trick or treat?'

'Treat,' said the Doctor. 'I think I know what you want from me. You want me to ask you the right questions. So my treat is this. Who are you?' Then he pointed at the guy. 'And who is he?'

The four boys broke out in relieved grins. 'Well, we're

you of course,' said the tall boy with curly dark hair, the one who'd asked about jelly babies. 'And so is he.'

The shortest boy pulled the mask off the guy. There lay a dummy of an elderly man with long white hair.

'Now, my last question: why Hallowe'en?'

'Because it's still Hallowe'en, silly,' said the boy with straight blond hair, munching on a stick of celery. 'It's been Hallowe'en forever. It was the only way we could get to you, let you know, by becoming part of the Hallowe'en party ourselves. Yourselves. It's been you who's been trying to let you know this all along. *You're still at the Hallowe'en party.*'

'But at the same time, you're not,' put in the shortest boy, and the boy with curly blond hair rolled his eyes and told him to stop confusing things.

'We've landed,' said the boy with curly blond hair, and the Doctor realised that he was right. He operated the scanner. It was dark outside, but nearby he could see a single flashing blue light. A very familiar light. As he made out the shape of another police box in the darkness, it faded into nothing. The other TARDIS had left. 'Was that –?' he began. But when he turned round, he found he was alone again. No boys, no guy.

The Doctor never admitted to anyone, least of all himself, that he was even the slightest bit nervous of anything.

He certainly wasn't about to tell anyone that he didn't want to leave the safety of his ship, and to prove how much he wasn't worried about it he took a deep breath, opened the door and strode right out.

A path of jack-o'-lanterns led the way to an old mansion. The Doctor followed the trail without the least hesitation. He didn't knock on the mansion doors, despite the prominent lion-head door knocker; he pushed them straight open and burst across the threshold.

Inside, a gypsy violinist was playing while a group of children in fancy dress danced around. It jogged some far-distant memory in the Doctor's mind – as did the figure dressed in a mandarin costume who came forward to greet him.

The Celestial Toymaker.

'Doctor! What an unexpected pleasure.'

The Doctor looked at him. 'Unexpected?'

'Oh, yes. And quite a paradox.'

'In what way?'

The Toymaker chuckled. 'You mean you haven't worked it out? I assumed you must have done. Why – and how – else are you here? Come with me.'

He led the Doctor through a door on the far side of the hall. A giant blue box stood in the room – a replica TARDIS, much bigger on the outside than the real one, but instead of having double doors its entire front swung open on hinges. Inside, it was divided into rooms, floor to ceiling, and the Doctor realised what it resembled – no, what it *was*: a dolls' house. A TARDIS dolls' house. And it was filled from top to bottom with dolls. A girl doll with dark nylon hair sat at a tea table, permanently pouring non-existent tea from a plastic teapot, while next to her a boy doll proffered a plate of painted wooden cakes. Rag dolls, plastic dolls, even dolls carved from clothes pegs, all could be found inside the house. Some were sitting on chairs, some lying on beds, some just in piles on the floor. There was another girl doll in red-and-white striped dungarees, and a pink-and-white plastic boy doll in a kilt. A knitted penguin was perched on a sofa and a poseable doll with sticking-out nylon hair and dressed in scraps of fake leather menaced it with a plastic knife. Some of the figures seemed almost familiar . . .

'A TARDIS toy,' said the Doctor, deliberately dismissively. 'Well, it's very nice, but I prefer the real thing.'

The Toymaker burst out laughing. 'The real thing? Doctor, you haven't been in the real thing for hundreds of years.'

The Doctor was disconcerted, but refused to show it. 'Nice try, Toymaker. But I've just come from the TARDIS.'

'Oh, you think you have. Of course you do. That's the

whole point, Doctor. Don't you realise? You thought you had beaten me at the Hallowe'en party, but the truth is you lost. You failed to choose between Dodo and Steven and thus forfeited the game. Since then, you've been my puppet. I've amused myself by playing games with you. Sending you off into space, pitching monsters against you . . . It's been *great* fun.'

The girl doll with the teapot, the boy with the cakes . . .

'Dodo,' said the Doctor, their long-gone images conjured up in his mind. 'And Steven. They were with me . . .'

'Of course, when you lost, so did they,' the Toymaker said. 'At first, I kept you together. But Steven was a bright boy. He started to figure it out, so I had to take him away to a game of his own. But that turned out to be a good thing, because it gave me the idea that I could replace your friends with other dolls – those who'd once been the people who'd fought hardest, those who'd nearly won their own games. I was going to keep Dodo. She never struck me as being particularly insightful, but I misjudged her and had to get rid of her rather quickly. Never mind. It's been a joy to see you paired off with some of my very favourite dolls over the years.'

'And what of me?' asked the Doctor. 'That's where your story falls apart, Toymaker. I've regenerated five times since I met you here. This is just a story, a trick.'

'No trick! You forget, I am the Toymaker! The maker of toys!' He flung back the lid of a large wooden chest. 'Do you not think I can also repair toys when they are broken? Replace an arm, a leg, a head . . . at what point is it not the same doll? At *no* point!'

The Doctor looked into the chest. A jumble of doll parts lay inside. A head, still with a floppy hat on top of its curly woollen hair. A plastic foot sticking out of the bottom of a single torn cream-striped trouser leg. A sewn white hand with a large blue-stoned ring on a cotton finger.

'My rag box, Doctor. The remaining scraps of old puppets. Would you like to see my current puppet, though?'

He led the Doctor through another door. A large, three sided box stood inside: a replica of the TARDIS control room, with photographic roundels on its three walls and a plastic console stuck in the middle. Inside, leaning against the console to keep it upright, was a rag doll with curly blond hair and a patchwork coat. A string was attached to each arm, each leg, the head, all fixed to a wooden crosspiece.

'Did you think it was all real, Doctor? Truly? I'm the first to admit I got it wrong sometimes. The reality filters cut out every now and then, but you never seemed to notice the plastic Daleks or the bendy dinosaurs or that quite ridiculous giant plush rat. Did it never cross your mind to wonder why

that time tunnel you fell into recently was actually, literally decorated with Christmas tinsel? A total failure on my part. I tried to distract you by bringing the Daleks out again, but now I'm beginning to wonder if I need have tried so hard. You were obviously completely oblivious to the whole thing.'

Waves of doubt. Could this all be true? Could everything that had happened to him – every person he had met, every monster he'd fought – have sprung from the mind of the Toymaker? 'You're saying all my adventures were *made up*? By *you*?'

'Well, it's hardly plausible that so many things would happen to one person, even a time and space traveller. I mean, look how many times you run into the Daleks. The trouble is, they're my favourites – perhaps because they're one of the few monsters I didn't make up myself. If ever I find myself getting bored, I just set up another Dalek battle. Totally implausible that you'd keep meeting like that – but again it clearly never bothered you.'

'But if I'm your toy, being controlled by you – if I'm that very doll there – how can I be here too? You're bluffing. It makes no sense.'

The Toymaker smiled, obviously enjoying the note of uncertainty that the Doctor hadn't been able to stop from creeping into his voice. 'I expect it's hard to get your head around, yes,' he said, folding his arms, 'but the answer is simply that you're not here. You only think you are. Just like in all of your adventures since you became my toy. You've managed to create a degree of self-awareness, of autonomy, for yourself, but all I have to do is play with my puppet and you'll be mine again.'

'Why don't you do it then?' demanded the Doctor, also folding his arms in a gesture of defiance.

'Oh, I will – eventually.'

The Doctor walked over to the console-room set and looked down at the marionette. Was that all he was – all this incarnation of himself had ever been?

No. Even if it were true, he had been the Doctor once, and he was the Doctor now. His thoughts were his own, his decisions were his own, his actions were his own, even if the situations he was placed in were the creation of someone else. Well, hadn't they always been?

A soft voice came from behind. 'I propose a game.'

The Doctor spun round. 'Well, of course you do! You're the Toymaker! Games are your meat and drink. Is there a prize?'

'Naturally. If you win, my power over you will be broken.'

'Not that I will live to enjoy it – your world and everyone

in it perishes when you're beaten, I know. And, if I lose, I remain your puppet for all eternity, I suppose?'

The Toymaker inclined his head. 'As you say.'

'Games with you are a no-win situation, as my friends from Earth would put it. I suppose I have no choice but to accept – but on one condition. I get to choose the game.'

'Very well.' A light had come into the Toymaker's eyes. This was what he lived for, the Doctor knew. Oh, the Toymaker wouldn't entertain the idea of losing – but to toy with his victims, to make them think they had a chance, that was everything to him. The first time they had met, the Doctor had both beaten the Toymaker and survived his wrath – perhaps the only person ever to do so in the eternity that this strange man-outside-time had existed. He'd made a bad enemy then. No wonder the Toymaker had lured him to his Hallowe'en party all those centuries – or was it all those minutes? – ago. His motive had been revenge.

'There's a very simple game I came across on Earth. It's called two truths, one lie. I give you three statements. Two are true, one is a lie. You have to say which is the lie. If you get it right – you win. Should be easy, really, for someone who's been in charge of almost everything I've ever done.'

'Oh, you're going to try to trick me!' said the Toymaker. 'How delightful. You suggest it will be easy, which means you've come up with something you think is impossible for me to know. Now, go ahead, Doctor. Play your game.'

'These are my statements,' said the Doctor. 'Statement one: I am a toy of the Toymaker. Statement two: I am not a puppet controlled by the Toymaker, so he must let me go free. Statement three: This is an elaborate trap designed to put me under the Toymaker's control. Which one of those is false?'

The Toymaker gaped, as the Doctor smiled. It was the smile that many of his opponents had seen: the smile of someone who had successfully set a trap. It was a smile that had been on the Toymaker's own face a thousand times, but that he had rarely seen on others' faces.

'You were wrong,' said the Doctor. 'I didn't want to play this game because I'd come up with something it was impossible for you to know. I'd come up with something you knew only too well. None of this is real. I did win the game back then. Dodo, Steven and I did escape from you, and one of the reasons I know that for a fact is that I saw their TARDIS leave as I arrived, which wouldn't have happened if you'd kept them here as toys – and which you couldn't have fabricated and put in my head if I had temporarily obtained autonomy, as you claimed. Your world was destroyed. All of this –' he swept a hand around, indicating the entire mansion, the trappings of Hallowe'en – 'has been rebuilt by you.'

He went back to the previous room and stood in front of the toy TARDIS, staring at the companion dolls. So much trouble taken. He had no doubt that the Toymaker had found a way to watch him over the years, waiting to find a good time to spring his trap. A time when the Doctor had no friends travelling with him, a time when he could be psychically manipulated without anyone there to pull him back to reality.

As the Toymaker joined him, he continued. 'Oh, the trick-or-treat boys were an excellent touch. Making me think I was trying to give myself a message, making me think I'd found a clever way to break through. You fooled me for a while. Although not for as long as you thought. This whole charade was to build up to another game: I was supposed to think a loss would merely lead to an extension of the status quo and therefore I really had nothing to lose, whereas in reality the loss would turn me into one of your playthings for the first time. So tell me: what is your answer? Which of my statements is false?'

But the Toymaker couldn't answer. To give the correct answer would have been an admission of the truth and would have handed victory to the Doctor. To give an incorrect answer would have been to lose the game.

'Remember that thing I was talking about called a no-win

situation?' said the Doctor. 'I think this might just be one. But for you this time, not for me. Goodbye.'

He looked again at the dolls, wishing for a moment that they were capable of becoming real people, that he could see again all the friends he had lost.

But no. Dwelling on the past was what had brought the Toymaker to this situation. The Doctor had to look on, to the future.

So, leaving the Toymaker trapped, forever unable to end the game without losing it, the Doctor returned to his TARDIS.

THE SEVENTH DOCTOR

THE LIVING IMAGE

Written by Scott Handcock

Fear gripped the city. Elliot Matthews was running for his life.

Until this point, his day had been the very definition of routine. He'd got up at the crack of dawn, headed out for work, and set up his stall in Old Spitalfields Market. The day had been slow to start, but they usually were. He took a break for lunch around midday, a few sly drinks, a bit more work, then, as the October dusk began to fall, he shut up early. Nobody wanted to be out in London after dark. Now Elliot understood why.

He'd heard all the stories, of course. He and the lads had taken ghoulish glee in sharing them with one another, often embellishing the details, competing to tell the most terrifying tale they could. They talked of monsters and demons, phantoms and spirits, creatures that stalked in the dead of night. But not one of them ever believed that these creatures might be real.

Elliot didn't stop running. He wasn't entirely certain what it was that was pursuing him; all he knew for sure was that it wasn't a man. He cried for help and banged on doors, but nobody came to his aid. They'd heard the stories too.

He ducked round a corner, pausing slightly to catch his breath, then darted off down an alleyway. He had thought, at the back of his mind, that he might know London better than whatever was trailing him did. He hoped that maybe he could lose it, or tire it out, or perhaps it might even lose interest. Unfortunately, Elliot Matthews was wrong on all counts.

In his haste to get away, he made a fatal mistake: he began to run even faster. Almost immediately he slipped on a mulch of leaves and lost his footing, falling to the ground with a smack. He picked himself up from the cobbles and tried to steady himself, to carry on running, but it was far too late for that now.

A presence appeared behind him and time seemed to slow.

Elliot knew in his head and his heart that it was over. This was the end.

Slowly, finally, he turned to face his pursuer . . .

And he screamed.

In a dark converted studio just a few streets away, Nathan Gough remained oblivious to Elliot Matthews' plight. He'd been staring at the same sheet of canvas for most of the day, willing inspiration to strike him. A couple of times each hour, he picked up a paintbrush. Sometimes he simply waved it in phantom strokes; more often he'd mix up colours on a palette, idly combining oils he'd never use.

He sighed and sank back in his chair. He couldn't remember the last time he'd struggled so hard to paint. Painting had always been something he loved, something he had *excelled* at. Now, however, it was nothing more than a means to an end, a way of making money by selling commissions.

Not that he was working on a commission at the moment. He hadn't taken on any paid work since the death of his mother a few weeks earlier. Instead, he was focused on completing a project of his own, a personal piece: a portrait of his mother, something to remember her by, maybe even help him through his grief. Perhaps it was rather too soon for him to be thinking about such things, but he felt compelled to paint the portrait. He could hear his mother's voice in the back of his mind, urging him not to forget her, to find a way to keep her spirit alive . . .

The night of her funeral, Nathan had even thought he'd

seen her in his studio. She had been just an abstract shape at first, reflected in the shards of a broken mirror. The figure never moved, so to begin with he didn't notice it at all. It was only as the hours drew on that he became aware of a strange sensation, almost as if there was somebody else in the room. Someone watching him. His mother.

Since then, he could feel his mother's presence growing stronger with each passing night. He knew, somehow, that she was always standing over him, observing him work. At first it was almost comforting. His very own guardian angel, come to protect him! Then, as the weeks drew on, he couldn't shake the notion she was judging him.

Even now, he could hear her, clear as day: sometimes encouraging, often criticising, but always forcing him to carry on with his work. 'I gave you life,' she reminded him. 'Now you will grant me mine!'

Nathan wasn't quite sure what she meant by this. He stared blankly at the canvas, hoping for an answer. Then, when it was clear that none was coming, he leaped out of his chair and, with a yawn, grabbed a coat on the way to the door.

'I need some air,' he told the empty room, slamming the door behind him.

As the chimes of Big Ben struck seven, a 1950s London police box materialised on the city's Embankment, shrouded in a haze of mist and drizzle. Its door snapped sharply inwards and a young girl stepped out. She wore a jacket adorned with badges and with her nickname, 'Ace', emblazoned in large, stark letters across the back. She shivered, taking in the dismal sight in front of her.

'You're on to a right winner here, Professor!' she huffed, yelling back inside the TARDIS. 'This place is cold, dark, dreary *and* damp!'

'Good job I brought a brolly then, isn't it?' replied the older man who stepped out after her. He wore a light cream linen jacket, checked trousers and a distinctive question-mark-decorated pullover. He popped a straw hat on to his head to finish off the ensemble. Neither one of them had dressed for the weather, or the period.

'London, 1887!' The Doctor grinned, raising his voice above the sound of the falling rain. He opened his umbrella and held it above Ace's head, offering her what precious little shelter he was able to. She smiled and huddled closer to him as they strolled gently off along the river.

It occurred to Ace that London never really changed. Even now, a century before she'd grow up there, it all seemed weirdly familiar. True, the lamps were ablaze with gas instead of electric, and there was a distinct lack of modern skyscrapers on the horizon, but there was still the inimitable bustle of Londoners, the unmistakable stench of the Thames, and of course the awful British weather. Even the Tower of London hadn't changed much. Though, in fairness, that was probably to be expected.

'You have to appreciate this city's ambition,' the Doctor said cheerily. 'Just look at it all: the people, the sprawling architecture! Difficult to believe that this is a London still in its infancy.'

'Yeah, I guess,' Ace conceded a little reluctantly, 'but it's not exactly London's heyday, is it?'

The Doctor looked puzzled. 'How do you mean?'

'Well, you know . . .1887? It's a bit of a dark period, isn't it? All smog and slums and street urchins and, oh yeah, wait! Jack the Ripper!'

'The Ripper murders won't take place for another year,' the Doctor replied. 'Unfortunately, there's nothing we can do about them. Or rather, nothing we can do *now* . . . or not that I've already done . . . or perhaps even will do. Time travel's funny like that.'

Ace groaned. She hated when the Doctor mangled his tenses. It was one of the few downsides to travelling with a Time Lord. 'So what you're basically saying is that it's not all bad?' she said.

'Oh, Ace.' The Doctor sighed. 'Nothing's ever *entirely* bad. Just as nothing can ever be entirely good. Lifetimes spent travelling the universe have shown me that much.' He offered her a reassuring smile. 'But no. Right here, right now, London isn't such a terrible place to be. Trust me.'

Ace was almost ready to relent and take his word for this, when an anguished cry echoed abruptly through the streets. She couldn't help raising an eyebrow. 'You were saying?'

But the Doctor didn't respond. Instead, he licked the tip of his index finger and held it up to the chill night air. If he could work out which direction the wind was coming from, he might just be able to pinpoint the victim's whereabouts. He closed his eyes and focused on the voice, blotting out all other sounds around him.

'This way!' he barked. 'Just up beyond the Tower!'

Ace didn't need telling twice.

Together, they ran towards Whitechapel as fast as they could and, since the horrible screaming never stopped, they didn't either.

As they rounded a corner on to one of the side streets, they stumbled upon a wholly unexpected sight. A dishevelled young man was lying in the middle of the road, curled up on his hands and knees, crying out for someone – anyone – to help. However, it was immediately clear why nobody had.

'Gordon Bennett!' Ace blurted under her breath.

Above the stranger's body, suspended in the air, a host of abstract figures spiralled round him. Occasionally, they even looked like people, though when they did it was only for the briefest of moments. For the most part, they were more like the embers of a fire caught on the wind: abstract sparks picked out in unusual patterns, threatening to resemble a far larger, more sinister form. Each of them glowed a sickly, eerie green, burning crisply through the murk of London's smog. They howled like a building gale, hounding their victim.

The Doctor hurried towards them. As he advanced, their wails grew louder, and the specks of spectre vanished into the air.

A dread silence fell across the street.

'Are you all right?' the Doctor asked, softly resting a hand on the young man's shoulder.

It took the stranger a moment to register the Doctor, his head still buried firmly in his hands. When he finally looked up, he seemed both relieved and haunted.

'Thank you,' he said quickly, catching his breath.

'Don't mention it.' The Doctor smiled and offered the young man a handkerchief. 'I'm the Doctor, incidentally, and this is my young friend –'

'Ace!' she interrupted, a little too keenly. 'Nice to meet you . . .' she trailed off, and gave the slightest cough, prompting the man to finish her sentence.

'Oh, er, my name is Nathan,' he replied a little unsteadily. Then, as if they might have heard of him, 'Nathan Gough?'

'Nice to make your acquaintance, Mr Gough.' The Doctor helped the man to his feet. 'I hope we didn't disturb anything just now?'

Nathan glared at him incredulously. 'It wasn't you I was disturbed by!'

'Yeah, bit freaky, wasn't it?' Ace agreed. 'What *were* those things?'

'What did they look like?'

'I, er . . . I don't know.' To Ace's surprise, she found herself hesitating. She knew full well what the things she'd seen had *looked* like – to her, they'd looked like ghosts – but she didn't want to say that. Not in front of the Doctor. She'd been travelling with him for long enough that she knew such things weren't real. If it looked like a ghost and sounded like a ghost, chances were it wasn't anything of the sort. No, she knew better than that. There was bound to be a rational explanation.

'If I didn't know any better,' the Doctor said, 'I'd say

they looked like ghosts.'

Typical, Ace thought. *Of course he'd say that!*

'No such thing,' snapped Nathan. 'The dead do *not* come back. When they pass, they are lost forever. We have to accept that. We *have* to!' Anxiously, he dusted himself down, brushing dirt from his sleeve. He looked about him, getting his bearings. 'Now, if you don't mind,' he told them politely, 'I really ought to be on my way. Thank you both again for your . . . assistance.'

'The pleasure was all ours.' The Doctor doffed his hat. 'Have a good evening, won't you?'

Nathan didn't say another word. Instead, he began to walk in the other direction, stopping only once or twice to make sure of his location. Ace instinctively moved to follow him, but the Doctor held her back.

'Professor!' she protested. 'What are you doing? Shouldn't we follow him?'

The Doctor pressed a finger to his lips. 'Not yet,' he whispered. 'He's nervous enough as it is without us adding any more to his troubles. Besides which, he keeps checking over his shoulder – he'd be bound to spot us.'

'So what do we do then?'

'We wait a minute, give him some distance . . . and *then* we follow him.'

Ace nodded. 'So there *is* something going on here after all?'

'Oh yes.' The Doctor smiled. 'Indubitably!' He had a mischievous twinkle in his eye. 'Come on. Keep to the shadows and follow me.'

When Nathan returned to his home, he poured himself a very large glass of something 'medicinal', followed by another, then finally slumped into one of the armchairs by the window holding a third. He felt his entire body shudder in that moment – partly due to the temperature of the room, but mostly because of what he'd experienced out on the street. If it hadn't been for that strange little man, the Doctor, and his friend . . .

Nathan dismissed the thought quickly. He didn't want to consider what might have happened if they hadn't found him. And yet it all seemed even more hopeless now. He'd gone out to clear his head, perhaps even forget about his troubles, but it seemed there was no escaping them. His demons followed him everywhere he went . . . and now something worse had joined them.

He heard his mother's voice inside his head, still tinged with bitter disappointment. 'What about your work?' she rasped.

'I can't,' Nathan protested aloud, feeling more than a

little sorry for himself. He drained the contents of his glass and set it down. 'Painting's not that easy. It *shouldn't* be easy. It requires time, and thought, and above all else passion.'

'You used to find painting easy. What's changed?'

Nathan choked back his reply. He didn't want to tell her it was her fault, that her death had had such an impact on him. He didn't want her to feel guilty for holding him back. Or, worse still, he didn't want her to think that he blamed her for his own shortcomings. Not that she was actually there, of course; she couldn't be. Nathan knew that. And yet . . .

'I'll finish the painting soon,' he said, more to himself than to her.

'Tonight,' his mother insisted.

'I . . .' Nathan hesitated. 'You don't understand. I can't. I physically can't!'

'Oh, but you can,' she urged. 'You can do anything you put your mind to. Isn't that what I always used to tell you? You, my boy, you can achieve the impossible.'

Nathan shuddered again, as though he could feel the chill caress of her hand on the back of his neck.

'You have to carry on working at this difficult time. You *know* that.'

'But thinking of you, trying to paint you . . . not enough time has passed!'

'Then you must paint something else,' his mother instructed. 'A self-portrait, perhaps? That handsome young face of yours, captured forever in pigments and oil. What a masterpiece that would be!'

Nathan considered this for a moment. He'd been so consumed with grief that it hadn't occurred to him that he could use that sense of loss, he could exploit how he was feeling, and pour all those dreadful emotions into his work. After all, art didn't need to be happy to be good.

He sprang from his chair with a newfound sense of purpose, gathering his tools up from around the room, and began to think of his new composition.

That's when the tapping started.

'Is it me, or is it getting colder around here?' Ace shivered as she and the Doctor arrived on Nathan's street.

The Doctor pulled a fob watch from his pocket, then flipped it open and held it up in front of him. It chirruped a sequence of strange mechanical trills.

'You're right,' he confirmed, interpreting the watch's burble of data. 'There's been a recent drop in ambient temperature . . . some atmospheric disturbances . . . not to mention instances of temporal distortion. All of which suggest we're in the right place!' He snapped the case of the fob watch shut. 'Now we just need to work out which of these buildings our young friend Mr Gough resides in.'

'If you mean "Where does he live?" I think I've a fair idea.'

'Oh?'

'Yeah.' Ace pointed up to a third-floor window a few doors down. 'Look!'

Obediently, the Doctor did as he was told. There was a light in one of the windows. Not the golden, reassuring flicker of candlelight, however, but the unnatural, sickly green sparks that they'd seen above Nathan Gough in the alleyway.

'I mean, it's just a hunch,' Ace continued a little smugly, 'but I'm guessing it's probably that one.'

The Doctor hurried over to the house, then bounded up the steps that led to the porch and rapped his knuckles four times on the door. He waited a few seconds for a response, then knocked again. This time, he heard footsteps coming down a staircase, followed by the sound of a key turning in the lock. The door swung suddenly open, revealing an extremely flustered Nathan.

'Mr Gough, what a coincidence!' The Doctor beamed, trying a trifle too hard to sound surprised. 'We had no idea you lived around here!'

Nathan eyed the Doctor warily.

'You remember my young friend, Ace?' the Doctor said.

'Hiya!' She waved, bouncing up to greet him. 'Mind if we come inside? It's a little bit wet out.'

Nathan wasn't sure that was a good idea; he wasn't very sure of anything any more. 'I'd rather you didn't,' he said, keeping his voice low. 'Now is . . . now is not a good time.'

'Oh, I know all about time!' the Doctor blustered, barging past Nathan and into the hallway. He shook the rain from his umbrella and started marching up the staircase, calling back behind him. 'Strictly between you and me, the *bad* times tend to be my speciality! I take it upstairs is where you'd rather we didn't go?'

Nathan's dumbstruck silence could only mean yes.

'Splendid. I thought as much!' The Doctor stomped from step to step. 'Come along now, Ace. No time to lose!'

Ace smiled apologetically at Nathan. 'Sorry about him,' she said. 'If it makes you feel any better, he knows what he's doing. Most of the time.'

Ace could see from Nathan's expression this wasn't helping, so she tried a different tack.

'Last one up's a Ratkin!' she cried, tagging him on the shoulder and dashing upstairs.

'You really don't want to go up there!' he shouted, but he had no choice but to follow them.

When the Doctor entered Nathan's studio, he instantly knew something was wrong. A foreboding atmosphere permeated the room, the air tasted oddly stale and the hairs on the back of his neck were beginning to prickle. He tried to make out what detail he could, but, aside from a couple of half-burned candles on the mantel, the room was wreathed in darkness.

'I'm afraid I'm unused to house guests,' Nathan explained, following them both hurriedly into the room. He immediately threw open the curtains, not that it helped much. The moonlight was struggling to break through the rain clouds.

'Interesting place you have here,' the Doctor said, wandering casually around the room, picking up ornaments.

'Creepy, more like,' Ace muttered, flicking through a discarded sketch pad. 'You like drawing, then?'

'I'm an artist,' Nathan admitted. 'Though I'm not sure "like" comes into it. Rather, I'd consider it my calling.'

'Ah, the temperamental type!' The Doctor chuckled. 'That would explain why it's been targeting you.'

'Why what has? What are you talking about?'

'You tell me, Mr Gough.' The Doctor tapped the handle of his umbrella against his chin. 'You . . . tell . . . me.'

Before Nathan could answer, a low, hard thump sounded

from the corner of the room. It was as though something large and solid had hit the other side of the wall.

'What was that?' Ace instinctively turned in the direction of the noise.

Another thump boomed, followed by another, then another.

'Hey, I think it's coming from over here!' Ace moved awkwardly into the corner of the room, shifting the paints around Nathan's easel. 'Can't see where though.'

The Doctor and Nathan moved to join her.

There came another thump.

'I think,' the Doctor said, 'that it might be coming from the canvas itself.' He pointed towards the easel Ace was crouched beside, where a broad frame had been suspiciously covered from view with a tattered old dust sheet. 'Care to tell us what you're working on, Mr Gough?'

'It's nothing. Just a personal piece,' Nathan answered quickly. 'A portrait of my . . . of my mother. She died recently.'

'Did she indeed? Well, let's take a look, shall we?'

Before Nathan could stop him, the Doctor had whipped away the dust sheet with a magician's flourish, revealing the image that lay beneath. If it had once been a loving depiction of Nathan's mother, it had drastically changed. Her features lacked the warmth she'd had in life, and the face was hard and sallow; it was most definitely not how Nathan would have chosen to remember her.

'Either that's not your mother,' whispered Ace, 'or you really didn't like her very much.'

Nathan shook his head in disbelief. 'I don't understand.'

'I think I do,' said the Doctor, plucking the fob watch from his pocket. 'This area's rife with temporal instabilities.'

The others looked confused.

'Put simply, that canvas is now a weak point in the fabric of space and time. Like a doorway, a portal, to another aspect of reality altogether. Something's breaking through. Those things we saw outside? Those ghosts?'

An angry thump punctuated his words.

'In truth, they weren't ghosts at all, but something else.'

I knew it! thought Ace.

'There are all manner of abstract creatures we don't even know about yet. Entities that stalk the gulfs of the Space–Time Vortex, beings unlike anything you'll have ever known here on Earth. They exist in five dimensions all at once; they're here and yet they're not here.'

Another thump. This time it shook the easel.

'But how can that be?' asked Nathan. 'How can we not see them?'

'Because they exist in a different dimension,' explained

the Doctor. 'Think of it this way: we're *three*-dimensional beings, yes? We exist. The pictures you paint are only *two*-dimensional. They also exist. And yet, the subjects you depict in your paintings couldn't even begin to conceive of a *third* dimension, never mind a fourth or even a fifth!'

'So you're saying we're basically stickmen?' Ace suggested, not very helpfully.

'But no, those phantoms . . .' Nathan was struggling to process what the Doctor was saying. 'They came for *me*. They *know* me!'

'Not at all. Just insubstantial glimpses of a dimension beyond our own. But the fact we can see them means they're getting closer. They're growing stronger, minute by minute, and I think it's thanks to you, Mr Gough.'

'Me?'

'Of course. Entities like this feast upon the abstract. They devour concepts and emotions, meaning creative talents like yours are the perfect target. Add to that the death of your mother and you become the perfect puppet. They're using her to manipulate you.'

Nathan heard his mother in his head again, warning him not to heed the Doctor's words. Who was this stranger, anyway? She knew him better than this 'Doctor' ever could! After all, he was *her* special baby boy and always would be.

Thump!

'I don't know what to do.' Nathan sighed, pulling up a chair.

'Then listen to me!' The Doctor grabbed Nathan's arm as he reached for the easel. 'You can't allow them to get any closer. You have to stop this.'

Thump! Thump! Thump!

Ace recoiled as the portrait started to shift. Its features twisted horribly.

'HE WILL CONTINUE!' the image rasped, its green eyes rolling to the back of its head. 'HIS WORK MUST BE COMPLETED!'

'Mother?'

'Nathan, no, it's not your mother!' the Doctor warned. 'You know it isn't. It's using your talent, exploiting you to establish a link. These things, these *monsters*, they feed off abstract concepts. Works like this, they capture a specific point in time – in this case, a time *before* your mother's death, but that time has well and truly passed. I'm sorry, but that's how they're doing it. They're leeching off the abstract years that never were, between how she used to be in the image and how she is now. Reliving happy times: it's the most basic form of time travel, and they're exploiting that through you to travel here.'

Nathan's mother's face snarled, and the canvas creased around it. 'PAY HIM NO HEED, CHILD,' it hissed. 'GIVE ME LIFE!'

Suddenly a spectral hand tore through the canvas, ripping at the fringes of reality and grabbing Nathan firmly round the throat. 'GIVE ME *YOUR* LIFE!'

The Doctor tried to wrest the hand away, but the creature was far too strong. Nathan had formed a link between dimensions, and the monster was beginning to take his place. Nathan could hear its voice inside his mind now, screaming in triumph, its supernatural life force coursing through him. He tried to scream but couldn't. His will was already being crushed from inside his body.

'YOU HUMANS MAKE THIS SO EASY!' the creature gloated.

Then Nathan heard another voice cry out. It was Ace.

'Oi, grotbags!' she yelled, picking up a jar of murky liquid. 'Get out of his head, yeah?'

Ace threw the liquid at the canvas, smearing it with her hands and distorting the image. Immediately the force's influence started to wane. Nathan's senses were taking hold again, and the creature's grip round his throat was beginning to weaken. It howled at Ace in fury, releasing its hold on Nathan, then punched back through the canvas, leaving behind nothing but a smear of muddy oils.

It was as if it had never been there.

'Ace!' The Doctor's voice cut sharply across the room. 'That was extremely irresponsible of you!'

She looked like a wounded puppy. 'Oh.'

'But also extremely resourceful and really rather brilliant,' the Doctor continued. 'I wish I'd thought of it!'

'What did she do?' asked Nathan, getting his breath back. His neck was stained with dark paint from the creature's claws.

'She disrupted the link, with the help of a handy jar of paint thinner,' the Doctor replied. 'As I said, it needed that painting of your mother to form a link with you, to feast off the years between life and death. Spoil the image and you spoil the link, giving it no choice but to retreat back to its own dimension.'

'So that's it now – she's gone? My mother's gone?'

'Your mother has been gone for a long time, Nathan,' the Doctor told him solemnly. 'But *it* hasn't gone. It's just not here any more, but it won't be long before it finds another victim, another target much like you.' He sighed and considered his options. 'We need to draw it back here.'

'I'm not sure I like the sound of this,' Ace muttered.

'All we need to do is give it a target.' The Doctor smiled,

taking up a seat next to Nathan. 'Mr Gough, I'd like you to paint my portrait, if you'd be so kind?'

'I . . . I'm sorry?' Nathan stammered. 'You'd like me to do what?'

'I know how it sounds, but trust me, I know what I'm doing.' The Doctor removed his hat and struck a pose. 'Remember, it needn't be perfect. Just enough of a likeness that it can force a link through me.'

'If you're certain?'

'Absolutely.' The Doctor nodded.

Ace watched as Nathan frantically mixed together oils on his palette, sweeping vague shapes of colour across the canvas. Within seconds, the image of his mother had all but gone, replaced instead by the indistinct face of the Doctor.

Quickly, Nathan worked up detail – the sharp, steely eyes, the furrowed brow – and the Doctor felt his senses slipping away from him. He could just about make out Ace, encouraging Nathan as he worked. Then silence fell, and the Doctor realised he was not in his own dimension . . .

He had travelled across to the creature's realm and found himself surrounded by a host of fierce intelligences. Now, their minds were linked. Their thoughts were inside his thoughts; he could see what they saw, feel exactly what they felt . . . and he became aware of their intentions should they ever arrive on Earth. He knew in that moment what they would choose to do to the human race: things that must never be allowed to happen. So the Doctor made them an offer.

'I know you can hear me,' he yelled, his voice echoing through the void between dimensions. 'Our minds are linked, which means you must already know who I am.'

The creature's voice lashed out. 'YOU CALL YOURSELF "DOCTOR"!' it growled.

'Yes, and I'm here to make you an offer.'

A ripple of mocking laughter swirled around him.

'Right now, you're trying to break into our reality through a painting. You're harnessing a young man's talent, using all his energy and emotion, to feed your own ghastly ends. I can feel you trying to force access, using me and my image as the bridge.'

'IT WORKED BEFORE. IT SHALL WORK AGAIN!'

'I'm allowing you the chance to walk away,' the Doctor said. 'You don't need Earth. You don't even need our dimension. You have the entire Vortex at your disposal: the fourth and fifth dimensions of space and time!'

'THESE DIMENSIONS ARE INSUBSTANTIAL!' raged the creature. 'WE SEEK PHYSICAL FORM!'

'Then I'm sorry for you, because I cannot allow that to happen.' The Doctor sighed. 'I really did hope you might change your mind when you realised what you were up against. Believe me when I tell you that I'm sorry.'

Suddenly the entity started to struggle to contain the Doctor's will. The more it fought to maintain control, the less it had.

'I'm a Time Lord,' the Doctor explained with a voice of quiet steel. 'I'm afraid I don't age like human beings. In fact, I barely age at all. Even when I die, my image changes completely. So, you see, there's nothing for you to exploit here; no abstract differential between the me I am right now and the me I might one day become. Meaning *you're* trapped inside *my* mind. There's no way out for you.'

The creature tried to move, but found it couldn't. It was like an insect caught in amber. In fact, it could scarcely think.

'Luckily for me, a Time Lord's mind is more than enough to contain a feeble little being like you,' the Doctor continued cheerily. 'I'm afraid there's probably a fair bit of clutter in there – my apologies – but I'm certain you'll soon make yourself at home there, given time.'

The entity didn't respond. It *couldn't* respond. All of its power had been lost through the Doctor's image.

In that moment, it knew this was the end. It tried to scream, but it couldn't.

■

At that very same instant, back in Nathan's studio, just as the artist completed his final brushstroke, the Doctor groggily returned to his senses. He breathed a great sigh of relief and patted Nathan gently on the shoulder.

'Excellent work, Mr Gough.' He smiled, hiding his exhaustion. 'The painting's not bad either. Now, I don't suppose you'd happen to have a kettle?'

Half an hour later, having said their farewells and indulged in a pot of restorative Earl Grey, the Doctor and Ace were back on the night-time streets of London, heading in the direction of the TARDIS. The rain had finally stopped, the clouds had parted and, even though there was still a heavy fog, suddenly all seemed calm.

'Is that it, then?' Ace asked chirpily, skimming stones into the Thames. She waited for each satisfying plop before throwing another.

'For now, yes,' said the Doctor, thinking it over. 'But others like it are still out there. They always will be. That's how the universe works.'

'But they can't break through, yeah? Not like that, I mean. Not again.'

'I might have deterred them for a while, but when has that ever stopped anything? I'm sure one of them will try again at some point. All they need is an image, after all. It doesn't even have to be a painting. It could be a simple sketch, a Polaroid, a selfie –'

'A what-now?'

'Never mind.' The Doctor chuckled, taking Ace's arm in his. 'Come on. Let's get back to the TARDIS.'

THE EIGHTH DOCTOR
ORGANISM 96

Written by Paul Magrs

Marie hadn't been singing on cruise ships for long, but she already knew that some very strange things could happen at sea.

It all began on the day they fished Miss X out of the Mediterranean.

'What's all the fuss about?' asked a man on a sun lounger who was wearing a striped Edwardian swimming costume and a huge fluffy robe. As he spoke, he stared at her over his sunglasses.

'Hm?' Marie hated tearing herself away from the drama, but she was already late for the afternoon show. She was performing twice daily in the theatre and she couldn't afford to be late again.

'Have I missed something exciting?' he asked her.

'Oh, yes,' she said, flustered. 'It's all been happening down on Deck Six. On the starboard side. Hang on, is that right? Or was it the port side? I should know, really. I'm part of the crew. I've done the safety training and everything . . . Anyway, down there on the left.'

The stranger sat up in his sun lounger. 'Is there an emergency?' He started at once to gather up his belongings: his towel, his milkshake, his science-fiction paperback. 'I never heard an announcement over the tannoy.'

'Oh no, it's nothing like that. Not an emergency. They just had to fish someone out of the sea.'

The man took off his sunglasses. He had chestnut curls and his eyes were extremely blue. 'Someone fell overboard?'

'Well, no, as it turns out,' Marie said. 'She wasn't even a passenger on this ship. She was just bobbing about in the sea, on her own, in the middle of the day.'

'How extraordinary,' said the man softly. 'Is she all right?'

'Oh, yes. She wasn't in any distress or anything. I saw her first. I was looking out for the coast of Italy and next thing there she was. Rather smartly dressed. Over-dressed, really, for the weather.'

The man frowned. 'Tell me, Marie – it *is* Marie, isn't it?'

She blinked. 'Er, yes.' How did he know her name?

'Where do you think this lady came from?'

Marie felt dazed. Perhaps she had been staring at the
spangling silver of the sea for too long. That's what she'd
thought when she had first seen the floating lady: *I must be
hallucinating . . . or have seasickness.* But then the old lady had
waved and Marie had started calling for help.

Right now, she was feeling dizzy again, as the man
quizzed her.

'I've been trying to figure it all out,' she told him.

'Yes,' he said. 'I can tell you enjoy mysteries, and this
sounds like a good one. The Mysterious Miss X of the
Mediterranean.'

'Perhaps she fell off another cruise ship?'

'It's possible. We could check that out. There'll be a
timetable somewhere. Captain Letts will know. Shipping lanes
and all that. Also, we could probably ask someone to have a
look at the radar and see what other vessels are nearby. Yes,
perhaps I'll go and do that right now . . .'

He started walking away, clutching his things and
chewing on the end of his milkshake straw. Marie hurried
after him. 'Are you a detective?'

'Not really. I'm the Doctor. Usually I'm the sort of
person who is right at the heart of very strange and unusual
events, only this time *you* were that person. I was napping on
a sun lounger some twenty yards away. But you can help me

now if you like?'

Suddenly she remembered where she was supposed to be. 'I'm meant to be performing in *The Sounds of the Seventies* right now!' With that she dashed off in the direction of the lifts.

'I'll see you later, then,' murmured the Doctor, and he headed off to confer with the captain of the *W. H. Allen.*

Marie saw the Doctor again later that night in the bar on Deck Ten. He was talking with another passenger: a spry old gentleman in a military blazer who was drinking a whisky and soda. The Doctor was sipping ginger pop through a curly straw.

'Doesn't surprise me that the captain's not very helpful,' the older man was saying. 'Surly-looking chap. But I shouldn't worry. I'm sure there's a perfectly simple explanation.'

The Doctor smiled. 'That's hardly ever true. Haven't you noticed that?'

The man in the blazer went on, 'I haven't actually clapped eyes on the lady in question. Have you?'

'No,' said the Doctor, noisily finishing off his pop. 'That's my next port of call, as it were.'

'I gather she's been in the sickbay all afternoon. Getting a check-up and whatnot. Touch of amnesia, from what I hear. It's a wonder she's still alive. I'm not sure I'd be up to a swim in the briny at my age.'

'Quite,' said the Doctor. 'Though I'm sure you found yourself in much more dangerous situations in your former career, eh, Colonel Hulke?'

'What do you know about my former career, sir?' said the old man sharply.

The Doctor feigned innocence. 'Oh, you look like the kind of fellow who's been in a scrape or two.'

The elderly gent seemed rather cross now, and he glared at the Doctor.

Marie, too, was staring at the Doctor. She was impressed by his evening wear, which included a raffish green velvet coat and a silver cravat, even though it was as warm now as it had been all day.

She caught him as he left the bar. 'I was ear-wigging.'

'Oho!' He smiled. 'That pompous old spy is pretending he wasn't in MI5. Well, never mind. How was your cabaret show?' He eyed her Abba-inspired catsuit.

'It was okay,' she said. 'Was he really a spy?' She was keen to keep up with shipboard gossip, and having a genuine retired secret agent in their midst was a novelty. 'What does he know about our Miss X?'

'Only that she's forgotten her name and that she's in the sickbay.'

'How very convenient.'

'I thought so too,' said the Doctor. 'Your curiosity is just as piqued as mine, isn't it?'

'Of course,' she said. 'There's something fishy going on here. Who is she? And what was she doing in the sea?'

'I'd like to know that too,' agreed the Doctor.

'Why don't you pretend to have a funny turn?' she suggested. 'Right now.'

'What? Oh, yes! All right.' He started moaning theatrically and clutched at himself as if he was in horrible pain. He kept up the amateur dramatics all the way to the sickbay, where the ship's Doctor Marter gave him a cursory once-over and frowned at Marie. 'He'll have to wait. I'm in the middle of a childbirth.'

'What?'

'Sudden arrival in the Hawaiian Cocktail Lounge. Wait here.' He filled his bag with emergency supplies and dashed off.

The Doctor stopped moaning as soon as Doctor Marter had disappeared. 'Now to find our Miss X.'

'Get back, Marie! Keep away from it!'

She stared at him incredulously. 'Doctor, what are you on about? You're embarrassing me.' She turned to the old lady, who was sitting on a bench in the consulting room. 'I don't know what's come over him. I'm so sorry.'

The Doctor was still shouting. 'It's not safe! Just look at its venomous tentacles! Get away from it at once!'

The old lady looked utterly dumbfounded. She turned to Marie and murmured, 'Is your friend quite all right in the head?'

'I hardly know him,' Marie explained, glaring at the Doctor.

The lady pursed her lips. 'He's not being very respectful, I must say.'

Marie poked the Doctor in the ribs. 'What's the matter with you?'

He grabbed Marie by the shoulders and stared into her eyes. 'Is there something wrong with your eyesight?'

The old lady was on her feet now and pulling on her coat. She bustled past them, muttering crossly, 'Strangers saying horrible, insulting things. I'm not staying here. Good day to you!'

The Doctor stepped aside for her, looking aghast as she left the sickbay.

'How did that *beast* get aboard?' he demanded once the old lady was out of hearing range. 'Seriously, I have no idea what that creature is. Some kind of mutant. And how come you don't look a bit more shocked? Is this an everyday event?

Do you often have horrible mutations on board the *W. H. Allen*?'

'What do you mean?' Marie snapped. 'She seemed like a perfectly ordinary old lady to me.'

The Doctor frowned. 'Then we definitely aren't seeing the same thing. And, judging by the lack of terrified screams from other passengers on the deck she's just wandered on to, I'm guessing that no one else is seeing her as she truly is, either. How intriguing!'

Marie was gawping at him. 'But that was Miss X. The lady I saw in the sea . . .'

The Doctor shook his head. 'No, that was a heinous monster, Marie. And monsters are my business!'

There was every chance that the man who called himself the Doctor was crackers. Marie decided she had to concentrate on her job and, even though the Doctor was rather intriguing, it might be best if their paths didn't cross again.

She was singing in the *Sounds of the Seventies, Eighties Extravaganza* and *Hits of the Nineties* twice a day, and it was during the matinee of the third of these that she noticed him sitting in the audience, eating crisps and singing along. What was the Doctor up to now?

Over the next few days she kept noticing Miss X, too,

though this was less surprising, since the old lady had become something of a celebrity on board the ship. The captain had generously provided her with a cabin with a balcony, and a smart wardrobe from one of the designer boutiques. The old lady's memory still hadn't returned and she constantly wore a slightly vague look.

'Hello.' Marie bumped into her on purpose. 'I'm Marie Blenkinsop. I'm the one who spotted you the other day, when you were in the water.'

Miss X's face brightened considerably. 'My dear, then I must thank you. I owe you my life!'

'It was nothing,' said Marie, though it was nice to be thanked for her efforts. She'd screamed herself hoarse that day. 'Anyone would have done the same.'

'I must think of a suitable reward for you.' Miss X smiled.

Suddenly Colonel Hulke was standing beside them in his blazer with brass buttons. 'Good afternoon.' He executed a stiff little bow.

'Colonel Hulke is treating me to lunch today,' Miss X explained.

'I want to hear all about your ordeal at sea,' he said. Then he added gallantly, 'Though not if you'll find it too upsetting.'

'Of course not. Lead on, Colonel. The sea air has given

me quite an appetite.'

As Marie watched the two elderly people amble towards the first-class dining room, she was aware the whole time of the Doctor standing by the railings and watching over his newspaper.

'Why are you spying on them?' she asked him. 'They're perfectly ordinary.'

'You know that isn't true.'

'Don't start this again!' Marie made to hurry away.

'Look,' said the Doctor, producing a clunky Polaroid camera from one of his coat pockets. 'I snapped some pictures to prove to you that she's the hideous creature I say she is.'

The instant print was still developing. He shook it and the grey square clarified to show Marie talking to a perfectly innocuous and respectable Miss X.

The Doctor was astonished. 'What? *That's* how you see her, is it?'

'Of course. That's how everyone sees her.'

'I don't,' he said, almost sulkily. 'She must be using a very powerful form of mind control if she can even fool my camera.' The Doctor's thoughts were racing.

'You're really worried, aren't you?'

'Well, of course I am! That mutant squid creature has

got razor-sharp tentacles! I don't think it's come aboard simply to have lunch and hear you singing in *Eighties Extravaganza*, good as your show is.'

'Then what do you think it's here for?'

'Ah, you're starting to believe me!' He smiled.

'Not really,' she said. Then added, 'Well, perhaps . . .'

There was just something very convincing about his manner.

'We're in grave danger,' he said.

A body was found early the next morning. The victim was floating face down in the hot tub on the top deck, and identified as the rather tipsy middle-aged man last seen drinking martinis in the Over-the-Rainbow Cocktail Bar.

'He was found by early-morning bathers,' Captain Letts solemnly informed the Doctor, as they watched the body being hoisted out of the bubbles. 'Never in all my years have I had a murder on board my ship. This is a bad business.'

'Very bad.' The Doctor crouched by the sopping corpse. 'Strangled, of course, though look at those red burns on his flesh.'

The captain bristled. 'I'm sure Doctor Marter will give him a thorough post mortem.'

'They look like jellyfish stings,' mused the Doctor.

'Look, who are you?' demanded the captain. 'You're not part of my crew. Are you a passenger? We don't want news of these deaths getting out and causing panic on the ship –'

'Aha! So this *isn't* the first murder then?'

Captain Letts glared at him.

'You look like a man who knows he has a serial killer on his hands, Captain,' the Doctor said. 'Let me help. Who else has died this week?'

The captain passed a weary hand over his face. 'One of the entertainment troupe.'

The Doctor asked, 'Who?'

'The young woman's name was Tamsin.'

'I'll need to examine both bodies for clues. Do they have the same markings?' he said, hurrying along the deck, with the captain struggling to keep up. 'Don't let panic spread throughout the passengers, or you'll have a mutiny on your hands . . . Now I must find Marie!' Then he was haring off, and the captain was left staring at his green coat tails.

Who the devil is he? the captain wondered. There was a rumour that there was a secret-service man aboard. Perhaps that's who this eccentric fellow was?

Marie emerged from the staff quarters and was shocked to come immediately face-to-face with the Doctor.

'I'm so glad you are safe, Marie. I just heard about Tamsin.'

'Do you know where she is?' Marie asked anxiously.
'No one's seen her since yesterday morning. She missed last
night's shows and the matinee.'

'Ah. I'm afraid there's some bad news.' The Doctor
gently took her arm and led her up to Deck Six, where they
could talk privately.

Marie tried to take in what the Doctor was telling
her. 'But I sang with her just two nights ago! We did our
Bananarama medley. And now she's dead? But who would
murder Tamsin? And why?'

'She was the first, and there's been a second victim
already. They found a dead man in the hot tub this morning.'

Marie looked ill.

'There's a savage maniac on board killing
indiscriminately,' said the Doctor, with steel in his voice. 'No
one is safe.' Then he smiled reassuringly. 'Luckily I'm here to
unmask the killer!'

Marie stared at him. 'Unmask?'

'I've a very good idea who's behind this.'

'Right . . .' Marie was giving him a funny look. A
terrible thought had just gone through her mind. Who was
this man, really?

'Wait, Marie! Where are you going?'

'I've . . . I've got to get back to work.'

'You don't suspect *me*, do you?'

'No, of course not!' Now she was running back the way they had come, her slippers slapping on the wet deck.

'Just because I showed up right when dead bodies started appearing. It's a coincidence, Marie!' he called after her, attracting the attention of other deck strollers. Then he remembered his promise not to let the news slip. 'Marie?' he called once more, but she was gone.

Later that morning the Doctor stole into a dingy storage area deep in the hold of the ship. Here among the packing crates hid the solidly reassuring shape of the TARDIS. He nipped inside to collect the bits and pieces of electronic equipment he needed in order to build the device he had in mind.

He was humming to himself as he emerged from the blue box balancing a pile of parts in his arms. *I'll call it my . . . De-mesmerisor*, he was thinking happily when all at once he realised that he wasn't alone in the hold.

A hulking, jagged silhouette stood in a shaft of murky light before him.

'Aha!' said the Doctor, staring hard at the creature.

It hissed at him menacingly.

'It *is* you, isn't it?' the Doctor called out in challenge.

'There's no use denying it. You're the little old lady they fished out of the sea.'

The creature slithered closer, inching further into the light and revealing a jumble of suckered tentacles and a mass of bulbous eyes.

'You know my true form,' said the creature from the sea. Its voice was a hideous gurgle. 'You are the only one who can see me as I truly am.'

'I know that you are responsible for two murders,' said the Doctor.

'I need to kill. I need to eat,' the creature said as it slithered closer. 'I have been programmed to kill.'

'Who by?' The Doctor frowned. 'Who programmed you?'

The tentacles quivered, as if the creature was distressed by the Doctor's question. 'No, no . . . leave me . . .'

'Perhaps I can help you?'

'No one can help me. I was made to be like this – to hide my true nature and to kill!'

'You're somebody's unfortunate experiment, are you?' the Doctor asked.

Froth was forming on the fleshy folds and scales of the creature's hide. 'I can't help killing . . . but I wouldn't stop myself, even if I could! I can live among humans looking just like an innocent old lady, while taking my pick of which brains to eat. I find I love the taste.' Each of the creature's yellow eyes fixed on him at once. 'You will do nothing to stop me. Not if I make *you* my next victim! Those brains of yours would make a particularly delicious meal . . .'

The Doctor gasped and took a step backwards, as the creature burst forward with a surprising turn of speed. A single tentacle lashed out and paused for a second in mid-air, just in front of the Doctor's face.

'Doctor?' a female voice called out.

The creature hissed with fury and retracted its tentacle.

'Marie?' the Doctor replied. 'Marie, is that you?'

She walked hesitantly into the dimly lit room. 'Are you there, Doctor? I followed you down here and got lost. Who are you talking to?' She was squinting into the dark.

'Oh, it's Miss X!' Marie said, spotting the elderly passenger. 'Hello! What are you doing down here?'

The old lady composed herself and smoothed down the silk ruffles of her blouse. She smiled simperingly at Marie. 'Why, I was just having a little chat with the Doctor here. We had a minor . . . misunderstanding.'

The Doctor wasn't putting up with her lies. 'Rubbish! She was just about to attack me with her razor-sharp tentacles and poisonous suckers!'

'What?' cried Miss X. 'Oh, very amusing! What a strange sense of humour you have, Doctor.'

Then she turned and smiled at Marie once more. 'I must not dawdle. Colonel Hulke has asked me to dine with him as his guest at the captain's table, and I need to go and get ready.' With that, the old lady tottered away.

Marie turned to look at the Doctor, who was still clutching his armful of parts for the De-mesmerisor.

'I came looking for you to apologise for earlier,' she said. 'I'm sorry I doubted your sanity and ran away.'

The Doctor shrugged. 'That often happens. No hard feelings.'

'Do you still maintain that Miss X is a monster?'

'Yes. You can't see it, but she's really a ravenous, tentacled creature that's acquired a taste for human brains.'

Marie looked pale but determined. 'To my eyes she still looks like a nice old dear. But I *heard* her, Doctor. When she was talking to you and she thought you were alone. I heard the terrible things she was saying!'

He grinned broadly. 'So you do believe me now?'

Marie nodded. 'I think I have to. It's the most bizarre thing that's ever happened to me, but I know it's true.'

'Excellent!'

'But what can we do about it?'

'Well,' the Doctor said, 'help me carry all these bits up to the bridge. I have a very brilliant plan to carry out!'

The grand dining room was splendidly decorated in gaudy shades of orange and purple for Hallowe'en. Miss X seemed at first surprised by the profusion of fake cobwebs and paper bats, but as he escorted her to the captain's table Colonel Hulke assured her it was all quite customary. 'Don't you have Hallowe'en where you come from?'

She smiled. 'My memory is still on the blink.'

The captain's table was in the very centre of the opulent room and there was a great deal to take in. When he took his own seat, the captain made a courtly nod in Miss X's direction, then the meal began in earnest. Smartly attired waiters brought in silver platters of smoked salmon.

Miss X ate hers in one bite.

'Hungry, my dear?' the colonel enquired, raising an eyebrow.

'Ravenous,' she replied.

A string quartet played classical music while champagne was served to all the guests. The captain held up his crystal flute and the whole table toasted their new guest of honour.

'To our mysterious Miss X!' they chorused.

I could quite get to like this life, thought Organism 96. The

creature's true name came back to it all at once: the name –
hardly a real name at all – that had been bestowed upon it
by the Soviet scientists who had genetically engineered it for
warfare. *I am Organism 96*, it thought. *I was created in a Petri
dish and lived for seventy years in an underground lake. Dark, cold
and all alone.*

'Are you all right, my dear?' asked Colonel Hulke,
looking concerned by Miss X's far-away expression.

At that very moment the ship's tannoy speakers whined
harshly with feedback, gaining everyone's attention.

'Good evening!' came an amplified voice. 'This isn't your
captain speaking. This is the Doctor. I've tied up the purser
and taken over the tannoy system, all for a very good reason!'

Captain Letts was on his feet, looking furious and
barking orders at members of his crew. Diners at other tables
were looking confused, trying to work out if this was some
form of bizarre entertainment.

'You're all being hypnotised and you don't even know it!
A genetically modified, mutated murderer has scrambled your
senses in order to disguise itself,' continued the Doctor. 'And,
because I am amazing, I have built a machine that will un-
hypnotise the lot of you!'

His voice was immediately drowned out by a rising
cacophony that came crackling over the airwaves.

'W-what's that noise?' cried Miss X, looking alarmed. She grasped the colonel's arm. 'What is that man talking about?'

'I'm afraid I don't know.'

Miss X stood up, swaying, feeling as if the air and light around her were turning into quivering jelly. That horrible sick-making noise; why couldn't they just shut it off?

Then she realised that everyone in the dining room was staring at her.

People were getting up out of their seats.

Ghastly looks upon their faces.

There were even screams.

'What's the matter?' she bellowed at them.

Captain Letts shouted and now sailors were running towards her.

All at once Miss X knew what was happening. They were seeing through her disguise. They were seeing Organism 96. The Doctor had managed to do exactly what he had threatened.

Organism 96 swung round to face the colonel. He looked disgusted, but not as fearful as the rest of them.

'I am sorry,' the creature gasped, and turned to flee. It slithered from the room, paying no heed at all to where it was going. Passengers screamed at it wherever it went. Its tentacles

flailed and its suckers flinched, spitting hot venom as it went. Its hybrid heart beat falteringly inside its chest. *Where to go? What to do?* Just moments ago it had been enjoying the toast to its new life! To being human! Now it was all ruined. All of it.

More screams rang out as Organism 96 emerged on to the deck. The sun was going down and many passengers were enjoying an evening stroll. Most scattered at the sight of the creature. Some cowered as it swept past, and others remained frozen to the spot in mute horror. It slobbered along the railings and howled its rage and frustration at all it met. Bloodlust filled its thoughts.

'Oh my god!' said Marie in disbelief.

She had been running from the bridge towards the dining room. In the golden Mediterranean light, the creature swung round and Marie saw at last what the Doctor had been seeing the whole time. The organism was truly terrifying, like a squid standing on two sturdy legs, glistening with fetid slime. It quivered with spite and rage, showering the deck with droplets of stinking ichor.

'You pretended to be a poor old lady, and this is what you really were?'

'Who's to say,' gasped Organism 96, 'that underneath this monstrous shell my true self isn't like Miss X after all?' It wheedled and inched closer to Marie. 'Being among humans,

I could have learned to *become* more human and fit in!'

Marie gagged. The closer the monster came, the worse it looked. She stared at the greasy slime dripping off each shining scale and the quivering suckers on every swaying protuberance.

Organism 96 was close enough to make a grab for the singer. A single tentacle wrapped itself neatly about Marie's throat, before she had the chance to scream.

As he hurtled into the dining room, the Doctor was intercepted by Colonel Hulke.

'What have you *done*?' exclaimed the former spy.

'I revealed its true appearance, didn't I? Where has it gone?'

The elderly man looked furious. 'You blundering idiot! I had the whole situation under control!'

'Steady on,' said the Doctor. He was tuning out and listening to the sounds of pandemonium from the deck, attempting to pinpoint their source. 'I fear she's running amok!'

'There'll be a massacre,' said Hulke, hurrying to keep up with the Doctor's purposeful strides. 'The captain's gone ballistic. He's arming the whole crew. Shoot on sight!'

'Oh dear. I thought I was doing the right thing bringing

everything out into the open.'

'You did, did you?' the old man snarled. 'I was working on her so carefully, gaining her trust.'

The Doctor stopped and stared at him. 'You mean you *knew* she was a monster?'

'Of course!'

'Marie and I thought you were having a holiday romance!'

'Don't be disgusting. I knew what she was all along. MI5 have been tracking that creature for weeks. We knew it was still in this area, following its escape from the subterranean Soviet base. There are agents all over the Mediterranean looking for it, on board every vessel from here to Majorca.'

At that very moment there came a much louder burst of screaming from the deck outside. Screaming from healthy, well-trained lungs.

'She's got Marie!' gasped the Doctor.

News of Miss X's terrifying transformation spread quickly throughout the ship. Warnings were broadcast advising all passengers and crew to avoid contact with the monstrous being that was now holding Marie Blenkinsop hostage on Deck Six.

It was a very dicey situation.

The Doctor stood several yards away, trying to appear jaunty and unconcerned. 'Do you prefer to be addressed as Miss X or by your official Soviet-designated name?'

The creature produced rancid blue froth from both its mouths. 'I'd rather *you* didn't address me at all!'

Colonel Hulke stepped smoothly forward. 'My dear, allow me to apologise for my reaction to your . . . erm . . . altered appearance at the dinner table. My manners were dreadful.'

The creature tightened its grip on Marie. 'You're being kind to me. Trying to trick me, I suppose?'

'Not at all. I know you're a civilised person, despite outward appearances. In the past week I believe I have been getting to know a very special lady.'

Each veiny, globular eye swivelled to study the old man. 'Do you really mean that?'

'I do.'

'Marie,' said the Doctor in a stage whisper. 'You know that high note you do at the climax of the Whitney Houston song? The one from the nineties show?'

'What about it?' she hissed back.

'Do it now,' he suggested. 'I've had some experience in dealing with deep-sea monsters. Trust me. Sing like Whitney!'

Luckily the colonel and Miss X were paying this exchange no heed whatsoever. The creature's attention was entirely on the old man, as he took a cautious step towards her. It watched him reach into a pocket of his blazer and produce a small padded-velvet box.

Organism 96 gasped. A jewellery box! Its mind dared to imagine what might be inside.

'*Now*, Marie!' cried the Doctor.

Marie looked up to see that every deck above her was crammed with faces staring intently at her. Something inside her snapped to attention. The potent force that had possessed her all her life was the need to sing, and right now – with slimy tentacles slowly squeezing her – she needed that talent more than ever.

Marie opened her mouth and sang like Whitney with all her might.

The effect was immediate and remarkable.

Organism 96 shrieked in pain and loosened its shining coils at once. It shoved the noisy young woman away from it with a gurgling cry of rage.

Marie was sent sprawling to safety, and the Doctor caught her.

'Make her stop!' gibbered Organism 96.

The Doctor said, 'I guessed its delicate ears wouldn't be able to take that!'

'What?' Marie was dazed and vaguely insulted.

Colonel Hulke was still holding the jewellery box out to the creature on the deck. Everything was quiet again. 'Take it. Open it,' he commanded.

'Is it . . . a ring?' asked Organism 96, picking up the box with the tip of a tentacle.

The old colonel sighed. 'I have my orders, I'm afraid. You are a rather dangerous organism. Much too deadly to be around human beings, no matter how much you'd like to be.'

'Oh no,' murmured the Doctor.

'What is it?' asked Marie.

'We need to move now, Marie,' the Doctor insisted. 'We haven't got much time.'

Suddenly Marie was being dragged backwards along the deck and the Doctor was yelling at the top of his voice, 'Everyone, get back!'

Organism 96 stared at its elderly gentleman friend with confusion in all of its bulbous, bloodshot eyes. 'I don't understand. If it isn't a ring, then what is this ticking, bleeping, glowing device you've handed me?'

Colonel Hulke replied gently, 'It's a small bomb, my dear. I'm afraid our time together is over.'

Organism 96 looked in disbelief at the velveteen box. 'Why? Why have you done this thing?'

'My duty to queen and country. I'm very sorry, my dear.'

'But –'

And with that, both Organism 96 and the man whose final mission was to locate her at all costs exploded in a bright blue flash.

For a few seconds their frozen silhouettes hovered in the sunset at the prow of the ship. Then they faded, leaving nothing but a hole in the side of the *W. H. Allen*.

Klaxons sounded. Garbled instructions blared through every speaker. Footsteps thundered along platforms and decks. Lifeboats were winched into position and passengers wearing lifejackets milled about in confusion.

'I must go and help,' Marie told the Doctor. 'The entertainers have to help in the event of an emergency at sea. I've had the training and everything! I must go to the assembly point.'

'Of course,' said the Doctor. 'You've got work to do. Best get on with it.'

'Well, you'll have to get aboard a life raft, too.'

He smiled, unperturbed by the crush and kerfuffle all around them. 'I've got my own life raft, as it happens.'

'That unfortunate woman,' said Marie. 'Or whatever she was. And that old man! Sacrificing himself to fulfil his duty . . .'

The Doctor took a deep breath. 'A little drastic, really. I was hoping to find another way. Perhaps, with help, the creature could have broken the conditioning of its masters. But at the same time it seemed to enjoy the killing and all that business about eating human brains. That's not a very forgivable trait in nice old ladies.'

'I guess not,' said Marie. They were both shouting over the noise of the wailing klaxons and the general panic. 'Look, I need to help with the life rafts. Are you sure you know where you're going? Will you be all right?'

'I'll be fine!' The Doctor grinned.

'Will I see you again?' Marie asked.

'Oh, somewhere,' he said lightly. 'Some other time, perhaps.'

He started to hurry off and find the TARDIS, then at the last moment he turned back to shout, 'Well done on the singing, by the way! You've got a fantastic talent there! Keep it up!'

Then he was gone.

Marie shook her head, then dashed off, heart racing, to the life rafts.

THE NINTH DOCTOR

THE PATCHWORK
PIERROT

Written by Scott Handcock

It was a cold November morning when the carnival came to town. Autumn had descended across the landscape a few weeks before, bringing with it a chill, foreboding air, but still the people went about their business. They had jobs to lead and lives to live, and nothing was going to change that, least of all the weather.

At first the noise sounded like thunder, except the skies were completely clear. The source of the rumbling was a ramshackle convoy of vehicles rattling along the dirt tracks on the horizon. They thundered through the tiny Nebraska town and set up camp in a nearby field, bringing with them a storm of curiosity.

In the wake of the Civil War, people yearned for

distraction, and carnivals like this one promised exactly
that: a glimpse beyond the ordinary world they thought they
knew. People flocked from miles around to take in new and
sensational sights, to feel a sense of wonder. Sometimes they
just wanted to believe in something more, even if they knew it
was a con.

Within a mere hour of the convoy's arrival, the circus
began to sprawl out across the field. The Big Top billowed
from a central scaffold, while all manner of strange
mechanical structures were erected around it. Exotic beasts
and animals slumbered patiently in their cages, seemingly
oblivious to the wall of noise around them.

At another time, on another day, an altogether different
noise might have been heard, too: the sound of the universe
tearing itself in two as the Doctor's TARDIS wheezed into
existence. Today, however, the TARDIS's arrival was lost
beneath the clamour of hammers and wind, mangled in the
tuneless dirge of a hurdy-gurdy.

Seconds after its materialisation, the doors to the
TARDIS opened, and a tall, broad figure emerged. He
sported close-cropped brown hair, a battered old leather
jacket, and a stern expression on a face that didn't seem used
to smiling. His eyes darted round and up and down, taking
in his new surroundings and trying to process the assault on

his senses. Aside from the sounds of labourers, there was
the sickly-sweet tang of cotton candy in the air, and almost
everything he saw was garishly vibrant.

'A carnival.' The Doctor tugged the TARDIS door
closed behind him. 'Fantastic.'

He ventured out into the busy crowd of labourers and
performers, striding through them as if he owned the place.
In spite of all the life and colour around him, there was
something unnerving about the place, though he couldn't
quite put his finger on what it was. Everywhere he turned,
trunks were being unloaded from their wagons, tents were
being pitched and posters had gone up promoting all kinds
of weird attractions. Many of them were what he might have
expected – acrobats and fire-eaters, lion tamers and clowns
– but there were also a couple more curious personalities.
The Reptile Girl, for instance, seemed remarkably familiar,
and there was an apparently 'notorious' Tattooed Man, who
claimed to 'see your fortune in the stars!'

The Doctor scoffed, craning his neck towards the crisp
autumn sky above him. 'Not quite how the future works,
mate,' he muttered quietly to himself. 'Still, keep trying.'

Very soon, an entire community had appeared as if
from nowhere, flooding the field with people: managers,
performers, stagehands and labourers, men and women

old and young, individuals from every possible walk of life imaginable. The Doctor smiled at this. Even after the horrors of the war, the human race thrived. If only he could have said the same of his own kind.

'You okay there?' A stranger's voice interrupted his train of thought.

'Always,' replied the Doctor, spinning on his heels.

A young woman was standing behind him, wearing one of the gaudiest outfits he'd ever seen. A surprisingly bushy beard covered her face.

'You must be the bearded lady.' The Doctor grinned, extending a hand. 'I'm the Doctor. What's your name?'

'Mona,' replied the woman, taking the Doctor's hand and shaking it firmly. 'Oh, and it's a fake, just in case you were wondering.' To prove her point, she snatched at the beard and tugged the whiskers cleanly from her chin, then stashed them into one of her pockets.

'Your secret's safe with me,' the Doctor promised.

'I should hope so!' she teased. Mona couldn't quite place the Doctor's accent, despite having travelled across most of the United States. 'I don't think I've ever seen you here before. Where do you come from?'

'Oh, here and there,' the Doctor answered. 'You know how it is . . .'

Mona nodded sadly. She knew *exactly* how it was. Everyone in the circus had a similar story. Each of them had been forced to flee their homes, and most knew they could never go back. They were outsiders through and through. Now, they looked out for each other and the people like them.

The Doctor was one of those people, Mona thought. Even behind his obvious swagger and bravado, she detected a sense of loss, as though his entire world had fallen away beneath him. She would never know how correct her perception was.

'Well, whether you plan to stay or you're passing through, it's a pleasure to know you,' she said, dropping her voice down to a whisper.

It was then that the Doctor realised what had been troubling him. 'No one's talking,' he said, a little too loudly. 'Well, no one except for you.'

For all the noise and music, Mona's was the only voice he'd heard since he'd arrived. True, the labourers mumbled and grumbled here and there, but never loud enough to be heard above their work. Even the stallholders stood impassively in their stands, hoping to tacitly drum up business with nothing more than smiles and gestures.

'A silent circus,' the Doctor mused. 'Why *is* that?'

'You wouldn't believe me even if I told you,' Mona replied.

'Believe what?' the Doctor asked a little impatiently, producing a small brown leather wallet from his pocket. Quickly, he shot Mona a flash of psychic paper, then thrust it back inside his jacket. 'I'm the Doctor,' he repeated, more reassuringly, 'and I promise you I can help.'

Whatever she had seen in the psychic paper, Mona trusted him.

'They say people keep going missing, everywhere we go.' Mona paused for a second, gauging the Doctor's reaction; he seemed to be taking her seriously. 'Don't get me wrong,' she continued, 'people come and go all the time – always do in places like this. But I mean properly disappearing.'

'What, like kidnapped?' The Doctor seemed suddenly energised.

Mona shook her head. 'I don't know what it is. But you hear stories on the road, you know? People vanish when the circus comes to town.' She sighed, then looked around at the wagons, checking that no one could overhear them. 'They say we bring something with us,' she hissed. 'Nobody's quite sure what it is, or where it came from, but that's what they believe. People claim they've seen things. Terrifying things.'

'What sort of things?' the Doctor asked. He looked concerned.

'A figure dressed in white.' Mona shuddered. 'Not a person like you or me, but something other – something supernatural. They say it never speaks; it only screams. Not that anyone's ever tried talking to it, that I know of – if it's even real, of course.'

The Doctor paused, letting the silence hang between them. On the surface, it sounded just as Mona told him: a ghost story, nothing more. You could find legends such as this one right across the universe, and they were rarely ever grounded in fact. Though 'rarely' didn't mean 'never'.

'Has anyone around here seen this figure?' the Doctor asked.

'Sure.' Mona grabbed him by the hand. 'Let's go!'

'Where to?'

'To the only other person who'll talk,' she said. 'At least to you.'

In the space behind the Big Top, a scruffy young man was lugging trunks from tent to tent. He was dressed in a dusty cream tunic and cut-off trousers. He was well built, slim, with a mop of chestnut hair, and even though it was mid-November he'd broken into a sweat.

'Jacob!' Mona said, startling the young man. He wiped a sleeve across his damp forehead, apparently trying to look a lot more collected than he was, but it was clear to the Doctor that he was just as on edge as everyone else.

'Where'd you find this one then?' Jacob asked, looking the Doctor up and down, unable to stop a hint of jealousy creeping into his voice.

Mona shot him a reassuring smile. 'This is the Doctor,' she said, dropping her voice again. 'Something to do with the sheriff's office, only sort of a maverick. He's here to help, whoever he is. That's what matters.'

Jacob nodded. 'God knows we could use a doctor around here, with some of the stuff that goes on. Turns out sword swallowing's not as easy as it looks.' He gave a short, grim laugh, and the Doctor couldn't entirely tell whether or not he was joking.

'Mona here tells me you might have heard something,' the Doctor said, 'about what's been happening around here?'

Jacob flicked his eyes at Mona, and she nodded back at him. The gesture spoke volumes: Jacob could trust the Doctor.

'I only know what I've seen,' Jacob said.

'Which is what, exactly?'

Jacob hesitated, then pulled the Doctor closer to him,

either so as not to be heard or for dramatic effect.

'None of us knows for sure,' he whispered. 'It just stands there, in the shadows, all billowing shirts and pantaloons. You know the kind of thing. A Pierrot. But, trust me, this ain't no clown. There's nothing funny about it.'

'Any idea who it could be?' the Doctor asked.

'Nope. Never once shown its face. Just wears this sort of mask thing. Not a mask like all the others, mind; this one is different. I mean, I only ever caught a glimpse of it myself – and that was more than enough – but it was wrong somehow . . .' Jacob trailed off. 'I guess Mona's told you why nobody talks around here?'

'She hasn't.'

'Well, it's because it's blind – blind cos it has no eyes. Just this blank, dead stare.' Jacob felt a chill run down his spine at the thought of it, this inhuman creature stalking the carnival, night after night. 'It's funny, I didn't even notice it at first. It just sort of appeared out of the darkness. Like it was watching me. Never knew how long it had been there.'

'And where was this?' demanded the Doctor.

'In the Big Top, a couple of months back. I'm not the only one who's seen it, either. Word gets about. Can't not in a place this small. You know how it is.'

'Has it ever been seen anywhere other than the Big Top?'

'Not that I know of,' Jacob said. 'People say it lurks there after dark.'

'And none of you have ever thought to go looking for it?'

A sharp burst of laughter from Jacob told the Doctor all that he needed to know.

'Thought not,' the Doctor muttered. 'Still, thanks for your help, Jacob. Much appreciated.' He patted the young man warmly on the shoulder, then strode off in the other direction.

For the rest of that afternoon, the Doctor wandered aimlessly around the carnival, taking in all manner of sights and sounds. He tried to make small talk with some of the stallholders and labourers, but they all maintained an unsettling silence.

When dusk began to fall, the Doctor quietly watched as lamps were lit throughout the field and cast a gentle orange glow across the landscape. The coloured canvas of the Big Top seemed to dance in the gaslight, throwing the workers' shadows on to the walls. It was like a large-scale shadow theatre, only instead of a play the Doctor was watching the silhouettes of labourers packing up tools.

'Haven't you got a home to go to?' a familiar voice enquired.

The Doctor looked up. 'I'm a traveller,' he replied, making room for Mona to sit down beside him.

'And how long are you staying?'

'Usually I stay for as long as I'm needed,' the Doctor replied. 'Why, you trying to get rid of me or something?'

'People say you've been asking questions,' she said.

'It's what I do,' the Doctor huffed.

'No one is going to talk to you about it.'

'Can't hurt to ask. And, anyway, I told you: I'm here to help. I think you are too.'

'I don't know what you mean,' Mona lied.

'Oh, come on! Don't give me that. It's why you're here right now.' The Doctor rose to his feet. 'I saw it on your face the instant Jacob spoke about that Pierrot. You know what I'm talking about – how he said it lurks about the Big Top after dark. You knew I'd still be here and that's why you came and found me.'

Mona sighed. There was no point pretending the Doctor wasn't right. 'You want to go there? You want to find out what's been doing all this?'

'Course!' the Doctor exclaimed. 'Don't you?'

Mona simply smiled.

They both knew that question didn't need an answer.

■

An hour later, the circus had all but closed. A cold fog had descended, and everyone had retreated either to their tents or to personal wagons. Everyone except for the Doctor and Mona, that is, who used the cover of darkness to sneak inside the Big Top.

To their surprise, the gaslight from outside made little impact other than to accentuate the uneven nature of the dye within the canvas. It was darker inside the tent than either of them could have anticipated. They struggled to make out their own hands in front of their faces, never mind each other.

'Stay close to me,' the Doctor whispered gruffly.

Mona had other ideas. 'How about *you* stay close to *me*,' she countered, stepping in front of him.

The Doctor followed obediently; Mona knew the place better than he did, after all. She traced a route between the walls and the makeshift scaffolding, following the curve of the canvas round, leading them deeper into the structure that hadn't even been there twelve hours earlier. Occasionally, Mona would twist her body inwards, ducking her head, whispering warnings back to the Doctor.

Eventually they emerged into the open. It was still dark, of course, but already the Doctor's eyes were becoming accustomed to their surroundings. He pulled out his sonic screwdriver and aimed it into the air. The lanterns round the ring burst into flame.

Mona's jaw dropped.

'What have we here, then?' boomed the Doctor, gesturing around the empty auditorium they found themselves in. There wasn't a single living soul to greet them; instead, there was just row after endless row of empty seating. It was a far cry from the ring's daylight alter-ego.

Mona realised she'd never seen the Big Top like this before. Usually, it was a place that brimmed with life, awash with noise and laughter. But now? Now it simply felt hollow and dead, as though they'd stumbled upon a tomb of entertainment. She didn't care for it.

'That's interesting,' murmured the Doctor.

He shuffled towards a marking in the sand just a few feet ahead of them. It looked like footprints, but made by feet of two different sizes: one footprint was large and elongated, the other much smaller and daintier.

'What is it?' Mona asked.

'I'm not sure,' replied the Doctor, crouching down for a closer look. 'That's what makes it interesting.'

It wasn't only the difference in size that made the footprints intriguing, but also the fact that they faced away from one another, as if they'd each been going in different directions. To the Doctor's surprise, this pattern continued as he followed the trail of ill-matched footprints through the sand until eventually they vanished entirely.

The Doctor looked up. He'd reached the edge of the ring. Ahead of him, there was just a shallow wooden barrier, designed to fence off the currently non-existent audience, and a ladder that towered up to a platform above him.

'Mona, come take a look at this!' he called, pointing to one of the ladder's lower rungs.

'Is that . . .?'

'Sand,' confirmed the Doctor, blowing it away with a single puff. 'Someone's been through here. And recently, too.'

'But who?'

'More likely *what*,' the Doctor corrected, gesturing back to the mismatched footprints. 'You know, I'm starting to believe in this Pierrot of yours.'

An unearthly wail echoed around the Big Top.

'What was —'

The Doctor pressed a finger to his lips, cutting her off, and Mona couldn't help but back away. The Doctor stayed put.

The creature howled again, this time with greater fury, and two things crossed the Doctor's mind: first, the scream reminded him of something, but he wasn't quite sure what;

and second, and frankly more urgent, where was it coming from?

Whatever the answers to those two questions were, one thing was certain: the thing that was making these noises most definitely wasn't human.

The Doctor threw out his arms, gesturing up to the darkness above. 'Come out and show yourself!' he demanded.

This only seemed to make the howling stutter, reducing it to a terrible, gurgled laugh. It was a sound that chilled Mona's blood, prompting her to back even further away.

'Where are you?' the Doctor repeated, searching for his invisible prey.

It sounded like the wails were coming from somewhere above them, hiding in the shadows of the rigging. The Doctor aimed the sonic upwards, when suddenly the laugh screeched louder. A dreadful, inhuman image darted in front of him, moving at speed: a tall, lithe silhouette, hurtling through the gloom, suspended upside-down from a trapeze.

What happened next happened all too quickly. In a single, swift, slick movement, the figure swung past the Doctor, out into the centre of the ring, snatched Mona round the waist and hauled her skywards.

She felt its breath on the back of her neck, followed by a short, sharp scratch at the top of her arm. It hurt at first, but within seconds she felt her senses starting to blur. She could just hear the Doctor shouting up at her, promising that he'd save her. Then the darkness swallowed her up . . .

When Mona recovered consciousness, the very first thing she became aware of was an almost overwhelming stench of rotting meat. She took short, shallow breaths, resisting the urge to retch. Then, as she regained her composure, she realised she couldn't move.

She was bound to a chair, forced into an upright position. Her wrists and feet were strapped to the chair's arms and legs. She cocked her head from side to side, scanning the area for any clues as to where she might be. A shaft of moonlight fought to be seen through a small, grimy window, which made her think she must still be inside. As she tried to move, she felt the floorboards rock beneath her and guessed she must be in one of the trailers.

'Hello!' she called quietly, her voice catching at the back of her throat. 'Can anybody hear me?'

She waited for a moment – a moment that felt like a lifetime – but nobody answered.

Fine, she thought. So she was on her own – at least she knew that much. She also knew she was in a trailer, which meant she couldn't have been taken far, even if the trailer was on the furthest edge of the field. And, of course, she was still alive . . . for the time being, anyway.

She peered into the moonlit gloom, scouring the shadows for further clues. In one of the corners there seemed to be a mass of filthy rags, heaped up like some kind of bedding. Above that, hanging from a set of rusted hooks, she could just make out the glint of metal: a dozen or so different objects gleaming beneath what little light there was. Tools, perhaps?

Before she had time to focus, the door of the wagon slammed inwards. In the frame of the tiny doorway, she could now clearly see the silhouette of the Pierrot. It looked much like any other clown, except its costume was tattered and grimy, the once-pristine white of its tunic stained with flecks of red and yellow.

It lumbered clumsily into the wagon, stinking of rotten flesh and iodine. It ran its fingers through Mona's hair and she flinched, recoiling as it then made to stroke her cheek. She thought she heard the Pierrot sigh appreciatively. Of course, it was impossible for her to know precisely what the creature was thinking; it hadn't yet spoken a word, if it even *could* speak. Its breathing was slow and laboured, wheezing unsteadily through a now-decrepit processor. Its face gave nothing away, hidden beneath the permanent grin of its mask.

Mona once more resisted the urge to gag as it leaned in even closer.

'Knock knock!' a familiar voice sounded, and someone rapped on the wood of the open door. 'Sorry to have kept you. Is this a private party or can anyone join in?'

The Pierrot jerked round to face the intruder, and Mona saw the Doctor leap into the trailer.

'Of *course*.' The Doctor sighed the moment he saw the Pierrot's face. 'I thought you looked familiar. Then there were the readings from the sonic: electromagnetic signals way too advanced for this period.'

'Wait,' Mona interrupted. 'You *know* this thing?'

'I've seen things like it, yeah,' confirmed the Doctor. 'It's a Cyberman – or at least it *was* a Cyberman, once. This one's a little crude, even by their standards.'

'Cyberman?' Mona repeated, and the Pierrot cocked its head upon hearing the name. Then, to her surprise, it started talking.

'WHY – are you – HERE?' it asked the Doctor in a strangely sing-song voice. 'WHERE have you – COME from? WHO – who – who – WHO are YOU?'

'Never mind who I am!' snapped the Doctor, aiming his sonic screwdriver at the Pierrot.

'What IS that – DEVICE?'

'This? Just a trick of the trade,' the Doctor replied. 'Funny, I don't remember you lot being quite so chatty.'

Mona watched as the screwdriver's tip glowed blue, accompanied by an unnatural, high-pitched whine. The Pierrot looked on impassively, as though it was processing this development.

'Doctor!' Mona hissed. 'What the heck is a Cyberman?'

The Doctor checked the readings from his sonic, considering whether to answer, then a solemn expression fell across his face. He knew he had very little time before the Pierrot designated him a threat – or worse, a potential resource.

'The Cybermen were once people like you and me,' the Doctor started, slowly edging closer to Mona. 'They lived on a world much like this one. The only difference was, that one drifted out among the stars. The planet grew steadily colder and harsher, more and more inhospitable, until eventually their only option to survive was to reinvent themselves. Literally.'

Mona stared at the Pierrot. It seemed somehow sadder now, though it still grinned with that blank, impassive face.

'Their bodies grew weak,' the Doctor continued, 'so they replaced them bit by bit, swapping organs for machine parts. The only trouble was, doing that drove them mad. So guess what? They sacrificed their emotions, too.'

'So what are you saying? That thing's a machine?'

The Doctor shook his head. 'Part machine, part human. This one must have fallen through a breach in space–time and ended up here: nineteenth-century America, an era without technology. Normally it would upgrade itself with whatever technology it had to hand, but here?' He glanced at the metal tools – surgical instruments, it was now clear – hanging neatly from the hooks. 'Here it's had no choice but to regress. If it can't replace its machine parts when they fail, it replaces the flesh instead. Hence the missing people. This place is the perfect cover. People go missing everywhere you go, and no one ever stops to ask questions.'

The Cyberman turned back towards Mona and stumbled forward. 'I WILL become – LIKE YOU!' it boomed, and Mona felt suddenly sick. As the creature moved, she noticed it was horribly lopsided. One leg was long and muscular, the other about two inches shorter, and looked like it had been attached to the body backwards. Its arms were similarly mismatched, with one hand a completely different colour from the rest of its body.

'That's why it brought me here, isn't it?' Mona realised. 'It wanted me for . . . for . . .' She couldn't bring herself to finish the sentence.

'I WANT – your HEART,' the Cyberman told her matter-of-factly.

'No!' The Doctor stepped between them. A quiet fury burned in his eyes. 'You want a heart, you'll have to go through me. I've got two of them, after all. But I'm warning you, leave her out of it!'

'I want – HER heart,' it repeated.

'Well, you can't have it!'

'You DO NOT – underSTAND,' the Pierrot Cyberman persisted. 'I WANT – her – heart. I WANT – her heart. I WANT – I want – HER . . .' It paused before continuing. 'Mona. I WANT – MONA.'

Suddenly the Doctor understood. 'But that's not possible.' He stared into the Pierrot's blank expression. 'I think . . .' The Doctor hesitated, then turned to Mona. 'I think it has feelings for you!'

Mona looked appalled. 'That thing? Don't be revolting. It's a monster!'

'All those upgrades must have overridden its Cyber heritage,' the Doctor said, turning back to confront the Pierrot. 'This isn't right. Can't you see? She doesn't want this! You have to let her go.'

The Pierrot shook its head. 'I KNOW – what she – WANTS!' it rasped.

'No,' protested Mona. 'You don't know at all! The Doctor's right. I *don't* want this. I don't want you. I don't want *any* of this. I love someone else!'

'CORRect!'

The Cyberman didn't seem at all surprised by this revelation. It simply raised its hands, released two clasps at the side of its head, and gingerly removed the mask that had covered its face.

Mona screamed.

Even the Doctor struggled to deal with the sight of what now faced them.

It had been human, once – there was no doubt about that – but all trace of humanity had long since been discarded. A ring of metal instruments had been welded into its scalp, connecting to a unit on its chest. Its eyes were just empty sockets, and the right-hand side of its jaw had apparently failed, exposing a terrible mouth of gaping flesh beneath. And the face – if you could still call it that – the face had been stolen from someone else. Thick black thread crisscrossed round the edges, fixing new skin awkwardly to old. It was a face that Mona recognised all too well.

'Jacob?' she whispered, horrified.

The Cyberman nodded. 'You HAVE – AFFECTION for this – VISAGE,' it said coldly.

Mona couldn't bear to look any longer. That awful voice, coming out of those beautiful lips. It was all too much for her. She closed her eyes.

'Okay, enough's enough!' the Doctor barked. 'This ends now!'

He wielded the sonic screwdriver squarely at the Pierrot. It looked at him from Jacob's lifeless face, then reached out and casually plucked a bone saw from one of the hooks.

'I WILL become – like YOU,' the Cyberman told him.

The Doctor stood his ground. 'You've killed too many innocent people,' he warned, still brandishing the sonic. 'You cannot be allowed to carry on!'

'YOU cannot – STOP me!' The Cyberman raised the bone saw slowly above its head.

'Doctor, please!' Mona yelled. 'You're going to get yourself killed! Just go, please. You heard what it said. It's not going to hurt me.'

'Oh, Mona.' The Doctor smiled sadly. 'It already has.'

Without another word, he activated the screwdriver and drove it firmly towards their foe. The Cyberman instantly started to scream: a horrible electronic wail mixed with feedback. It clawed at the sides of its head and dropped to its knees.

'WHAT – have you – DONE?!' it demanded feebly, a

series of sparks erupting from its chest.

'You're more human than machine now,' the Doctor told it, working at Mona's bonds. 'Didn't take much to shut down your systems – including your emotional inhibitor. Thought it was time you realised you can't just pick and choose what you want to feel!'

'But it – HURTS!' the Cyberman screamed at him.

'Yeah, I know. That's part of being human!'

The Cyberman started to sob, crumpling in a heap on the pile of rags.

The Doctor released the final strap and within seconds Mona was free again.

'Thank you.' She hugged him tightly.

The Doctor shrugged it off. 'Don't mention it,' he replied. 'Now come on. It's about time we got you away from here!'

He ushered her out of the door, casting one last glance back at the prone, pathetic figure of the Pierrot. It made no attempt to follow. It simply whimpered, struggling to comprehend the pain it was feeling.

'I'm sorry,' said the Doctor. 'Truly, I am.'

Then, without another word, he closed the trailer door.

It was now the dead of night. The Doctor and Mona returned to the carnival, and Mona was silent as she tried to make sense of what had happened. She wasn't sure how she'd ever explain Jacob's fate to those who hadn't seen him for themselves – or even *if* she should explain it. All she knew was that she'd managed to survive, but Jacob hadn't. Jacob was *gone*. At that thought, a wave of nausea swept through her body, and her chest suddenly ached. It just didn't feel *real*.

The Doctor offered to stay with Mona, but she was insistent; he should go. She didn't need anyone. That was part of why she had joined the carnival in the first place: she wanted to fight her own battles, to look out for herself. And besides, if the Doctor could save others like Jacob from such terrible monsters and terrible fates, then the last thing she wanted was to stand in his way.

The Doctor soon returned to the trailer, knowing he couldn't just leave the creature there, suffering. But the Cyberman was nowhere to be seen. It couldn't have ventured far – it was too badly damaged – though with its life support disabled, he couldn't even track it with the sonic. Perhaps it had already shut down? In any case, it couldn't have survived for much longer. Not in the state it had been in. He left the carnival as Mona had asked, thinking sadly of the young man whom he had been too late to save.

Time passed, and the creature did not reappear. It seemed that it had simply vanished without a trace, like so many of its unfortunate victims, and all that had survived of it was its story.

Though sometimes, carnival folk will spy something from the corner of their eye. The quick movement of something pale, flitting past them in the darkness. Or they'll hear a soft echo of a scream, and suddenly feel that they are being watched from the shadows. And just for a second, they'll wonder if the Patchwork Pierrot ever really left after all . . .

THE TENTH DOCTOR

BLOOD WILL OUT

Written by Richard Dungworth

Nancy hurried along the narrow, gleaming corridor towards the next junction. With only her intuition to guide her, she turned left . . . and found herself face-to-face with a grotesque mockery of a human child. Its body was outlandishly long and thin, drawn out like stretched dough. Lank, spindly arms drooped at its sides. The features of its bizarrely long face were ghoulishly misshapen.

Nancy halted in front of the mirrored wall that blocked her path. She paid little attention to her distorted reflection. Instead, her eyes darted anxiously around the edges of the mirror's warped image. She was seeking what she thought she had seen out of the corner of her eye in several of the other mirrors: a flicker of movement at the very edge of her vision;

a fleeting glimpse of something blood red, right behind her.

There's nothing there, silly, she told herself firmly. *Just me.*
But the unpleasant sensation of being watched still prickled
her skin. She turned away from the dead-end and tried her
luck in the other direction.

Nancy dearly wished she had spent her pocket money
on any one of the fair's many other attractions. Right now,
it seemed that only she in the whole of Farringham had
opted to experience the MIRACULOUS MIRROR MEGA-
MAZE. She had done so because of a strong sense that she
was *meant* to. As she had walked past the sideshow, images
of its glittering, labyrinthine interior had flashed across her
mind's eye. Nancy knew better than to ignore her mind-
pictures. Grandpa – the only one who knew about them
– had told her to treat them as a kind of guidance; her own
special sixth sense.

So Nancy had bought a ticket and entered the mirror
maze, unsure why she was supposed to, but hoping that its
'Mind-bending, Rib-tickling Reflections!' might make her
laugh – *and* give her the opportunity to admire her brand-
new dress.

In reality, wandering the deserted maze alone was
proving more frightening than amusing. All Nancy wanted
was to find her way out, as quickly as possible. She wanted

her big sister. Ruthie should have finished her ride on the dodgems with that boy from the posh school by now. She had promised to take Nancy for some candy-floss.

As she picked a random path through the corridors of silvered glass, Nancy found it impossible not to glance into each of the mirrors she passed. A host of weird and wonderful Nancy Latimers peered back at her. A freakishly short, squat Nancy. A scrawny beanpole Nancy. A Nancy whose face sagged and drooped like melting wax. At one spot, a pair of facing mirrors on opposite walls created two infinitely receding lines of identical eight-year-old girls in canary-yellow dresses.

To her relief, none of the mirrors held what she feared they might.

I imagined it, she thought, feeling a little reassured. How could anything live in a mirror?

On a hunch, Nancy took another left turn . . . and pulled up short, her heart suddenly in her throat. A smooth silver wall blocked the way ahead: a plain, flat mirror. Her true reflection stared back at her from it – as did that of the little girl standing right behind her.

Nancy spun round. The corridor was deserted. Pulse thumping, she turned back.

The girl in the mirror looked about Nancy's own age.

She was dressed for winter, in a rather old-fashioned woollen coat, scarf and gloves. There was a pretty silk bow in her hair, and she was clutching the string of a bright red balloon. She had the forlorn look of someone lost, lonely and frightened.

Reason dictated that the mirror-child must be just another of the maze's clever optical tricks – but all Nancy's instincts told her otherwise. Her initial swell of fear gave way to pity. Screwing up her courage, she approached the mirror. Slowly, she reached out and laid a hand flat against it. Both girls in the mirror reflected her nervous movement, the stranger's hand merging with that of Nancy's reflection. They stood palm-to-palm. The glass between them felt icy cold.

'Are you . . . trapped?' asked Nancy, wide-eyed.

Needles of pain suddenly stabbed into her outstretched hand. With a cry, she tried to jerk it away from the mirror's surface – but found she couldn't. It was stuck fast.

The little-girl-lost look had vanished from the mirror-child's eyes. She smiled a slow, sly smile.

'Not any longer,' she replied.

With a grating, splintering sound, a crack split the mirror's length, running through the point where the girls' palms were bonded. Nancy watched in helpless horror as the child behind its fractured surface closed her eyes and let out a deep, satisfied sigh. A long wisp of luminous green vapour came snaking from her mouth. It spiralled towards the crack in the glass and began to seep through.

'Right – I've got one!' said the Doctor, at last. 'And it's a belter!'

'About ruddy time!' Donna sighed. 'So – animal, vegetable or mineral?'

'Nope!' The Doctor beamed. 'Next question.'

'What do you mean, "no"?' Donna gave him a look. 'It must be *one* of those, you numpty. Or do you mean it's a mixture?'

'Another no! Two down, eighteen to go!' Folding his arms, the Doctor leaned back against the TARDIS's console, looking even more pleased with himself than usual. Behind him, the time rotor rose and fell in its luminous central cylinder. 'You'll never get it.'

'But it *has* to be animal, vegetable or mineral. That's how the game works.'

'Really?' The Doctor's smug smile slumped into a sulky frown. 'Well, that's rubbish!' he protested. 'That's ontological incorrectness gone mad! I mean, if we're restricted to primitive Earth-bound classification categories like those, I can't use *any* of my best ideas!'

Donna gave another sigh. She'd thought a game of Twenty Questions might help to pass the time, as she and the Doctor passed *through* time. She hadn't expected it to prove quite so problematic.

'Maybe we should try I Spy.'

Before the Doctor could reply, his entire demeanour underwent a sudden and alarming change. He lurched forward, one hand grabbing for the handrail at the edge of the console platform. The other flew to a sideburned temple. Grimacing, eyes screwed shut, he let out a grunt of pain through gritted teeth.

'Doctor?' Donna laid a hand on the stricken Time Lord's arm – and could feel the tension in it. 'Doctor! What is it?'

A moment later, the spasm passed. The Doctor's body visibly relaxed. His eyes flew open – wide with shock. He met Donna's anxious gaze.

'A scream,' he told her shakily. 'Proper blood-curdler.'

Donna frowned. '*I* didn't hear anything.'

'Wasn't on the audible spectrum.' The Doctor shook his head, as if to clear it. 'It was a mind-cry. Only perceptible by those with psychic sensitivity.'

Donna's frown became a scowl. 'Not blockheads like me, you mean?'

'Human minds are remarkable, Donna,' the Doctor said

earnestly. 'Even psychically latent ones like yours –'

'Even mine? Well, thank you so much,' Donna huffed.

'– but, however splendid Homo sapiens might be, only a handful of your generation are telepathically mature.'

'So now I'm immature as well as insensitive?'

The Doctor had already turned to the control console, and was consulting its unique hotchpotch of dials, gauges and indicators.

'I've never known a mind-cry of such intensity. Looks like it came from the Vortex itself. The telepathic circuits picked it up. Relayed it to my brainstem, full blast.'

'A cry for help?' suggested Donna.

'It didn't *sound* like a scream of fear. Or of pain. More like a mental ululation.'

'Excuse me?'

'A wild psychic howl. Of triumph, I'd say.' The Doctor frowned. 'And there was something familiar about it.' A spark lit his dark brown eyes. He pushed up the sleeves of his suit jacket. 'If I'm right –' his fingers began to dance across the console's primary interface – 'I should only have to isolate a telepathic signature . . . cross-reference it with any psychic profiles archived in the databank –' he entered a final command – 'and we *ought* to get . . .'

With a toast-popping alert sound, the viewscreen flashed

up a positive search result.

'A match!' The Doctor beamed.

A moment later his smile evaporated. He stared at the displayed data.

'What? Nooooo. No-no-no. That's not possible.'

He lunged to his right to release a tiny brass catch. Something sprang from the console like a cuckoo from a clock – a small, Bakelite-framed vanity mirror on a concertina-style arm. The Doctor hurriedly dragged it in front of his face. His eyes eagerly searched the reflection within.

'Come on, come on . . .' he muttered anxiously. 'Where *are* you?'

'Doctor?' Donna was looking on in bemusement. 'It's a *mirror*. The only one you're going to see in there is *you*.'

The Doctor continued to study the mirror for several more seconds before pushing it aside with a look of grim resignation. 'I'm sorry to say you're right, Donna. Which is *not* good. Not good at all.'

Hurriedly turning his attention to the flight controls, he commenced a rapid and energetic sequence of dial-twists, crank-winds and lever-pulls.

'Hold tight, Ms Noble . . .'

A final expert switch-flick with his right sneaker completed his urgent resetting of the TARDIS's space–time destination. The craft lurched violently as the course change took effect.

'We're jumping the tracks!'

PC Mallik was sure he had just caught the sound of breaking glass. To a police officer's mind, it was a noise that spelled likely trouble. It was hard to pinpoint its exact source, thanks to the hubbub all around him – the blaring pop music of the thrill rides, the yells of sideshow hawkers, the piping of the antique carousel's fairground organ, and the whoops and screams of high-spirited fairgoers – but Mallik had an idea of the rough vicinity. He made his way through the throng in the direction of the MIRACULOUS MIRROR MEGA-MAZE. It wouldn't hurt to take a look.

The weather – which, for late autumn, had been glorious all day – was fast taking a turn for the worse. A chill north-easterly breeze had picked up, and an ominous bank of grey cloud was advancing across the darkening sky.

Shame, thought Mallik. Nothing quenched the fun of the fair quite so fast as a downpour.

As he approached the mirror-maze sideshow, a little girl in a bright yellow dress emerged from its exit. It was the youngest granddaughter of old Timothy Latimer, the Farringham veteran who played poker with Mallik's elderly father once a week – and was a devil to beat, by all accounts.

Mallik gave her a warm smile. 'That's a very fine balloon you've got there, Nancy. Having a good time?'

Nancy Latimer didn't reply. She returned his friendly look with an intense, searching stare. Mallik found it peculiarly disconcerting – even more so when she tilted her neck sharply to one side and continued to appraise him, unblinkingly, with her head at a most unnatural angle.

'Everything all right, young lady? You don't look quite yourself.'

The little girl's mouth slowly curled, as if she found this remark somehow amusing. Her strange smile – it was more of a sneer, in truth – only increased Mallik's sense that something was amiss. It struck him that when he'd last spotted Nancy, at the Hook-a-Duck stall, she'd been with her elder sibling, Ruth.

'Have you lost your sister?' he enquired gently.

The cold, scornful tone in which the girl replied was as out of character as her unpleasant sneer. 'Sister?' she hissed. 'I have no sister.'

Mallik's concern deepened. She was clearly confused. With his best reassuring smile, he held out his hand. 'Come along now – let's you and I go and find your family.'

Nancy regarded the proffered hand with obvious disdain,

then fixed him with that unnerving stare once more.

'I do not require assistance.'

She took a sharp, hissing intake of air through flaring nostrils, as if seeking a scent. Her mouth curled unpleasantly again.

'I know *precisely* where to find them.'

Before Mallik could respond, Nancy turned and headed away through the crowd. The baffled police officer watched her go, wondering whether he ought to follow, but strangely reluctant to do so. The little girl's red balloon bobbed wildly after her in the stiffening breeze. Mallik told himself that the same chill wind was responsible for the icy shiver that suddenly ran through his body.

There was definitely a storm coming.

'Doctor! Slow down, will you? Where are we going?'

The raging wind drove cold, stinging rain against Donna's face as she fought against it to catch up with the Doctor, who was pressing on up the slope ahead, oblivious to her yells.

'If you insist on dragging me on some midnight hell-trek to God knows where –' Donna's soaking hair lashed across her face, and she flicked it away angrily – 'till I'm half drowned and up to my ankles in cowpats –' in light of her growing sense of dread, she was employing her preferred coping strategy: get steaming mad – 'the *least* you can do is to have the decency to tell me *why*!'

Donna liked to think she didn't scare easily these days. Since travelling with the Doctor, close encounters with a wide variety of terrifying alien creatures, from war-mongering Sontarans to fire-breathing Pyroviles, had left her little choice but to toughen up. It wasn't so much her present circumstances – the dark, the storm, the deserted countryside – that had set her nerves on edge, though. It was the Doctor's brooding mood. Since the baffling business with the vanity mirror, he had been grave-faced and withdrawn. Donna knew that if *he* was worried, there was something serious – and probably terrifying – to worry about.

The gusting gale had stolen her tirade. It brought something tumbling across the rutted field, out of the darkness, to bump against her leg. As she looked down to see what it was, a fork of lightning stabbed from the night sky. Its electric flash momentarily lit the gloom, eerily illuminating the thing at her feet.

It was a grisly imitation of a head, made of straw-stuffed sacking. Hollow black eyes and a grotesquely stitched mouth leered up at her.

A violent crack of thunder, following close on the

lightning flash, drowned out Donna's scream.

'*Doctor!*'

The Doctor had finally come to a halt, not far ahead. With a shudder, Donna kicked the straw head away and hurried to join him. As she saw what he had led them to, she felt another wave of foreboding.

It was a tall wooden cross; two rough timber stakes lashed together. It stood in the field like a vacant crucifix. Scraps of hessian sacking and spilt straw littered the ground around it. Recognising a rudimentary arm, Donna realised that she was looking at the remnants of a straw-built human figure. She thought of the grinning head. The bare stakes must originally have held a scarecrow, now reduced to scattered body parts.

The Doctor had already drawn his sonic screwdriver from his overcoat and was busy scanning its flickering blue tip along the timbers. He seemed oblivious to the wild forces of nature doing their best to batter and drench him. The fierce intensity behind his eyes suggested he was a far greater force of nature himself.

'What is it, Doctor?' asked Donna, raising her voice over the wind and rain.

The Doctor deactivated his sonic screwdriver.

'She must've released him after she freed herself,' he

shouted back. His frown deepened. 'And if she has the power to do that – to break open a temporal suspension envelope . . .' With renewed urgency and purpose, he turned back the way they'd come. 'Come on!'

'Not so fast!' Donna grabbed his arm. '*Who* released *who?*'

The Doctor turned a grim face to hers. 'It's the Family, Donna,' he told her. 'They're loose again.'

'The family?' Donna assumed the Doctor was *not* referring to Mafia mobsters. Or his own Gallifreyan relations.

Another flickering lightning bolt forked across the sky.

'The Family of Blood.'

A thunder crack rumbled through the cold night air.

The Doctor set off back across the dark, storm-lashed field towards the spot where his TARDIS waited. Donna hurried after him, her mind brimming with questions – including whether all Time Lords had such a flair for dramatic timing.

Back in the quiet, dry haven of the TARDIS's console room, the Doctor swiftly set about programming their next destination.

'Where now?' asked Donna.

'Not far. Tiny spatial hop. We could've gone on foot, but I want the old girl close.'

In the turquoise glow of the central column, the time rotor began its rhythmic rise and fall. The craft's cavernous frame vibrated as its ancient engine extracted it from normal space.

Donna pressed for more information. 'This Family of Blood – who are they?'

The Doctor squatted and dragged aside a segment of the console platform's grilled floor, revealing a storage area below.

'Four sociopathic predators acting in psychic union,' he answered, as he delved through a jumble of equipment. 'Mother, Father, Son and Daughter.' He hauled out a coil of rope with a grappling hook at one end. 'In their native form, they're green, gaseous entities – but they have a nasty habit of hijacking the bodies of others. Their last hosts were human.'

He slung the rope over one shoulder, replaced the grille, then hastily checked the instrument readings.

'You'll have seen one of them before. Many times.'

'What?' Donna's brow creased. 'When?'

'When was the last time you looked in a mirror?'

Donna flushed. 'Well, *that's* nice, I must s–'

'Never noticed anything odd in the reflection?' the Doctor pressed. 'Someone *behind* you?'

Donna fell silent. She stared at him, wide-eyed.

'You mean . . . the sweet little girl? With the balloon?'

'That sweet little girl was the Daughter's host,' said the Doctor grimly.

Donna had long ago decided that her glimpses of a child in the mirror could only be her imagination playing tricks. The news that the girl was real was a bombshell.

'The Family will stop at nothing to extend their own fleeting lifespans,' the Doctor told her. 'And there's only one reason they crave more time: to create more bloodshed and chaos. Given the chance, they'd spread war across the stars.' Anger burned in his eyes. 'That's why I locked them away.'

Donna raised an eyebrow. 'I might not be psychic, but I'm picking up a strong "this is personal" vibe.'

It was a moment or two before the Doctor replied. 'It was my fault they ever came to Earth,' he said bitterly. 'To England, in 1913. They were hunting me – for my Time Lord lifespan. They went on the rampage.'

'But you stopped them, right?'

'Not before precious human lives were lost.' A shadow of grief crossed the Doctor's face. 'Including mine.'

His last words baffled Donna. Before she could seek an explanation, the jolt of a heavy landing shook the TARDIS. Its double doors sprang open. The Doctor went bounding down the ramp towards them. Donna followed, hoping their 'tiny hop' had taken them somewhere rather less wet and windy.

The TARDIS had rematerialised in a deserted tunnel. Square in cross-section, it had a variety of pipes, ducts and cables running along its walls. Weak strip lights in the ceiling cast a sickly glow. From the pressure in her ears and from the chill, musty air, Donna had the strong impression that, wherever they were, it was deep underground.

As the Doctor set off purposefully along the tunnel, she kept pace, quizzing him as they went. 'If you locked the Daughter in a mirror –'

'In *every* mirror,' the Doctor corrected her.

'– what about the other three?'

'I suspended the Son in time,' said the Doctor. 'Inside that scarecrow back there. His sister must have found a way to free him. The Mother I trapped in the event horizon of a collapsing galaxy.'

'And Dad?'

The Doctor came to an abrupt halt. Just ahead, there was a large square void in the tunnel floor: the mouth of a vertical shaft.

'He's the reason we're here.'

He unslung the rope, secured its hooked end to a sturdy section of ducting, then tossed the rest down the shaft. Donna watched the rope tumble away into inky blackness.

'You left him down *there?*'

The Doctor's expression was without a trace of pity. 'Bound in unbreakable chains.'

Not for the first time, Donna felt somewhat awed by her alien friend's quiet, righteous wrath. 'Remind me not to get on your bad side.'

At the foot of the shaft, the darkness was absolute. The glow of the Doctor's sonic screwdriver reached only a few metres. Beyond that, all was pitch black.

Casting the light around revealed no sign of the chained Father – only the opening of another tunnel.

'Stay close,' whispered the Doctor as he led the way. Donna didn't need telling.

After only a few paces, the Doctor stopped, crouching down to examine a vague shape against the wall. It was a heaped coil of heavy chain. The link at one free end had been sliced cleanly through so as to be parted from the other.

'Not *that* unbreakable then,' observed Donna.

The Doctor frowned at the severed link. 'This was cast in the heart of a dwarf star,' he muttered. 'What cuts through star-forged alloy?'

As he continued to pore over the broken chain, Donna noticed something odd. Her own shadow was visible on the wall before her. That meant a light source *behind* her . . .

A noise made her blood freeze.

Both she and the Doctor spun round to find three figures silently observing them from the gloom. The smallest clutched the string of a red balloon, which glowed with an eerie crimson light.

As Donna took her first horrified look at the three members of the Family of Blood, they, as one, fixed their cold eyes upon her. All three inhaled vigorously through flaring nostrils. In uncanny synchronisation, they tilted their heads sharply to one side, appraising her malevolently.

The human unlucky enough to host the Father was a thickset middle-aged man with a large, bushy moustache. He wore the tweed jacket, waistcoat and breeches of an Edwardian gentleman farmer. The Son looked like he had stepped out of the same period drama. He had stolen the form of a tall, dark-haired, arrogant-looking young man in the smart wing-collared uniform of a public-school boy. There was a hint of madness in his fixed smirk and widened eyes.

But it was the Daughter who, despite being the youngest and smallest, had the aura of command. She stood slightly forward of the other two, who flanked her like henchmen. Balloon apart, she did not, Donna saw to her surprise, look like the little girl she had spied in her mirror.

'Got yourself a fresh body, eh?' growled the Doctor,

eyes narrowed. 'What about your last host? Young Lucy
Cartwright?'

'Expended.' There was no hint of remorse in the
Daughter's reply. 'These human shapes are *very* fragile.' Her
superior tone was wholly un-childlike. 'They do not sustain
us for long.' She smiled a malicious smile. 'I have changed in
many other ways, too, Doctor, since we last met.'

'So I see. Head of the Family now, are we?'

The Daughter did not reply – only extended her free
hand. A crackling bolt of blazing white light burst from her
fingertips. It hit the Doctor square in the chest. He sprawled
on to the floor of the tunnel. His sonic screwdriver skittered
away into the shadows.

'Doctor!'

As Donna crouched over him, the Doctor stirred feebly.
He was badly stunned, but alive.

The Daughter stepped forward, keeping her hand
trained on the Doctor. Donna turned on her, trying to
suppress her terror. 'Any nearer, missy, and I'll . . . I'll . . . pop
your balloon!'

'Brother of Mine! Father of Mine!' snapped the
Daughter. 'Bind them!'

Donna dared not resist as the Son and Father obediently
advanced, manhandled her and the semi-conscious Doctor

into a back-to-back position, and bound them tightly with the heavy star-forged chain. She recoiled as the Daughter let loose another energy blast – but its aim was precise. It fused the severed link of the chain into an unbreakable whole once more.

'Telekinetic hadron excitation,' murmured the Doctor, beginning to recover. 'Impressive. Where'd you learn *that* little party trick?'

'Thanks to *you*, Doctor, I have acquired many new powers.' The Daughter smirked. 'By locking me away, you set me free.' She moved to stand over him. 'I have watched, alone, from every mirror in existence, across all time – as you decreed I must,' she said bitterly. 'From the looking-glass of the Prime Imperator; from the mercury mirror-pool of an Ulgron arch-mage; from the blood-polished obsidian of a Ch'Sok spirit-glass; from the mirrored walls of the great Sanctum of Reflection; from –'

'Yada-yada. From a lot of mirrors,' the Doctor interrupted, scowling. 'We get the picture.'

The Daughter glowered back at him. '*Infinite* mirrors, offering windows on countless worlds,' she hissed. 'An eternity in an instant to watch – and learn.' Her eyes shone. 'I learned how to escape my prison. And in the moment of my release, while I still existed across all time, I sent a psychic cry into the

Vortex –' her mouth curled nastily again – 'and brought you running, Doctor, just as I'd planned.'

The Doctor held her vengeful stare. His strength was returning, his eyes filling with contained fury. 'So – which of you gets the big prize, eh? A Time Lord's lifespan. Or do I get to host the whole Family?'

It was the Son who answered this time – in a manic, mocking tone.

'Oh, dear, sir! *No*, sir! You mistake our intentions, sir!'

'We no longer need your shape, Time Lord,' snarled the burly Father.

'Through my watching,' the Daughter continued, 'I have seen more . . . *desirable* hosts. Creatures of the Vortex that can offer us eternal life,' she sneered. 'For you are mortal, Doctor. I have watched you die – many times.' She turned her chilling gaze on Donna. 'And seen this one's futures, too. The part she might play, at the End –'

Donna frowned. 'What end?'

'– were it not that *we* have determined a different destiny for you both.'

The Daughter turned expectantly to the Son. 'Do you have it, Brother of Mine?'

'Yes, Sister of Mine. I have it here.'

He gleefully produced and displayed a familiar brass

door key.

'Doctor!' cried Donna. 'The TARDIS key!'

The Son had evidently picked the stricken Doctor's suit pocket at the same time as binding him. He smirked tauntingly at his victim. 'You, sir, and your feeble human friend –'

Donna bridled. 'I'll feeble *you*, you stuck-up –'

'– will share the fate, sir, that you so *cleverly* devised for Father of Mine.'

'You'll rot here,' growled the Father. 'Slowly. Bound in the darkness.'

'While *we*, sir, will use your grubby little Vortex craft to liberate the last member of our Family –'

'And pursue our prey at will!' crowed the Daughter. With a sudden jerk of the neck, she threw back her head. Her upturned face glowed with a sickly green light as she voiced her wild psychic cry.

'We come, Mother of Mine!'

She cast a final, triumphant leer at the Doctor, then turned and led her family away, taking the balloon's crimson light with them.

Left in total darkness, bound so tightly it was hard to breathe, Donna struggled to keep panic at bay.

'What now, Doctor? What do we do?'

The light-hearted tone of the Doctor's reply threw her completely. 'How about that game of I Spy?'

Donna really couldn't see a funny side to their present predicament. 'Hilarious,' she hissed. 'Just to be clear, this is *not* my idea of a jolly lark. I'm not crazy about seeing out my days at the bottom of a miserable pit!'

'I've seen *worse* spots. Mulphlux Four, for instance. Now that really is –'

'Doctor!' Donna was baffled by his sudden lack of urgency. What had got into him? She felt a pang of dread. Had he given up? He never gave up . . . did he? 'We can't let the Family get away! "War across the stars", you said. We have to stop them!'

She felt the Doctor's body wriggle, heard him utter a soft grunt. The pressure of his back against hers released.

'Doctor?'

There was silence for a few heartbeats – then a familiar buzzing sound. Blue light blossomed in the darkness, and Donna found that the Doctor was now standing over her. His face, lit by the glow of his recovered sonic screwdriver, wore a steely expression.

'Oh, I'll stop them, Donna, don't you worry.'

Donna gawped. 'How did you . . .?'

'A little technique Harry Houdini taught me.' The
Doctor began loosening the chain looped round her. 'I might
not have spent eternity eavesdropping –' he helped her free
of the heavy coils – 'but you don't live to be nine hundred
without picking up a trick or two.'

Donna looked at him expectantly. He seemed in no
hurry to move.

'Well?' she prompted. 'Shouldn't we get after them?'

'All in good time,' said the Doctor. 'Let's give them a
decent head start.'

Donna stared at him, flummoxed. 'But . . . what about
the TARDIS?'

The Doctor smiled slyly, a glint in his dark eyes.

'It's her I'm counting on.'

Donna stepped gingerly over the Father's tweed-clad bulk.
He was lying flat on his face, out cold, at the upper end of the
TARDIS's entrance ramp.

The Doctor, a few strides ahead, was negotiating a
similar obstacle: the body of the Son's human host, sprawled
out on the console platform.

The Daughter was nowhere to be seen.

Donna scanned around anxiously, expecting to be
frazzled by an energy blast at any moment. Then –

BANG!

A shred of bright red rubber, with a length of string
attached – all that remained of the balloon that had just
popped against the vaulted ceiling – came drifting limply
down to land behind the console. The Doctor quickly ducked
after it.

'All clear, Donna!' he called. 'She's here!'

Donna hurried to where the Doctor crouched beside the
unmoving form of the little girl in yellow.

'What happened to her? To all of them?'

'They've been rendered unconscious.'

'I can see that! But *how*?'

Delving under a floor grille, the Doctor quickly withdrew
something from the storage area and held it out to Donna.
'Here. Take this.' It was an empty glass bottle labelled Zordn's
Original Astralberry Schnapps. 'It's already contained one
evil spirit . . .'

Kneeling over the girl, he gently pushed back her lower
jaw, then held his sonic screwdriver close to her face.

'The TARDIS's databank includes all the Family's
psychic profiles,' he told Donna, in answer to her question.
'They're still on the primary system, from when I called up
the archive earlier.' Slowly, he drew a thin wisp of luminous
green vapour from the child's open mouth. It hung limply

from the screwdriver's buzzing tip. 'The moment they mind-spoke to one another, the old girl's telepathic circuits would have tuned in. Matched the profiles. Recognised them as known enemies – key or no key.'

'So . . . the TARDIS took out all three of them?'

The Doctor gestured for the schnapps bottle. As Donna held it steady, he lowered the dangling gaseous strand into it. 'She knows how to handle herself,' he said proudly. 'And, with surprise on her side, she'll have given them a nasty shock. Literally.'

He deactivated his sonic screwdriver. Taking the bottle, he capped it, then held it up in front of Donna's fascinated gaze. The gaseous green entity within was beginning to stir, swirling restlessly.

'Animal, vegetable or mineral, would you say?'

Donna gave the Doctor a look. 'Okay. Point taken.'

She eyed the bottle warily as he put it aside.

'Will that hold her? With all those new powers she was bragging about?'

'Powers schmowers,' replied the Doctor dismissively. 'Without a host, she has no corporeal agent to exercise them.'

He turned his attention to the unconscious child. As he scanned for life signs, Donna looked on in concern.

'Is she . . .?'

'She'll be fine. She's a lucky girl. She didn't serve as a host long enough to sustain any permanent neural damage.' The Doctor removed his pinstriped jacket, folded it, and slid it gently under the girl's head. He stood up. 'Just needs to sleep it off. Then we'll get her home.'

He glanced at the other two bodies lying nearby, then at the schnapps bottle. 'In the meantime, we should tidy up around here.'

'What are you going to do with them?'

Moving to the console, the Doctor reached for the flight controls.

'Perhaps I *was* a little harsh, consigning them to solitary confinement. They did seem awfully keen to see Mother.' The TARDIS's doors slammed shut. 'I thought we might drop them off at her place.' The time rotor stirred into motion. 'Of course, with "her place" being the event horizon of a collapsing galaxy, they won't ever be able to leave again . . .'

As the thrum of dematerialisation filled the console room, the Doctor flashed a wicked, bright-eyed grin at Donna.

'But it's good for family to spend time together.'

THE ELEVENTH DOCTOR

THE MIST
OF SORROW

Written by Craig Donaghy

As holidays went, this one had been a total wash-out. From start to finish, the Martin family's camping trip had been ruined by rain. And not just one type of rain, but every sort of rain from light, sticky drizzle that coated every surface with perfect pinpricks of water to heavy slugs of rain that clumsily shook the tent. Now, all five of the Martins were on their way home, finally getting warm and dry in their old car.

'At least it's stopped raining now, chaps!' Mr Martin said, trying to lift his family's spirits.

Mrs Martin took her eyes off the road for a second, with just enough time to give her husband a stern look. She then went back to steering the car down the gravel track. Wherever they were driving through now was grey and quiet. The storm they had experienced earlier had passed. No more low growls of thunder or vicious scratches of lightning.

'I'm just saying.' Mr Martin was clutching at straws. 'Despite the constant wet weather and the flooding and the drizzle, we had a great time. Right, guys?'

In the back of the car, Evan shook his head.

Pip, his little brother, who was squashed in the middle seat between his big brother and sister, shook his head too. Evan was eleven and Pip was seven, and Pip copied *everything* his big brother did.

Their big sister, Roxy, kept her headphones on and her hood up and tried to block out everything. She thought camping was the uncoolest thing possible. But camping in the rain was just crazy. Hadn't her family heard of hotels?

Evan hadn't been troubled by the rainy holiday, but something else was bothering him and he couldn't quite put his finger on it. Something felt wrong. Like if you put a jumper on backwards, or remember you've forgotten to do your homework, or know you're about to be told off for breaking that purple vase in the kitchen even though it was totally an accident.

Then he spotted something in the sky above. A blue box. It was spinning quickly across the grey sky.

Evan jumped up in surprise and then ducked down to get a view through the car window. 'I just saw something . . . in the sky!'

'It was probably a seagull or something,' Mrs Martin said.

'It wasn't a seagull! It was like a blue box . . . spinning in the air, really fast.'

'You've been reading too many comics, Evan. You're always looking for adventure!' his mum replied wearily.

Evan sat back. He knew what he had seen. And there was no such thing as reading too many comics. The problem was quite the opposite – not reading enough comics. And looking for adventure? Well, everyone should be doing that, shouldn't they?

'I believe you!' Pip said, grinning at his big brother.

Roxy rolled her eyes at Evan. She loved winding her brothers up.

'Is this new, love?' Mr Martin asked quietly, pointing to the winding path ahead of them.

'Shhhh, I'm driving,' Mrs Martin warned, concentrating on the loose gravel road.

'I'm just saying it's new,' Mr Martin protested.

'I'm following the diversions. I don't just make up routes, like some people I could mention.'

Evan wiped the condensation off the window and

continued looking outside. He desperately wanted to see that spinning blue box again.

The family's car was making its way through a dramatic valley that looked like a giant had taken an axe and cut a V-shape from the mountains. The road twisted round a slanting patchwork of bright green fields that were separated by dark, leafy bushes and trees. Some lengths of the road may have been safe and flat, but ahead there were sections where the side of the road became a steep drop into a gully of boulders and brown shrubs.

Mrs Martin slowed the car down and pulled over.

'What are you doing?' Evan asked.

'Yeah, Mum, what are you doing?' Pip echoed.

'There's a car stopped up there. I'm just going to see if they need help.' Mrs Martin jumped out of the car and made her way towards a small blue car that seemed to be abandoned on the side of the road. Its lights were on and the door was left open. Mrs Martin leaned inside, looking around.

'Dad, go with her!' Roxy ordered.

'I'm no car expert like your mother is!' Mr Martin raised both hands in protest.

'Well, go in case there are weirdos about!' Roxy insisted.

Mr Martin was just about to open the car door when Mrs Martin came and got back into the driver's seat.

'Nothing,' Mrs Martin said, as she put her seatbelt on. 'There's no one there. Not a trace. They've left their lights on and everything.'

Mr Martin looked at his phone. 'Anyone got a signal? We should probably call someone just in case they've gone to get help and got lost.'

'Is someone in danger?' Pip asked.

'No, no, no. We're just checking in case someone needs help,' Mr Martin chirped.

Evan was suspicious. His dad was trying to reassure them, and that just made Evan more worried. And, when Evan became worried, Pip became worried too.

Everyone checked their phones – apart from Pip, who didn't have one. Nobody had a signal.

'We'll try when we're out of the valley. Must be because we're so low, you know?' Mr Martin said, still trying to sound calm and collected but fooling nobody.

No one said anything, but they all thought things were distinctly creepy.

The valley was becoming darker. A purple haze had filled the air and the greens and greys of the fields and rocks changed colour into something other-worldly. There was a certain static in the air. Mr Martin could always tell when a storm was brewing – something to do with pressures and temperatures and fly bites and curling leaves. But this felt . . . artificial somehow. Too warm. Too dry.

Mrs Martin carried on driving. Everyone was silent and alert. The purple haze was becoming stronger and thicker. It was so subtle and slow that it could have been perfectly natural – a rare phenomenon that occurred in the lowest part of a valley. Something that could be ignored. But it was so bizarre that it was impossible to ignore.

'What is it?' Evan asked.

'What is it?' Pip echoed.

'I don't know, love. Mist? Fog? I've never seen anything like it,' Mr Martin said distractedly. 'There has been an awful lot of wet weather recently. It could just be the after-effects of that . . .'

Roxy chewed nervously on one end of the drawstring on her hoodie. Something was definitely up.

Mrs Martin was driving very, very slowly. Everyone sat up straight, carefully watching the road ahead. The headlights seemed to be blocked by the ribbons of purple smog that twitched and turned in front of them before dissolving, then forming anew.

Suddenly Mrs Martin stopped the car. 'There's something in the road.'

'I can't see anything,' Mr Martin said.

'There!' Mrs Martin pointed through the windscreen.

Out of the mist appeared a figure. A solid, stony figure. With two hands covering its face, as if it were crying. Not just crying – weeping.

'Is it a statue?' Evan said, leaning forward, trying to get a better look.

'Why would someone put a statue in the middle of a road?' Roxy asked.

The car's headlights were just able to pick out the figure's key features. It looked like a woman. No, not a woman. An *angel*. It was definitely made of stone, that was clear, even through the purple mist. It looked ancient and unnatural, like it could have been there since the start of time, but didn't truly belong anywhere.

Mrs Martin looked at her husband. 'I'm going out there to see what it is.'

Mr Martin started to argue, but the radio burst into life with a sudden screech. Through the static came a man's voice.

'I wouldn't do that if I were you.'

The family looked at the radio, confused.

'Is this a joke?' Mrs Martin asked. She wasn't impressed.

'If this was one of my jokes, you'd all be rolling around on the floor. You'd be laughing so hard that you'd need to sleep for three weeks, and even then you'd wake up with a smile on your face,' the mysterious voice replied.

'Is this a radio show?' Mrs Martin started twiddling the dials.

Nothing happened.

'Tell her, Mr Martin,' the voice on the radio commanded.

Mr Martin stared at the radio for another second or two before turning to his wife. 'The radio's broken, love,' he said. 'Has been for weeks.'

'Not any more, it isn't,' the voice from the radio added. 'I fixed it, because I'm me, and because you need help!'

The family looked at one another, searching for a sign that this was a prank or that someone else understood what was going on.

'Let's just cut out the whole disbelief-and-shock thing and jump straight to the bit where you do exactly what I say to keep you all safe.' The voice on the radio was friendly but insistent.

Mr Martin and Mrs Martin sat there with their mouths hanging open.

An audible sigh crackled out of the radio. 'If you want something done, ask the ones with brains – the kids. Evan, isn't it? The middle child.'

Evan was shocked. 'Y-y-yes.'

'Good. Make sure all of the doors are locked.'

Evan took off his seatbelt, then climbed over his family to lock all of the doors.

'Roxy? The big sister.'

'Yes?' Roxy answered.

'Make sure all of the air-con units and any gaps in the car are shut, turned off, blocked, whatever. I don't want that mist getting inside the car.'

Roxy too undid her seatbelt and jumped into action, leaning over her parents to turn everything off and close all the air vents.

'Pip?' the voice asked. 'The littlest Martin.'

Pip straightened, ready for orders.

'Keep being cute.'

'Easy!' Pip smiled.

Evan looked around. The mist had grown so thick that he couldn't see anything at all outside. 'Who are you?'

'Good question,' the voice from the radio boomed. 'But a better question is: who are *they*?'

'They? There's just that.' Evan pointed at the strange statue in front of the car. Even lit up by the headlights, he could barely make out its shape now.

'It's not a that. It's a *them*.' The voice had lost its playfulness. 'I'm terribly sorry, Martins, but you're completely surrounded by Weeping Angels.'

Another figure suddenly appeared close to the window beside Roxy, making her jump in her seat. It had a stony face ripped by a ferocious anger and carved with sharp teeth and cold, dead eyes.

'OK, now, this is important. Everything I say is important, but this is right up there with the most important of things. They cannot move if you look at them. So keep your eyes on them at all times.'

The family widened their eyes and looked around.

'You cannot even blink. If you're going to blink, then touch someone next to you and let them take over. If you're going to look away, then whistle. I don't care what your system is, but use your eyes on the Angels and your ears on me.'

'Tell us who you are,' Evan said again, knowing that this time he'd get a response.

'I'm the Doctor. There's a lot I could tell you about myself, but there's more you need to know about the Angels right now.'

'That fog keeps hiding the statue,' Roxy said, staring at her Angel as purple smoke passed between them.

'That's not fog. It's no accident or natural occurrence. That's the Mist of Sorrow. It's artificial and it's on purpose. It's a personal black-out. It's a blindfold for you and your nearest and dearest.'

The lights danced on the radio.

'The Angels are clever and devious. They love to hunt and they can only do it when they can't be looked at. This isn't a mist; this is their portable hunting ground. I'm doing what I can, but you need to stay in your car and you need to keep looking at them. Don't even blink!'

Mrs Martin glanced at her children in the rear-view mirror. She forced a smile, but as soon as she looked back the Angel that had been in front of the car had moved closer to her window. She gasped in terror. Up close, the Martins could see that this Angel's pointy teeth were worn and tired, its mouth and eyes hollow and skeletal. Its bony hand was frozen, reaching towards the side window.

Then there was a buzz. The car's dashboard flickered and the engine and headlights turned off. All of the lights within the car, except for those on the radio, went off too, plunging the family into near-darkness.

'Do something to help us!' Mrs Martin yelled. 'Now!'

'All right, Mum!' the Doctor said. 'I'm working on it, but I'm not in charge of this weather!'

The Martins were all on high alert. Their hearts beat in their chests and they took it in turns to gulp. Mrs Martin and Roxy kept their eyes on the Angels closest to them. Evan, Pip and Mr Martin looked everywhere, not sure what they were really doing besides making sure that anything that moved behind the dancing fog was captured in their eyeline.

Evan leaned over the back of his seat and started reaching into the boxes in the boot. He searched through the camping equipment and pulled out two battery-operated lanterns. He turned them on to full blast with a couple of little clicks.

'Ahh, I can see some lights,' the Doctor said. 'That's some good thinking, Martins!'

'Where *are* you?' Evan was confused. Was the Doctor out there in the fog?

'I'm in a blue police box floating above your heads.'

Evan smiled. *I knew it!* he thought. *I knew I wasn't imagining it.* 'I saw it earlier!' he said. 'It looked like it was spinning out of control and about to crash.'

'Oh no! Not at all. It was all completely under my control,' the Doctor replied, but Evan wasn't convinced.

'Are you a police officer?' Pip asked.

'Hmm . . . a bit like a police officer, but with a bow-tie and a very strong chin.'

'Do you catch the bad guys?' Pip asked.

'Yes! I do. Pretty much most of the time.'

'What?' Mrs Martin said. '*Most* of the time?'

'Some things are as old as forever and they cannot be stopped. You just have to run away or wait for them to disappear. Victory isn't winning; it's surviving.'

'Are you saying you can't stop them?' Mr Martin asked, unable to hide the fear that was creeping into his voice.

'I'm trying to scan the area. I can see you and the Weeping Angels and quite a few . . . abandoned cars.'

'What do they do to you?' Mrs Martin asked nervously. 'Do they . . . Will they eat us?'

'No. Nothing like that . . . It's much kinder and crueller than that.' The Doctor paused. 'They send you back in time. One touch and you're zapped somewhere in the past.'

'That's impossible!' Mr Martin stated.

'Not a word I'm familiar with,' the Doctor's voice crackled.

Just then, the car rocked a little, like something powerful had breezed past.

'It's what they do. It's unjust and unfair, but it's what they do,' the Doctor continued. 'They feed off the life you would have lived.'

The car shook hard. It lifted up, then bounced back down on to the gravel track. The family screamed. As well as the purple mist, dark grey dust from the road bloomed around the car. Something was underneath the car, raising it off the ground.

There was a thudding noise. The sound of stone on

metal. A crunching noise followed by the rip of tearing metal. A stone hand shot through the floor of the car and tried to grab Pip's foot. By the time the family had turned to look, the clawed hand had a solid grip round Pip's shoelaces.

'Heeellllp!' Pip screamed in terror.

Evan and Roxy started hitting the stone hand with the lanterns and Mr and Mrs Martin tried to help.

'No, keep your eyes on the outside!' the voice on the radio screeched.

It was too late. The side windows were now full of stony shapes. The glass cracked as the Angels were frozen midway through clawing at the car.

The Martins were trapped.

'Doctor! One's got hold of Pip!' Evan whacked at the stone hand.

'OK, enough is enough!' The Doctor sounded angry. This might be what he did all the time, battling monsters and creatures, but there was something personal here. The Weeping Angels had done terrible things, but also some terrible things to him or to the people he cared about – Mrs Martin could hear it in his voice. She knew.

'Keep your eyes open and hold on to something,' the Doctor warned.

The car suddenly sprang into life and the engine roared.

The dashboard lit up. The headlights flared brightly.

'After three, pull Pip free.'

Everyone in the car shouted, 'OK!'

'One . . .'

Evan and Roxy held Pip's leg.

'Two . . .'

The car revved and the steering wheel twitched without Mrs Martin touching it.

'THREE!'

The car moved forward in a powerful and steady charge and Pip's foot slipped out of the shoe as Evan and Roxy pulled it hard.

Mrs Martin held up her hands. The car was rolling forward and the steering wheel was moving by itself.

'What's happening?' Mrs Martin asked.

'That's just me! I'm driving. Now, don't worry. I very much think of you as a remote-controlled car full of little, squashable people who I absolutely do not intend to squash or squish in any way. I'll take care of this, I promise. You keep watching out for Angels.'

The family kept looking around.

'How are you doing this?' Evan marvelled at the car moving, but remained focused on the threat.

'Not easily, I'll tell you. That mist, it's blocking

everything. I can hardly see or get a signal through it. But I found enough power in there to help you out. All of those other cars – the Angels took the owners, but they left the cars behind. Well, I can use their power.'

The headlights glowed and flickered, catching the rolling of the mist and snapshots of Weeping Angels in frozen postures. Some were covering their eyes or hiding their faces. Others were locked in the beginning stages of attack. The flashing headlights and the lamps from the Martin family's car combined with the Martins' watchful eyes were paralysing the monsters.

Though the car continued to move forward at a gentle pace, the sound of numerous Angels swooshing through the mist outside was anything but gentle. Their swooping was almost deafening, as was the screech of their nails scratching the glass of the windows and pulling at the door handles.

'They're angry!' Evan shouted.

Something heavy and solid hit the side of the car. The family yelled as the vehicle veered left off the road and headed straight down the steep valley.

'They pushed us off the road!' Evan cried.

'I've got you.' The Doctor sounded determined.

Through the purple fog, the family could see trees and rocks hurtling towards them as the car gained speed. The steering wheel turned quickly and violently, narrowly missing each potential collision. The car swerved left, avoiding a cluster of jagged boulders; it swerved right, only just missing a huge ditch full of thorny bushes. Each turn revealed Weeping Angels in the headlights. They hid among the trees or peered out from behind huge rocks. Some stood openly on the hill, with their claws held high above their heads.

The steering wheel turned violently and the car spun round several times, then screeched to a giddy halt in a whirlwind of dust and purple mist. The car was now at the bottom of the valley.

The radio crackled and the Doctor's broken voice tried to communicate. 'Martins . . . OK . . . tell . . . speak . . .'

Mrs Martin turned round and anxiously asked, 'Is everyone OK?'

Everyone was fine. Scared and shaken up, but unharmed.

Something heavy crashed on top of the car with a massive thud that made the roof buckle. Then came another crunch. The whole car groaned as the roof started to lower under the tremendous weight.

Another crunch.

More and more Angels were landing on the car roof.

'Can you hear me? Martins?' the voice on the radio

pleaded desperately. 'The Weeping Angels – they're above you.'

'They're on top of the car!' Roxy yelled.

'We're going to be squashed!' Mrs Martin cried.

'You need to get out of there. Now!' the Doctor said.

'But you said we had to stay in the car,' Mr Martin yelled. 'That's what you said!'

'I changed the rules. I tend to do that.'

The car creaked ominously. The Weeping Angels were shifting around.

'I've got a plan,' the Doctor insisted. 'But you're going to have to get out of the car and I won't be able to talk to you.'

'How can we get out?' Mrs Martin asked. 'They'll get us.'

'Do what you do best as a family: stick together.'

The Martins looked at one another. They nodded. They had to trust the Doctor.

'I need you to head in front of the car and keep walking in a straight line. Eyes open and always watching. Stay back to back.'

A huge dent appeared in the roof of the car as a powerful fist tried to pound through it.

'Go! Now!' the Doctor shouted.

'Dad, give me the mirror.' Evan reached out his hand.

Mr Martin looked at his son in confusion. But Mrs Martin understood and yanked the rear-view mirror from above the windscreen and handed it back to her son.

Another thud, and this time a clawed hand came through the roof and remained locked in a stony fist.

Evan opened his door. 'Someone watch behind me.'

He tilted the mirror so he could see the three Angels on the roof of the car. They were locked in poses of furious attack. He stepped out of the car and opened the front passenger door. Mr Martin carefully slid out and he and Evan stood back to back and shuffled round the front of the car. Evan kept his eyes on the Weeping Angels on top of the car, and Mr Martin scanned the rest of the area around them, leaning forward to open the driver's door and let his wife out.

'Be careful, Mum,' Evan warned.

Mrs Martin joined her family, with her back towards them and her eyes forward. She opened the back door and Roxy carefully passed Pip out as she kept her vision locked on the Angel's hand in the car.

'OK, my turn . . .' Roxy said, swallowing hard while finding her bravest face.

'I can't see what you're doing, but I bet you're doing just great!' The Doctor's enthusiasm sounded strained. 'Good luck, Martins. Get ready for the storm.'

Roxy joined her family outside the car. They formed a circle. With their backs against each other, they slowly walked away from the car, moving dead ahead, as the Doctor had ordered. They watched vigilantly through the dry, static mist, looking out for any movement, moving slowly and carefully. They could hear each other's nervous breathing. They held each other up as they stumbled over stones and tree roots.

Evan kept his eyes on the car, but a thick plume of mist passed in front of his face and, when he could see again, the Weeping Angels had vanished. He still held the car mirror. He gripped it tighter as they heard movement through the grass nearby, or the sound of stone scraping against stone, or the sound of trees shifting in the artificial wind.

The Weeping Angels were circling them. The whooshing of their movement grew closer and closer.

A quick, solid movement whacked the mirror from Evan's hand. He heard it hit the grass.

'Evan!'

'I'm OK, but they got the mirror.'

The family gripped each other tighter. For warmth, for security, for love. The Weeping Angels inched closer and closer and closer. The family could just see them through the patches of purple smoke.

Some of their fierce faces had become gentle smiles.

Their hands reached outwards, as if to claim the family.

Evan desperately wanted to close his eyes. They all did.

The mist made them want to blink; it dried and burned their eyes. But they knew they couldn't do it. They linked arms. Maybe if they all held on to each other, they would stay together? Together wherever the Angels sent them. It seemed hopeless.

Evan felt something hit his face. A drop of water. Then another. And another. It was raining.

Evan was sure he heard a shout. It sounded like 'Geronimo!'

'Typical.' Mr Martin laughed. 'It's raining again!'

The family couldn't help but smile, even now, at the scariest of times.

The rain became heavier, as if they were under a waterfall.

The mist fluttered and turned. The rain seemed to make each purple particle swell and fall. The view started to clear.

The rain powerfully pushed the mist down, washing it from the atmosphere. A purple oil started to form on the ground and a heavy wind started to blow the fog away. This was the storm the Doctor had promised.

The Martin family stood rooted to the spot with fear. They were soaked through. They could see everything now. They were surrounded by a circle of ten Weeping Angels, all of whom were frozen like statues, staring at them, reaching for them, ready to grab or claw or bite or whatever they did.

The family didn't take their eyes off their attackers. Not even when they heard something hitting the ground nearby hard. Not even when they heard a door creak open, spilling warm light across the valley floor.

'This is the good bit!' the Doctor's voice piped up. 'You can move!'

The family shifted on the spot, not quite believing the Doctor's words.

'Just don't touch them,' he added.

The Martins moved through the circle of Angels slowly and carefully. They avoided touching them at all costs, creating awkward shapes with their bodies and crawling along the ground in order to avoid them.

'That's him!' Pip said, pointing.

The Doctor stood in the doorway of an open blue police box. He was a silhouette in front of a thousand lights that mysteriously blossomed from behind him. He looked tall and thin and a lot more bendy than they had imagined. He moved forward and bowed, before lifting his head with a wide smile.

'Ahhh, the Martins! My favourite family that found themselves trapped in a car during a Weeping Angel feast.'

He had a young face but old eyes. He had floppy hair and a ridiculous bow-tie. There was wisdom in his features –

an angry, fierce sense of everything and everyone. Then he put on a fez and all of that lifted in a second.

'They're locked in each other's gazes,' the Doctor said. 'They won't be going anywhere for a long time. They can't hurt you now.'

'Why do they do that? Why do they freeze?' Evan asked.

'They're quantum locked. Some say it's a punishment. Some say it's evolution. Some say it's a curse from the gods to give the rest of us a fighting chance.'

'What do you say?'

'I say they deserve it.' His face became deadly serious. Then he exploded forward, and slapped his hands together and smiled nervously.

'You're making it rain?' Mrs Martin asked.

'Yes. Apparently I *can* control the weather! Not your holiday weather, though. That was just good old-fashioned Mother Nature.' The Doctor laughed. 'And, let me tell you, you shouldn't mess with her!'

Mr and Mrs Martin smiled, taking all of this wonderful madness in.

'It's just a simple atmospheric excitation. Well, not simple. That mist was causing all sorts of trouble. I had to find a way to amplify my sonic screwdriver to create some seriously heavy rain. Luckily I've got a TARDIS full of bits and pieces with which to build some amplification tech,' he said, gesturing at his strange blue box.

The Doctor pulled a small metal thing from his jacket pocket. It let out an electronic *Vreee!* and emitted a green glow. The rain stopped instantly.

The Doctor walked away from the TARDIS and Evan, Roxy and Pip moved closer towards him.

'You are all very brave. And very, very wet. Sorry.'

'What would have . . . What could have . . .' Roxy stammered.

'Best-case scenario, you would have all been sent back in time to roughly the same place and you would have lived your lives as normal. A little more carefully, perhaps. Always feeling like you had lost something you didn't quite understand.'

'And worst case?'

Roxy's question caused the Doctor to look down. He covered his mouth, removed his fez and brushed his floppy hair back. 'You would have all been scattered through time. Lost from yourselves and from each other.'

Roxy grabbed Evan and Pip and held them close.

'How do we thank you?' Evan asked.

'You just say thank you.'

'Thank you.' Evan smiled.

'Thank you.' Pip smiled.

'And keep doing this. The Martin family camping trips. Even when you're older. Even when you've got your own kids and grandkids. Even when some go and more come. Make it a tradition, a bond, a pact, a promise. Be the opposite of scattered through time.'

The Doctor smiled, then appeared to remember something super-exciting and spun round, giddy. 'I've heard the Martin family camping trip in 2048 is a hoot! Who even knew flying bears would make a comeback? Not me, that's for sure . . . Oops! I've said too much.' The Doctor put a finger to his lips. 'Spoilers, sweetie. As an old friend of mine says.' The Doctor looked round in a panic. 'She's not *old*. Don't tell her I said that. She's an old friend. A friend for a long time. Definitely *not* old.'

Mr Martin and Mrs Martin smiled at each other.

'Now, you chaps are going to need a lift back. I've got a garage in the TARDIS and a few visiting Ood who love to tinker with ancient domestic vehicles.'

'Ood?' Evan looked puzzled.

The Doctor spun round again. 'Aliens with no hair and big wiggly fronds. They mean well. Some say the more they salivate, the more they want to make you a cup of tea.'

Evan couldn't believe it. He had wanted an adventure

and he had got an adventure. As he and his family followed the Doctor towards the TARDIS, he felt like he could face anything. So long as he was with his family – and with a little help from the Doctor, of course.

THE TWELFTH DOCTOR

BABY SLEEPY FACE

Written by Craig Donaghy

They knew it was a stupid idea, but they could never say no to a challenge. They especially couldn't say no to a challenge that the other had set, even if it meant that they were now walking through the woods in the middle of the night. The weak beams of their tiny torches revealed a forest floor covered in muddy leaves and thorny bushes. The moon was out, bold and bright, but the ceiling of twisted tree branches above blocked out its calming blue glow.

Amber and Ross were twins. They both disliked this fact very much, because they were so different. Amber was quick and curious, always sniffing out mysteries and looking for answers. Ross was gentle and thoughtful, drifting in a cloud of his own stubborn ideas. Nonetheless, they had two very identical traits: they were both very competitive and both very tall.

'It's a competition,' their dad would say. 'They're racing each other to the stars, but keeping their feet on the ground!'

Now their feet were tearing through thorny tangles as they weaved between the dark, silent trees. Amber raced ahead, claiming she was the fastest, but Ross kept overtaking her, defiantly trying to prove he was the bravest. Both wanted to stop. Both wanted to turn round every time they heard a creak or a rustle. But this was a competition that they both wanted to win.

Three nights earlier, Amber had woken Ross up to show him something very strange. She led him to her bedroom window and pointed to the hill in the distance. Normally, they'd have seen the dormant silhouette of the abandoned doll factory on the edge of the woods, but now a grey smoke poured from the factory's chimneys and unnaturally white lights skipped past the shattered windows. It was the same again the following night, and the night after that.

'It's reopened, that's all. They're making dolls again or something,' Ross had said dismissively.

'But why not tell anyone?' Amber asked. 'We haven't heard Dad talking about it.'

Their dad had once worked in the doll factory. Everyone's parents had. Then the factory had been closed down, and everybody had lost their jobs. The factory closure had made things so hard for everyone in the town. Many families had left for the nearby city in search of work, and those who had stayed in the town struggled to find jobs and to feed their families. The town had become a sad, depressed place. If the factory was reopened, it could make everyone happy again. People would have work again, and they wouldn't have to leave. It could save the town.

'I'm going to go and find out!' Amber declared proudly.

'No. *I'm* going to go and find out!' Ross declared, slightly prouder.

The twins stood side by side outside the factory and watched the smoke spiral into the night sky. They could see flashes of light behind the dirty glass of the windows. Something was off. It was all too quiet. The huge concrete building, with its giant chimneys and tall windows, vibrated with an eerie . . . nothingness.

It wasn't long before the twins were inside the factory. A loose panel in a forgotten wooden door had led them straight into a storage area. The space smelled old, damp and forgotten. Their torches' tiny spotlights danced across boxes furred with dust and a floor covered in broken dolls' arms and legs.

Ross found a light switch and instantly regretted illuminating the single bulb that hung from the centre of the ceiling. Shelves of broken dolls watched them with empty eyes, silently poking their podgy fingers at the twins. Rows and rows of tiny toes pointed to the cobwebs on the ceiling. Amber stumbled backwards, bashing into a crate full of shiny glass eyes. The eyes spun around in confusion before settling back into place.

'This is seriously creepy,' Amber whispered.

'Are you scared?' her brother whispered back.

'*No.* I said it's creepy, not that *I'm* creeped out.'

'Whatever.'

The twins spotted a wooden door at the far end of the storage room, framed by floor-to-ceiling shelves of dusty, slumped dolls. Amber and Ross looked at each other and gulped nervously.

'Don't be such a baby, Ross!'

'You're the baby!'

They ran towards the wooden door and reached it at the same time, bashing it open.

What they saw on the other side left them open-mouthed with shock.

The factory was indeed up and running again. No –
more than that. It was brand-new. The ceiling and walls were
white and clean. All of the machinery and conveyor belts
were shiny metal. All the moving parts, the tipping vats, the
grabbing claws, the churning moulds and the spray guns
worked away silently with a ruthless efficiency.

'I came to visit Dad here one time,' Amber said. 'It did
not look like this.'

'This is like something from the future.' Ross gazed
around. 'Everything's so new. What are they making?'

The twins made their way through the factory, ducking
under metal pipes and pumping machines, and it soon
became very clear what was being made. Hundreds of pink
arms and empty heads knitted with yellow hair glided along
the metal assembly lines. At the end of the lines, plump baby
boys and girls in stripy red-and-white pyjamas slid off the
rolling chutes and into a packing crate.

Dolls.

Ross picked up one of the little boy dolls. It had sleepy
eyes, rosy cheeks and fluffy yellow hair.

'Extra creepy,' said Ross.

'I'm Baby Sleepy Face!' a metallic recording rasped from
inside the doll.

Both twins jumped. Then they couldn't help but smile at

each other. They were both a little creeped out, and there was no hiding it.

'They used to make these Baby Sleepy Face dolls here,' Amber said. 'They were huge. Even I had one.'

The doll suddenly opened its mouth to reveal big white teeth and bit Ross's hand. He yelled and dropped it on the floor, where it landed on its feet in an expert crouch. The doll then straightened up and started to walk towards the twins. It let out a wail – a long, screeching cry that seemed to split the air. The other dolls in the crate nearby joined in.

Amber and Ross edged backwards as a wave of pyjama-clad dolls climbed out of the crate and off the assembly line and advanced on them, screaming and shouting. Their chants began to synch and words formed. 'It's time to go to sleep! It's time to go to sleep!'

The dolls' faces began to change. Despite their rosy cheeks, dimples and sleepy little eyes, they looked angry and hungry for a fight.

'Evil dolls? Is this even happening?' Ross asked.

'We need to stop them,' Amber said, her voice determined.

With a nod to one another, they lunged forward. Amber launched a kick at the doll that had used its teeth on her brother and sent the bedtime biter flying into the crate. Ross took off his backpack and swung it round, bashing five of the dolls across the room. Another doll jumped on to Amber's back and started pulling her hair. She flipped it over her shoulder and whacked it on the floor. No matter how many dolls the twins kicked away, more and more kept appearing. Brand-new dolls continued to roll off the end of the assembly line, and rather than sliding along on their chubby bottoms they stood up and ran furiously down the chute, desperate for a fight.

'I know how to stop this!' Amber cried, turning to run away. 'I can turn off the machines!'

'Hurry!' Ross replied, grabbing dolls and jamming them into the crate. He pulled a heavy lid on to the box and sat on it to keep them all trapped inside. He could hear the dolls shouting from their prison. 'It's time to go to sleep! It's time to go to sleep!'

When she'd come to visit him here, Amber's dad had showed her where everything was in the factory. She remembered a small boxed area full of switches and levers: the control room. There had been a button, a big red one, that would stop everything in case something went wrong or someone got hurt. If that control room had been restored exactly like the rest of the factory had, then she had to hit it – and quick.

'Hurry up, Amber!' Ross yelled, trying to keep the captured dolls in the crate while fighting off the new ones that kept appearing. They seemed to burst into life the moment they were fixed together by the machines.

Amber spotted the red button, and hit it as hard as she could.

The production line stopped. The silent machines came to a sudden halt, although the dolls carried on shrieking and twitching.

Amber ran back to Ross and together they were able to stack heavy boxes on top of the crate full of dolls. They could hear the dolls clawing to get out, but the boxes kept them safely trapped inside.

'See.' Amber smiled. 'I did it.'

'I would have done it faster.' Ross smirked.

'Let's get out of here,' Amber said. There was no time to argue. 'We need to find help.'

The twins dived back into the stale storage room. The dolls that had sat silently on the shelves were now twitching as if waking up from a long, dusty sleep.

This time, though, Amber and Ross weren't alone in the room.

A man stood in the centre, under the single humming

light bulb. Except he wasn't really a man. He had a human body and human hands. He even wore a dark brown jacket and blue overalls. But he had a huge plastic doll's head with cold, glassy eyes and blushed cheeks. As he stepped forward, his plastic eyelashes fluttered. A metal headset was wrapped across the side of his face, connecting his mouth and ear to what looked like a small satellite dish.

The twins grabbed each other's hands, fear and instinct driving their movements.

'I'm the Foreman,' the figure said in a lifeless voice, stretching out his arms towards them. 'This is my factory. Trespassers will be eliminated.'

'What's going on? What is it that you're doing here?' Ross demanded, instinctively stepping backwards and pulling his twin with him.

'Building an army,' the Foreman replied, letting out a glitchy robotic noise. 'All of these Autons are built to fight. We've added essence of Sontaran to get them battle ready.'

The Foreman marched towards the twins. An unsettling metallic giggle sounded from the device on the side of his face.

'Now, why do the bad guys always feel the need to explain everything to the good guys?' a stranger's voice asked. A thin man stepped forward from the shadows. He looked angry – or at least his eyebrows did. He was smartly dressed in a buttoned-up white shirt and dark jacket. His curly grey hair was both tidy and unruly, and he looked both terrifying and kind, all at the same time.

'Who are you?' The Foreman turned towards the stranger, not lowering his arms.

'I'm not one of those idiots who tells everyone everything straight away,' the man said. He sounded Scottish. He thought for a second, appearing to process more thoughts than most people have in a lifetime. 'I guess, using simple logic, that makes me one of the good guys.'

The man quickly stepped forward and pushed the Foreman, who fell backwards over the crate of beady glass eyes and into a dark corner. The strange man seemed to be on the edge of losing his temper. He turned to Amber and Ross.

'Well, come on then, twins!' he said. 'You see each other all the time, so spend your time looking at something new and exciting. Me!'

Then he turned and ran through the forgotten wooden door that led outside. The twins raced to follow him, not quite knowing why, but feeling like it was the right thing to do.

'We're safe now,' Amber stated when they were outside the factory.

'Don't be ridiculous!' the strange man proclaimed.

'You're not safe. You never are. And in this case you're specifically extra not safe.'

'But we stopped them!' Ross replied.

'Do you two share a brain?' the man asked – but his insult then became a question. He curiously looked inside Ross's ear. 'Do you, though? I'd be very excited to run some tests if you do . . .'

'Who –' Amber started.

'Are you?' Ross finished.

'The Doctor. Ancient. Alien. Amazing.' He smiled. 'You're Ross. You're Amber. You're twins. You're caught in the middle of an alien plan to take over the world. Most people who know me are, to be fair.'

'I stopped the machine from making any more dolls.' Amber was defensive. She wasn't used to being criticised.

'And I put all of the dolls in a crate!' added Ross, eager to prove he had helped.

'Yes, yes. I know all of that. I was watching very carefully.'

'So,' Amber said slowly, starting to get frustrated, 'we stopped them.'

'Not at all. It was ineffective to the point of embarrassment.'

The twins looked a little hurt.

The Doctor impatiently rummaged in his jacket pocket and pulled out a bunch of small cards. He quickly flicked through them. 'Nope . . . Not this time . . . Save for later . . . No. Aha!' He started reading. 'Good work! You tried your hardest to stop an alien plot, invasion or mystery. Delete as appropriate. But this time you were unsuccessful.'

'What do you mean, we were unsuccessful?' Amber demanded. She didn't make mistakes.

'There's an alien called the Nestene Consciousness,' the Doctor replied. 'It controls plastic. All plastic. You stopped it building an extra-angry army of Auton dolls, but there's loads of things it can control already. Toys, dummies, mannequins, already formed in the most fighty of all shapes: the human.'

Before the twins could even begin to process what the Doctor had said, the ground started to shake.

'And your dumb-dumb species has been dumping plastic and burying it for years. This very factory was shut down because you lot buried so much right here.'

'We're on a plastic dumping ground?' Ross asked.

'You wish! We're on a graveyard of dolls,' the Doctor said with an excited smile.

The soil beneath their feet started to split. Clods of grass turned upside-down. Hundreds and thousands of discarded faulty plastic dolls began breaking through the dirt. The dolls,

missing eyes and limbs and with misshapen heads, clawed through the ground like mini plastic zombies, hungry for revenge. And their targets were the Doctor, Amber and Ross. Soon, the churned earth had become a sea of seething plastic body parts. There was no space left to step into. The dirty pink dolls marched in the moonlight, wearing tattered, stripy pyjamas. Their distorted voice boxes sang a chorus, telling the world they were all Baby Sleepy Face.

The Doctor pulled out a pair of sunglasses.

'It's night-time!' Ross exclaimed. 'There's no sun.'

'There's always a sun!' the Doctor cried in disbelief. 'What *are* they teaching you in school these days? This planet's really gone downhill . . .' He slipped the sunglasses on. 'Anyway, I don't need the sun right now. I need my TARDIS!'

Amber and Ross felt a huge rush of air – only, it wasn't air or like anything they'd ever felt before. A noise, as elegant and as powerful as whale song, hummed in their ears. Something bright and solid was forming around them, and they realised they were inside some sort of hi-tech control room. They looked around in awe, but the Doctor jumped straight to work, heading for a large console in the middle of the space. He began pressing buttons and pulling levers with all the verve and concentration of a concert pianist, then stopped and pointed at Amber. 'Hey, you! The one who loves hitting big red emergency stop buttons. Don't do that here.'

Amber nodded. She was so overcome by everything around her that she was speechless.

'What *is* this place? Some sort of classroom?' Ross was staring at all of the blackboards and books.

'Yes, in many ways.' The Doctor appeared to like this. 'Where others come to learn how completely stupid they always are. This is the TARDIS. It's a spaceship. It's a time machine. It's my home.'

He went back to work. He didn't look up, but he moved his hands over the console at break-neck speed. 'I've materialised it around us, so you won't get the whole "Wow, it's bigger on the inside!" experience, but, trust me, it's incredibly impressive.'

The TARDIS began to shake.

The Doctor looked at a screen on the console. He ran along a walkway to a small door, then flung it open.

'Oh dear, that's not good,' he said, peering outside.

Amber and Ross ran to the door of the TARDIS. There was a lot to take in.

'We're in a blue box? How can that be?' Amber said.

The Doctor slapped his forehead. 'I would be a bit more concerned about *that* if I were you,' he said, pointing up.

Looming high above them was one gigantic mega-doll, made from hundreds of smashed-up dolls, all piled together. The gigantic Auton creature stumbled around like a baby walking for the first time – clumsy but determined. It seemed to fall forward into each powerful step, making the ground shake.

A huge hand swooped down and picked up the TARDIS. Amber and Ross toppled forward, but the Doctor grabbed them both by their backpacks and pulled them back into the safety of the TARDIS.

He then peered closely at the doll's hand. Like the rest of the creature, it was made up of limbs, eyes, heads and torsos. A jigsaw of dolls. Some parts were old and discoloured – buried for years, rotten and forgotten. Some parts were the new dolls that had been made in the refurbished factory – pink and shiny and ferocious. Tiny arms and legs grabbed and kicked viciously at the TARDIS.

A booming robotic voice came from the giant doll. 'I'm Baby Sleepy Face.'

'Yeah? Well, I'm Doctor Angry Face,' said the Doctor, slamming the TARDIS doors shut.

'Doctor,' Ross pleaded. 'Can't we just get out of here? This is a time machine, right? And a spaceship?'

The Doctor held on to the rail as the TARDIS continued

to shake. 'Not as simple as that, Twin Two. I'm tracking a signal from out there – far away, even by my standards. I need to stop this thing being controlled by the Nestene.'

The TARDIS shook violently, knocking all three of them to the floor.

'Great. I just redecorated the library.' The Doctor dusted himself off grumpily.

'You've got a library?' Amber asked.

'I've got several. I don't like to boast, but I've got a garage, a gallery of oil paintings of cats, an observatory, a –'

The TARDIS shuddered again.

'Not the right time, Doctor Disco,' the Time Lord muttered to himself.

Something occurred to Ross. 'How's it getting a signal? If something's being transmitted –'

'Then something must be receiving it.' Amber finished for him.

'Good brain work, twins. Now let's keep it going. I was trying to look around that factory for some fancy metal stuff. A great big metal receiver. You see anything like that, Twin One?' The Doctor pointed at Amber.

'The control room?' she offered.

'Nope. Keep thinking . . .'

'The machines on the assembly line?' she tried.

'Wrong again. Twin Two?' He turned to Ross.

'What about the chimneys?' Ross suggested. 'Or something from the storage room?'

The twins were back in competition mode, both trying to think of everything, each of them in a race with the other to be first.

The Doctor walked over to them and raised an eyebrow. 'Do me and yourselves a favour and stop competing. Work together and you might be surprised at the results.'

The twins nodded sheepishly, then started again.

'How could they communicate?' Amber pondered.

'Were there phones?' Ross asked.

'Maybe in the offices? But there are no working phone lines . . .'

'They could have mobile phones?'

'Or hands-free kits? Or something like that?'

Then it hit them both.

The Doctor nodded. Had he already worked it out? Did it matter?

'Doctor!' Amber shouted. 'The Foreman had this metal thing on his head, like a hands-free kit with a little satellite dish on it.'

'It must be capable of receiving a signal,' Ross said.

The Doctor ran back across to the TARDIS console and

beckoned the twins over to look at a small screen. It showed
a scan of the giant doll. At the centre of its face, just between
the eyes, lay the green outline of a man. A man with a large
plastic head full of alien tech.

'Of course, he's part of the doll,' the Doctor said calmly.
'He's the brain of the beast.' He paced back and forth. 'I
need to shut that thing down. I can use my sonic sunglasses
to stop the receiver from working and block the signal, but I
need to get nearer to it. A teeny little satellite like that needs
fixing up close.'

'You're using those glasses? Haven't you got a
screwdriver or something?' Ross asked.

The Doctor grinned. If only they knew.

'How are you going to get up there? That thing's huge!'
Amber trailed after the Doctor as he paced around.

The Doctor pulled the TARDIS doors open once more.
'I'm going to climb up.'

'But you're an old man,' said Ross.

'You've got no idea,' the Doctor said.

'I'll do it!' Amber took off her backpack and stood proudly.

'Don't be stupid. I'm the better climber.' Ross took off his
backpack.

'That's not true. I can climb, *and* I'm better at not being
scared,' Amber retorted.

'Hardly. You've been a right chicken,' Ross said.

The twins' bickering was interrupted by a soft grunt. They turned to see the Doctor launch himself out of the TARDIS doors and on to the wrist of the huge Auton doll.

They gaped in awe, as they watched the Doctor scramble up the forearm of the plastic monster. He grabbed on to jutting limbs and fuzzy yellow wigs for grip. Loose hands scratched and pinched him, and the dolls' heads tried to bite him. Patches of the devilish giant doll were beginning to smooth out and form one solid creation. The Doctor had to move fast or it would soon be too slippery to climb. The Doctor gave it everything. The TARDIS swung around in the grip of the creature's hand, but the twins held on tight. They didn't want to miss a thing.

The Doctor made it to the giant doll's shoulder, balancing carefully on a row of heads with furious faces. Suddenly he slipped – first his legs, and then his body. He held on at the shoulder, but something was wrong. His sunglasses fell off. They bounced down the doll's torso as tiny hands tried to grab at them, and then landed on the churned-up grass.

'He needs those sunglasses.' Amber turned to Ross. 'I can climb down and climb back up to get them to him.'

'No!' Ross shouted, grabbing Amber's arm.

They shared a look. The Doctor was right: they had to work together to achieve their goal.

'You climb up and I'll climb down,' Ross said. 'I'll grab the glasses and throw them up to you. You're a better climber.'

'And you can throw further,' Amber said. 'Chuck them to me and I'll pass them to the Doctor.'

Ross nodded and jumped out of the TARDIS doors. He allowed himself to fall from the doll's pudgy hand, timing it so he landed on its chubby knee.

Amber followed after the Doctor. He turned and gave her a look of both fury and respect.

'I told you two to stay put,' the Doctor shouted, beginning to scramble up the doll's neck.

'No, you didn't!' Amber yelled, edging her way up the doll-beast's arm.

'Well, I should have,' the Doctor said. 'But I'd never tell anyone to do something I wouldn't do myself.'

Ross tried to slide down the plastic leg, avoiding spiteful pokes from blunt fingers. He made it down to the ground. Just as he was about to jump clear, the doll flicked its ankle, sending him across the dirty ground in a rough roll. Amber watched, panicked, as her brother lay there motionless on the ground. Then, a second later, he climbed to his feet and gave her a thumbs-up.

As Ross ran towards the sonic sunglasses, which lay in a heap of ripped-up grass, the doll's foot lifted ominously above them, then started to descend. Ross skidded across the ground to the sunglasses, grabbed them and dived out of the way just moments before the big plastic foot smashed down.

Amber gripped the doll with her knees and held out her hands. 'I'm ready!' she called to her brother. 'Throw them to me now!'

Ross hurled the sunglasses into the air and Amber caught them easily. She gave Ross a thumbs-up, but then the giant doll started moving violently. It threw down the TARDIS and used its hand to swat at her, as if she was an insect. An unearthly roar came from the plastic beast's delicate baby-pink lips. Amber moved quickly, heading towards the Doctor, who had now made it up to the face. He reached backwards and Amber stretched upward to pass him the sonic shades.

The Doctor nodded. 'Now, you two, move away as fast as you can!'

He scaled the giant's face. When it opened its mouth to roar again, he took advantage of the open lips and used them as stepping stones. Then he grabbed the big button nose and pulled himself up between the doll's huge eyes.

Ross helped Amber down the last section of the doll's ankle and they watched together from the ground. They nervously paced, ready to move away from the doll giant's lumbering footsteps at the same time as being ready to move towards the action so they could see everything.

The Doctor found what he needed. There, submerged in the broken doll parts of the face, was the Foreman. He slotted in perfectly, with his gigantic doll's head lying in the middle of the creature's forehead. His eyes were wide open and he watched the Doctor with loathing. The small satellite dish on the side of his head buzzed.

'You are an enemy of the Nestene,' the Foreman declared.

'I'm an enemy of anything that invades, bullies and controls. So you know what I must do.' The Doctor sighed, sliding on his shades.

The Foreman's face flashed with fear and anger, and he screamed. The doll giant's mouth stretched open once more and let out another tremendous roar. Every head that made up the creature also let out a scream.

The Doctor pressed the side of his sonic sunglasses. 'It's time to go to sleep.'

The signal was cut and the doll suddenly became still.

Amber turned to Ross, concerned. 'Did he do it?'

A low rumbling sound confirmed that the Doctor's plan had worked. Heads and limbs started to fall off the imposing figure, as it crumbled to a pink mountain of lifeless doll parts. The twins yelled out for the Doctor, as the creature collapsed in front of them, then they raced forward to search through the pile of plastic rubbish, frantically trying to reach the strange man who had saved their lives.

Amber suddenly felt something warm among all the hard plastic limbs – a real flesh hand. Ross ran over to help her and they pulled out the Doctor. He rose from the pile of body parts coughing, spluttering and shaking his head.

'That was ridiculous!' he said, brushing off his jacket. He began to head back to the TARDIS, which had fortunately landed upright, but at a slight angle. 'Even by my standards!'

'Where are you going?' Amber said.

The Doctor turned to look at her. 'It's the middle of the night. I'm getting you two home to bed.'

They didn't move, so he gestured impatiently. 'Come on then, twins. Hurry up!'

The twins ran into the TARDIS, this time entering into the surprisingly enormous interior through the small wooden doors.

'Wow! It really is much better this way!' Ross said in awe.

'Finally!' the Doctor said, grateful for the acknowledgement. He smiled, then remembered to look cross too.

'So, what about the Autons?' Amber asked.

'Just inanimate plastic now. Just dolls. I'm going to come back and tidy that lot up. There's a species I know that love that stuff. The Chekadarians. Gobble it up and poop out diamonds. Sounds amazing, but it's pretty gross. Actually, it doesn't sound that amazing. It just sounds gross.'

Amber and Ross stared at each other. Who *was* this man?

'But the Nestene thing, will it be back?' Ross asked cautiously.

'Almost definitely. They always come back,' the Doctor replied with a sigh.

'So, what do we do?' Amber found her backpack and started putting it over her shoulders.

'You do nothing. I'll do the worrying. You just get on with your lives. Dream your dreams. Eat your chips. Be kind and curious and the right sort of careful.' The Doctor's face darkened. 'And, for pity's sake, grow up and stop bickering. When you worked together, you helped to save the planet.'

Amber and Ross nodded.

The TARDIS started to make the same singing noise it had made earlier, humming and then wheezing. When it stopped, the Doctor headed to the doors and opened them to reveal they were in Amber and Ross's small back garden. They all stepped out.

'What happens now?' Amber said.

'You go to bed, fall asleep, dream your dreams, eat your chips, et cetera. Haven't I covered all of this already? Do pay attention.'

The Doctor walked back into the TARDIS and shut the doors. A second passed before they opened again and he popped his grey-haired head out.

'Check out that factory tomorrow. Take your dad. A few tweaks and it will be a fully functioning, eco-friendly, futuristic factory. Give everyone jobs. Make something fun and amazing that will save this town and change the world. But no plastic. Or dolls.'

The twins agreed. The TARDIS faded into the night, making that noise they had come to love, then Amber and Ross snuck into their house and went upstairs.

'Good work tonight,' Ross said, smiling at his sister.

'You too!' Amber nodded.

Back in her room, Amber put her backpack down and sat on her bed. She was still trying to get her head around everything. The Doctor. The TARDIS. Dolls. Aliens.

Suddenly she remembered something. She pulled a battered cardboard box from the top of her wardrobe and placed it on the floor. She crouched down and pulled out a

knitted blanket and some comic annuals, and there it was: her
old Baby Sleepy Face doll.

She picked it up and looked at it. She turned it upside-
down and shook it, but it was limp and lifeless. She was
taking no chances. Amber headed downstairs and opened
the back door into the small garden. She threw the doll into
the wheelie bin, then smiled and headed back into her room.
Now it really was time to go to sleep and dream of more
adventures with the Doctor.